SCARS LIKE WINGS

SCARS LIKE WINGS

ERIN STEWART

Delacorte Press

Text copyright © 2019 by Erin Stewart LLC
Jacket art copyright © 2019 by Jan Heur

All rights reserved. Published in the United States by Delacorte Press, an imprint of Random House Children's Books, a division of Penguin Random House LLC, New York.

Delacorte Press is a registered trademark and the colophon is a trademark of Penguin Random House LLC.

Grateful acknowledgment is made to Atticus for permission to reprint his poem "She conquered her demons and wore her scars like wings."

GetUnderlined.com

Educators and librarians, for a variety of teaching tools, visit us at RHTeachersLibrarians.com

Library of Congress Cataloging-in-Publication Data

Names: Stewart, Erin, author.
Title: Scars like wings / Erin Stewart.
Description: First edition. | New York : Delacorte Press, [2019] | Summary: One year after the fire that claimed her parents' and cousin's lives and left her severely disfigured, sixteen-year-old Ava faces the return to high school.
Identifiers: LCCN 2018039863 (print) | LCCN 2018048573 (ebook) | ISBN 978-1-9848-4884-0 (ebook) | ISBN 978-1-9848-4882-6 (hc : alk. paper) | ISBN 978-1-9848-4883-3 (glb : alk. paper) | ISBN 978-0-593-12381-2 (exp.)
Subjects: | CYAC: Disfigured persons—Fiction. | High schools—Fiction. | Schools—Fiction. | Self-confidence—Fiction. | Orphans—Fiction.
Classification: LCC PZ7.1.S7457 (ebook) | LCC PZ7.1.S7457 Sc 2019 (print) | DDC [Fic]—dc23

The text of this book is set in 11.5-point Adobe Garamond.
Interior design by Patrice Sheridan

Printed in the United States of America
10 9 8 7 6 5 4 3 2 1
First Edition

To Kyle.
You've made my life.

1

One year after the fire, my doctor removes my mask and tells me to get a life.

He doesn't use those exact words, of course, because he's paid to flash around lots of medical-degree terms like *reintegration* and *isolation,* but basically, the Committee on Ava's Life had a big meeting and decided I have wallowed long enough.

My postburn pity party is over.

Dr. Sharp examines my skin grafts to make sure I haven't inadvertently grown batwings in my armpits since our last monthly pat-down. Scars can be screwy little suckers, and since my body is 60 percent screwed up, it takes Dr. Sharp a full twenty minutes to check me over. The tissue paper covering the vinyl exam table crinkles beneath me as my aunt Cora watches attentively from the sidelines, scribbling notes in her gargantuan "Ava's Recovery" binder while her eyes follow Dr. Sharp.

He removes the bandana from my head and then my clear plastic mask, his fingers grazing my scars.

"Everything's healing beautifully," he says, without even a hint of irony. The coldness of his fingers registers above my eyes but fades as he moves to the thicker grafts around my mouth.

"Well," I say, "you can put lipstick on a pig, but it's still a p—"

"Ava!" gasps Cora, who is not only my aunt but also the self-appointed CEO of the aforementioned committee on my life.

Dr. Sharp shakes his head and laughs, revealing two deep dimples on either side of his smile, which only makes him even more like one of those McHottie doctors on TV who bang each other in the on-call room between saving lives. I blame his smoldering eyes and strong jawline for the butterfly swarm in my stomach every time he touches my grafts. It also doesn't help that I'm keenly aware he has seen me naked approximately nineteen times. Sure, it's on an operating-room table, but naked is naked, even covered with gauze and nineteen surgeries' worth of scars.

But we never address that awkward elephant in the room, just like I never mention the fact that he once literally took a chunk of my butt and stretched it across my face to make a new forehead.

Dr. Sharp hands me a small, salon-style mirror so I can admire his handiwork.

"No thanks," I say, giving it back.

"Still having trouble looking?"

"Unless I grew a new face overnight, I already know what I'm going to see."

Dr. Sharp nods while typing a note into my chart, and I sense a forthcoming committee meeting about my resistance to reflective surfaces. It's not like I haven't seen my face. I know how I look. I choose not to keep looking.

With a dimply smile, Dr. Sharp holds up my plastic mask.

"I think you'll be happy to hear that you can get rid of this little guy."

Cora squeals and awkwardly side-hugs me, careful not to apply too much pressure to disrupt the all-important healing process.

"You couldn't have given us a better gift today, Dr. Sharp. It's been a year, this week actually, since—" Cora pauses, and I can almost see her brain trying to come up with the right words.

"The fire," I jump in. "One year since the fire."

Dr. Sharp hands me the mask, which has been my constant companion every day, twenty-three hours a day for that year. Its one job: keep my face flat as it heals so my scars don't bulge out in fleshy blobs. The doctors and nurses reassure me constantly that the mask has made my scars heal so much better, although I'm unconvinced it can get much worse than the patchwork of discolored grafts I call my face.

"You'll still need to wear the body-compression garments until we're sure the scars won't interfere with your movements," Dr. Sharp says. "But I do have one more piece of good news for you."

Cora gives him the slightest nod, which tells me that whatever comes next is a direct result of an Ava's Life meeting. My invitation must have gone straight to spam.

"Now that you don't have to wear the mask, I am authorizing—and strongly recommending—that you return to school," he says.

I flip the mask around in my hand without looking up.

"Yeah, that's a hard pass," I say. "But thanks."

Jumping off the sidelines, Cora lays her massive binder by the sink and half sits on the patient chair with me, lightly tapping my thigh.

"Ava, I know you're bored with those online classes, and you're always saying how you wish things could go back to normal."

Normal.

Right. Old normal. Ava Before the Fire normal. Normal normal.

"That's Never. Going. To. Happen," I say. "I'm not going to waltz back into my old school and have everything be the same."

"You could go to the school by our house, like we've talked about. Or pick any school you want," Cora says, undeterred. "You know, a fresh start? Make new friends and begin a life here."

"I'd rather die," I mumble.

I've been doing fine at home taking classes online in my pajamas. Where no one can see me. Where no one can point and stare and whisper as I walk by like I'm deaf as well as deformed.

"I know you don't mean that," Cora says. "You're lucky to be alive."

"Right. I'm a human rabbit's foot."

Why am I the lucky one because I survived? Mom, Dad, and my cousin Sara are probably dancing through a celestial meadow somewhere or happily reincarnated as monkeys in India while I face an endless loop of surgeries and doctors and stares from strangers.

But I can't compete with tombstones. Death trumps suffering every time.

"If it were Sara, I'd want her to live a full life," she says. "And I know your mother would want you to be happy."

Her attempt to use dead people to win this argument irks me. "I'm not Sara. And you're not my mother."

Cora turns away from me, and so does Dr. Sharp, pretending to concentrate especially hard on the computer screen rather than acknowledge the tension that fills the exam room like smoke. I hate that Dr. Sharp is here for this embarrassing toddler tantrum, but he's partly to blame for blindsiding me with this development.

Cora sniffles quietly, and I wish I could take back my jab. She didn't ask to be my makeshift mother any more than I asked to be her understudy offspring. We're both trying to navigate this sick twist of "luck" the universe threw our way.

Dr. Sharp clears his throat. "Ava, the fact is, we're concerned about your level of isolation. Reintegration is a major part of your healing process, and we all think it's time to start," he says. I refrain from asking him who this mysterious "all" includes, since my concerning hermit status is news to me. "What if you go to school for a trial period, and then we reassess our reintegration strategy? Say two weeks?"

Cora looks at me hopefully, tears still wetting her eyes, as the guilt of the lucky creeps into my chest. The guilt of the one who lived.

This week marks one year for her, too. One year without her daughter. One year taking care of me, the girl who survived instead.

I can't give her Sara, but I can give her two weeks.

"Fine," I say. "Ten school days. If it's not a complete train wreck, then we'll talk about more."

Aunt Cora hugs me so tight that I act like it hurts more than it does so she'll stop.

"It's only two weeks," I remind her. "And it *is* going to be a complete train wreck."

"It's a start," she says.

I re-cover my scarred scalp with my red bandana as Cora and Dr. Sharp exchange a triumphant look. I toggle the transparent mask between what's left of my hands, fighting the urge to put it back on.

Cora stops at the front desk to haggle about unpaid surgery bills while I meander down the hallway of the burn unit, looking at artwork from some Hospital Arts Initiative to bring beauty to dying people. I don't even realize I've wandered into the regular hospital atrium until a little girl clinging to her mother's skinny jeans emits a high-pitched scream.

Her chubby little finger points at me.

At my face.

The woman flushes red as she mutters an apology and yanks her child away by her arm. The girl continues to wail and crane her neck back toward me as her mom scurries away. A man in a pleather armchair shifts his eyes quickly back to his newspaper, but I can feel him watching me as I inch my way back to the hallway, trying to act casual.

I wait inside the safety of the burn unit, where people are used to faces like mine. The man with the newspaper steals glances at me from down the hallway, making me wish Cora had let me bring my headphones so I could turn on my music and tune out everything—and everybody—else. Instead, I turn to a 3-D art display called *Starlight Reflections* hanging in the window, and pretend to be immensely interested in the broken pieces of glass shaped like little stars, each five-pointed mini mirror shooting rainbow fragments of light across the hallway.

The cascading Milky Way of tiny mirrors distorts me, reflecting a Picasso reality in the shards that hang together as if one touch will send them splintering to the floor. I find myself in the glass, my red bandana framing my fractured face.

For a second, I allow myself to believe the broken glass is to blame for the broken girl.

Once I step away, my face will be fine.

Normal.

That's what the committee wants. Go back to high school. Be normal again.

I know better.

Normal people don't terrorize small children.

Normal sixteen-year-olds look in mirrors. *Is my lipstick on straight? Is my hair doing that swoopy thing in the front?* Their reflections reassure them, and if they don't like what they see, they fix it.

For me, mirrors are a reminder.

I'm a monster.

Nothing in the world can fix that.

2

Cora spends the next week in a tizzy of back-to-school shopping, convinced that my successful return to normal teenage life hinges on whether I carry a backpack or an over-the-shoulder messenger bag.

The night before my official "reintegration," she spreads a lineup of bags on my bed. Bold-printed tote bags, floral canvas backpacks, and nylon crossbodies stare up at me.

"What are the kids using these days?"

I shrug. "I've been wearing hospital gowns and pajamas, so I may not be the best style source."

I don't add that I highly doubt anyone's going to be looking at my accessories. Cora's eyes flick from the bagstravaganza to me, her eyebrows pushed together with the same look she gets doing the Sunday crossword. Like if she can just focus hard enough, she can find the solution.

But for all Cora's efforts, I'm one puzzle she can't fix.

"I think this one," she says decisively, holding out a black messenger bag to me. "But try it just to make sure before I return the rest."

Rather than modeling it, I tell her whatever she wants is fine and remind her that in two weeks, when I return to my glorious hermithood, I won't need it.

Cora's mouth turns downward, and for a second, her CEO-of-Ava's-recovery mask slips and I see someone else, someone small and scared who wishes more than anything her own daughter were here, modeling backpacks and getting excited for new friends and rowdy sleepovers and all the other normal sixteen-year-old-girl things Cora wanted for Sara.

I sigh and take the messenger bag from her, slinging it over my head.

"It's perfect, Cora, thanks."

She adjusts the bag so it falls neatly by my side. The weight of it tugs on my already taut shoulders, but it's good to see her smile.

Cora plucks a navy blue bandana from my collection and holds it up next to the blousy blue shirt she bought me. "Now, *this* is an outfit." She doesn't have money to throw at new clothes right now, but I'm grateful not to wear Sara's hand-me-downs tomorrow. Luckily, it's February, so I can wear long sleeves and jeans to cover most of my compression garments.

"You're sure about no wig?" she says. "That nice lady from the hospital said we could call anytime. We could hop in the car right now and go get one."

I shake my head. "Definitely not."

A wig might cover my patchy scalp better than a bandana, but it's not going to fool anyone. The lady who came armed to the burn unit with wigs and makeup and all sorts of other hide-your-scars paraphernalia *was* nice, but for all her efforts, fake hair and foundation couldn't cover *this*. So why pretend?

After Cora leaves, I unzip my compression garments, carefully shedding the second skin that keeps my scars from puffing out like cotton candy.

I lie facedown on the bed in a tank top and shorts, the yarn from Sara's quilt tickling my nose. Cora returns and starts our nightly slather-me-in-lotion routine. We begin on my right side. She gently straightens my arm, which from this angle looks freak-ishly thin. Like skin-and-bones, back-from-the-dead zombie thin. Who knew fat cells could burn up?

Cora works the lotion into all my cracks and crevices as the fa-miliar medical/old-lady smell of the oily cream fills the room. My beige compression garments slump like snakeskin on my desk. After a year, they seem more me than the purply-pink swirling scars of my actual body.

I used to think of skin as one continuous unit, but mine is more like Sara's bedspread beneath me—a morbid quilt stitched together. Some pieces are original, some are scarred over, and some are grafted in from other parts of my body after the doctors played epidermal musical chairs. During the early days, I even had some pig and cadaver skin stapled in while we waited for a lab somewhere to grow more of me from postage-stamp-size cutouts from my back.

Cora works my arm like it's bread dough, her fingers pushing in and spreading the lotion. It's the one time Cora doesn't act like I'm an eggshell about to crack, probably because the nurses in the hospital told her the rougher she massages, the better for my scarring. And if it's "aiding recovery," Cora is all about it.

I lift my left leg before she even gets to it. After eight months of this full-body rubdown routine, we're like a synchronized-swimming duo. I'm flexible enough now that I could do my own lotion lathering, but honestly, it's nice to be touched by something other than Dr. Sharp's icy fingers. Besides, the massaging relieves the itching, which is a side effect of the dryness, which is a side effect of having no oil glands. That domino effect culminates in a constant buzzing itch beneath my skin I can never quite reach.

"So I read an interesting article," Cora says.

I almost laugh out loud at this utterly not shocking fact. *Burn Survivor Quarterly* comes to our house every few months to fill Cora's head with ideas on how she can help me. She reads every word of every issue, often leaving cutout articles on my bed.

"It said how important it is for burn survivors to have a support group of peers who understand them." Cora talks as she rubs. "And I just know tomorrow you will meet some new friends, and I think it's really going to help you, Ava. I can feel it."

I roll on my back so she can rub my knees.

"It's two weeks. Don't get your hopes up," I say, although it's clear her hopes have already rocketed out of the earth's atmosphere.

"Well, you're always saying how you don't need friends—"

"Which I don't."

"And I'm saying, stay open to the possibility. Don't let your fears stop you."

"I'm not afraid." I flex my puny arm muscles. "I've got my scar armor to protect me."

Cora's lips seal into a tight line as she rubs hard into my shoulders, working the lotion into my thickest scars. The wide bands of skin grafts pull in from my neck, my back, my arms, gathering like steel suspenders. Until recently, Cora had to help me put on my shirts because I couldn't move my arms high enough.

I hold my arms out to let the lotion air-dry before we begin the task of getting my compression garments over my tacky skin. I snake each leg and arm through the tight fabric, and Cora zips me up. She rubs lotion on my face last, using one finger to spread it across the graft lines that dissect me.

"I hear Crossroads does a musical every year," Cora says nonchalantly, like she didn't make sure the school I'll be going to has a stellar drama program. Like we both don't know I haven't sung a single note since the fire. Before, I couldn't stop singing. Pouring my heart out to the showerhead microphone. On the highway with Sara with the windows rolled down. At the dinner table, subjecting my poor parents to my latest Broadway obsession.

With all the smoke and tubes and surgeries, who knows if I even *can* sing now. Dr. Sharp says my throat has healed and all, but I have my doubts. Not that it matters. The girl who loved spotlights and solos doesn't exist anymore.

My eyes drift around the room where Sara and I used to have

cousin sleepovers every few months. Even though I lived an hour south, in Utah's farm country, we'd grown up in each other's rooms, sharing each other's lives. She called my mom Momma Denise, and I called hers Momma Cora.

Now I just call her Cora, and this room feels more foreign than familiar.

Most of Sara's things were gone when I arrived from the hospital, but a few haunting echoes remain—clothes in the closet that fit me, Sara's pointe shoes on a corner shelf as if she's going to sashay in at any moment, and, of course, the vintage Barbie collection that stares at me from behind the glass of a massive curio cabinet. Apparently, the dolls are super valuable. Not that Cora and Glenn would ever sell them or anything else in here.

Cora's tried in her way to make this space my own, though. Framed pictures of my parents on the desk. On the walls, Broadway musical posters like I used to have at home.

But this is not home.

And I'm an interloper—an impostor trying to fill the space of two girls when I'm barely even one.

Cora holds my chin so I'm looking right at her again.

"Promise me you'll give this a real chance. That you'll let people in."

Cora's earnest eyes search my face, and mine hers. Even in her pajamas with no makeup, she's beautiful. Mom used to joke that her little brother didn't stand a chance against Cora's looks, which lured him all the way up to the city.

I sigh. "Cora, the only way I'm going to survive the next two weeks is if I'm as thick-skinned as humanly possible, and lucky for me, hypertrophic scars are about as thick as it gets."

Cora's lips press together again as I ba-dum-ching an imaginary drum set.

"Oh, come on," I say. "I can either laugh or cry about it, and I'm about all cried out."

Cora does neither. Instead, she holds my hands, my purply skin particularly alien against hers. At least my right hand still has fingers. Calling the stumpy, clawlike structure at the end of my left arm a hand is unspeakably generous. It's more of a pincer now—fused fingers opposite a massive thumb that is actually my transplanted big toe.

Cora squeezes my hand—or claw, or whatever it is—tight. "It's your junior year of high school. Make some friends. Enjoy it."

I exhale long and slow. Cora doesn't understand: even my old friends back home didn't know how to be around me after the fire. Probably because I wasn't really *me* anymore.

I doubt many people at this new school are looking for that one special burn victim to round out their squad, either.

So instead of a clan, I have a plan: do everything in my power to disappear. Not like a magic act or anything but more like a melt-into-the-background camouflage. The only way to get through these two weeks of feigned normalcy is to minimize exposure as much as possible—mine and everyone else's.

"I almost forgot—" I grab my headphones off the desk and sling them over tomorrow's outfit draped on the chair.

Cora tenses, probably using every ounce of willpower in her

five-foot-three frame not to grab them off her perfect ensemble. She hates my headphones almost as much as I love them. Well, need them.

"You and your music," she says.

I don't tell her it's not about the music. Most of the time I don't even notice what's playing. I wear them to block out the world.

To help me fade away.

Uncle Glenn stops at my doorway to say good night. Standing there with his signature awkward smile and the top of his nose turning slightly upward, he looks so much like my mom. Sometimes it makes me so sad I can barely look at him. Sometimes I can't turn away. My mom was beautiful, too, but not in the porcelain-doll way Cora is. Mom's beauty was more unbreakable—crow's-feet by her eyes and calluses on her hands.

My own nose used to turn up like Mom's, too, a trait passed down from way back in her family tree. Dad used to slide his finger down the bridge and off the tip. "My little Swiss ski jumps," he'd say.

I touch my nose, which now ends in a round, bulbous cul-de-sac made of skin grafts. The fire was nothing if not thorough; it took all of Mom, even the pieces of her left in me.

Glenn steps into my room, his cowboy boots heavy on the carpet until Cora scolds him. He stops midstep to take off the pointy-toed boots that are as much a part of him as his skin, even though he hasn't worked a ranch since he moved to Salt Lake. He neatly sets the pair against the wall and helps me take off my bandana after I get into bed.

"Nice to only have to wear this at night?" he asks, adjusting the strap of my mask around my head.

I nod.

Glenn stands back, watching me wiggle the mask into place, the familiar pressure against my skin. "I'm proud of you," he says.

"For what?" I say through the small speech hole in the plastic.

"For being brave," he says. "Know what John Wayne used to say?"

I shake my head. "I barely know who John Wayne is."

Glenn laughs. "Well, then here's your first lesson: 'Courage is being scared to death but saddling up anyway.'"

I twirl my hand in the air like I'm whipping a lasso.

Glenn kisses the top of my head. "Good night, kiddo."

In the dim light, if I squint just right, I see my mom standing above me. I can almost believe she'll be right down the hall, waiting for me to crawl into bed with her and tell her I'm terrified to face tomorrow alone.

Glenn and Cora walk out together, his broad shoulders hulking over her tiny frame. He stoops to pick up his cowboy boots with one hand while holding Cora's slender fingers with the other. I watch them through my mask as they walk down the hallway.

I look down at my own hands, my claw on one side and my scarred fingers peeking out of my compression garments on the other.

Cora wants me to let people in. Problem is, no one's knocking on my door—now or ever.

So whatever high school launches at me tomorrow, I have to be ready.

Bulletproof.

I put on my headphones, turn up the music, and close my eyes under the stitched-tight grip of the compression garments and the weight of my face mask. Normally, my burn-survivor getup makes me feel like a creepy King Tut entombed in a sarcophagus.

But tonight, it feels good.

Like a protective layer between me and the world.

Like it's the only thing holding me together.

3

As Disappearing Act One, I ask Cora to drop me off thirty minutes early to avoid the crowded halls of my new school—Crossroads High, home of the Vikings.

I picked it because it's across town, where no one knew Sara. I've already stepped into the void formally known as my cousin at home; I don't need to slide into her shadow at school, too.

Cora's been a one-woman whirlwind since the Dr. Sharp visit, getting my school records and talking the Crossroads principal into a boundary exception so I can attend. She's been on the phone with all sorts of school personnel making a plan to best handle my "condition" this year, clearly having selective amnesia about the whole "only two weeks" deal.

When we pull into the parking lot, she tells me the principal's expecting me for a quick preclass meet and greet to "get to know me personally." She insists on parking and gets out with me in front of the school, bracing against the frigid February wind to hand me the messenger bag she's decided is my all-access pass to the social hierarchy of high school. I sling it over my shoulder and plug my headphones into my phone while Cora gives me a final rundown of How to Be a High Schooler, complete with instructions on "putting myself out there" and something about my medications.

I don't really hear this last part because (1) I know how to take my meds and (2) another girl gets dropped at the curb behind us.

She stops midstride when she sees me, eyes wide, like she's paralyzed. I look down at the phone in my hand, releasing her, and the girl power walks into the building, her quick footsteps disappearing into Crossroads High.

For a second, I almost run, too—back to the car, back to my room, back to my out-of-sight existence. Cora puts her hand on my arm. I can barely feel her touch through my compression garments.

"Are you sure you don't want me to come in with you?"

I shake my head. That is a big fat no. The last thing I need is a chaperone walking me through the halls of high school. As if my face doesn't draw enough attention to the fact that I. Do. Not. Belong.

That's a pretty big problem when the first commandment of high school is *Belong*.

I swallow my fears—a skill I've nearly perfected in the past year—and fake a smile. If you don't laugh, you cry, right? I hold out my arms wide, turning side to side.

"So . . . how do I look?"

I mean it as a joke, but Cora's eyes rove over me seriously.

"You look great."

"You know you're sending me into a full-on slaughterfest, right?"

She half smiles and adjusts my blue bandana, which is tied in a knot at the base of my neck so it covers my whole scalp.

"We'll pick you up right here, okay?"

"What's left of me."

Cora takes both my hands in hers with a firm squeeze. Does she wish I were Sara right now half as bad as I wish she were Mom?

"Think of everything you've been through, Ava. You're stronger than you realize."

I put my headphones on, making sure the left earpiece covers the spot where my left ear should be. With the music drowning out the world, I grip the shoulder strap tight and walk through the front doors, wishing I could believe as firmly as Cora does in the transformative power of the right accessory. The familiar smell of teen spirit (two parts dingy football pads and one part Axe body spray) wafts to me as I reenter the linoleum-floored, fluorescent-lit world of high school.

A huge cardboard cutout of a white guy with a Viking hat and a sword welcomes me to Viking Country: Be Bold. Be Brave. Be a Warrior. A handwritten banner hanging on the wall reads "Get your heads ready for piking! Here come the Vikings!"

Slaughterfest may have been an understatement.

It's not like I'm unfamiliar with how people react to me. I'm used to the stares from randoms at stoplights or the store. I don't blame them; I'm the human equivalent of a five-car pileup. You can't *not* look.

I'm quite the expert on these reactions, which I've narrowed down to several completely reliable responses:

1. Revulsion
2. Shameless staring
3. Fear
4. Pity
5. Frantic friendliness
6. Aggressive avoidance (like I'm invisible)
7. Condescension (like I'm brain damaged)

There's really no telling who will have which reaction, although kids tend to start out around the 1 zone, yelling to their mothers about why my face looks like bacon.

Adults are usually socially adept enough to skip the panic-stricken staring. Strangers at the store do an avoidance/pity combo, like the mothers who usher their loudmouthed little ones away from me, the real-life boogeyman.

And teenagers? Well, they land somewhere in between, which means I have no idea what I'll face today: pitchforks or pity party.

The unpredictability tightens my stomach as I venture through the lobby, making my way toward the office. I luck out—empty hallways.

Ava 1, reintegration 0.

In the safety of the quiet, carpeted front office, I pause the playlist and slide my headphones down around my neck while also tugging my bandana over my ear hole. I don't know where to go, so I kind of stand in the middle of the room, feeling as out of place as I'm sure I look. When the secretary behind the front desk looks up, her colossal grin falters for a split second.

"Oh." She exhales the word with more air than sound.

Her eyes dart to her desk as she tries to recover. When she looks up again, she wears a perma-smile, her voice loud and sing-songy.

"What can I do for you, dear?"

"I'm Ava Lee. I think I'm supposed to meet with the principal?"

"Oh, Ava, of course!" she half sings ten decibels too loud.

Classic frantic friendliness. *What scars? I'm too excited to even notice your deformed face! La la la!*

"Right this way!" she shouts, as if she's introducing me on a game show rather than ushering me into a tiny office with two men. One sits behind the desk in a polo shirt, the other across from him in a stiff, too-small dress shirt and tie that make his head red and bulgy, like a zit about to explode.

"This is Ava Lee! The new student!" the secretary half yells. Her message delivered, she shuts the door behind her and I can almost hear her sigh of relief. The polo-clad man gestures toward a chair.

"Have a seat, Ava. I'm Principal Danner, but most kids call me Mr. D or Big D. And this is Mr. Lynch."

"You can call me Vice Principal Lynch," the red-faced man says.

Principal Danner reaches out his hand, but pulls back slightly when I stick out mine. The fingers on my right hand peek out from my beige compression garments like wizened purple sausages.

"Is it okay?" he asks.

"It doesn't hurt, if that's what you mean," I say.

He smiles weakly and shakes my hand like it's a dead fish. I pretend not to see him wipe his palm on his pants as he sits down. His hair dips perfectly above his brow, and his expensive smile reveals a row of perfectly straight teeth. Behind him, a bookshelf shows off dozens of awards. He follows my gaze to a trophy topped with a gold football player.

"Used to be the quarterback here back in my day. Now I'm the boss. Life is funny, isn't it?"

I nod. Yeah, life's a real kick in the pants.

"Well, Ava, we are so pleased you are joining our school community," he says.

His eyes search my face for a resting spot. Good luck, buddy. He settles on staring just to the left of my head, so he's not really looking at me but kind of, sort of seems like he is. He might get away with it, too, if it weren't a tactic used by basically everyone who has to talk to me. Not like I blame them: I can't even look at me.

"Now, we understand that you are not the typical student. We want you to know that anytime you need extra help or someone to talk to, we are here. We also have a full-time nurse available. She will handle your medications throughout the day."

My skin buzzes up my arms.

"I can't take my meds on my own?"

The vice principal leans his pockmarked face so close to mine that a fleck of his spit ricochets off my cheek.

"This may be hard to understand, but the best thing we can do for you is treat you like every other student," he says. "No special treatment. No special rules."

Unlike Mr. D, Vice Principal Lynch stares directly at me when he talks, and his eyes stay glued to me even when I turn back to the principal. Shameless staring. Unusual for an adult.

I'd say he's swerving into tough-love territory, which is usually reserved for people like Cora and the nurses in the burn unit, whose jobs or bloodlines require them to spend time with me. They develop a whole separate set of coping-with-Ava strategies.

"What Mr. Lynch means is we do have some legal criteria we have to meet. Students can't carry pills with them. You can understand that, right?"

I nod even though I want to scream. I take a ridiculous amount of medicine like clockwork. It's going to be hard to fade into the back row if I have to march out the front of the classroom every two hours.

"We're already into our second semester, but your teachers have all been informed about you. About your situation. What I'm trying to say is we've tried to prepare everyone." He ekes out a smile as he trips over his tongue. "Enough logistics, right? Let's talk about you. We hear you're a singer?"

I shake my head.

"Your aunt Cora—"

"Is wrong." Should have known Cora would already have been here, sprinkling her optimistic pixie dust. "I don't sing."

Mr. D looks from me to Mr. Lynch, probably searching for some other get-to-know-you small talk. He fails.

"Then I guess that's that. Do you have any questions?"

Only about a million. What if I can't do this? What if I'm not strong enough? How did I get here, with this face and your eyes looking through me and your hands wiping on your pants like I'm contagious?

I shake my head. Nope. No questions. At least, none you can answer.

Mr. Lynch points to the headphones around my neck. "Those will have to go in your bag until after the final bell."

I look from him to Mr. D, hoping for some sort of intervention, some exception to the no-exceptions rule. "They're just for the hallway. I won't use them in class."

Mr. Lynch shakes his head. "School rule."

Both men watch as I take the headphones off my neck, the slight lifting of weight off my skin making me feel instantly more exposed. A ball of panic rises in my throat as I stick them in my bag. How will I disappear now?

As they escort me from the office, Mr. D goes to pat my shoulder but changes his mind at the last second, his hand floating awkwardly in the air.

"Ava. The students have also been warned—told—they've been told about you. But your aunt suggested you might want to take a few minutes in each class to tell your peers about yourself. Meet this thing head-on."

This thing? My melted face? My messed-up life? What *thing* are we talking about here?

"Yeah, that's a definite no," I say.

I don't need people to understand me. I don't need to answer questions or make friends or be an inspirational mascot. All I need is to get through the next two weeks.

"Well, it's up to you," Mr. D says as the bell screeches overhead. Boisterous voices and bodies flood the hallway. "My door is always open. I like to think of myself as more of a friend than an administrator."

He shoots me a winning smile with his bleached-white teeth, and I can't help but picture the Viking at the front door.

"You're gonna love it here, Ava. I guarantee it."

Mr. Lynch offers no such encouraging words. He points to the clock on the wall.

"Class starts in five," he says. "Don't be late."

I hesitate on the threshold between the relative safety of the office and the melee of students quickly filling the hallway. The words *running the gauntlet* come to mind, conjuring up images of medieval Britain where criminals walked half-naked in a line, flanked by men with whips.

Facing the crowded corridor now, I'd prefer to take my chances with the British.

My new bestie, Big D, starts high-fiving hulking boy-men in letterman jackets. Mr. Lynch yells at a student to walk.

Clearly, Principal Danner is here to relive his teenage glory days. Mr. Lynch is here to avenge them.

Me? I just want to survive.

4

A group of boys sees me first.

A skinny one with zit-ridden skin jumps back with a "whoa." His buddies turn to me, then do an about-face to the lockers, doing a truly terrible job of hiding their laughter. They peek sideways at me with quick head jerks. Real supersleuths.

I sense eyes on me—a feeling I should be used to by now. Whispers and gasps are the background soundtrack to my life, but in this small hallway surrounded by kids my own age, the heat of so many eyes creeps up my neck. My legs and arms start to itch as the familiar buzzing spreads through my body. My face burns as I cast my eyes to the ground.

Don't look up.

I force myself not to react, even when I hear a group of girls break into nervous giggles and whispers, followed by "Shhhhh . . . shhhh . . . stop. She's coming."

A girl at her locker pretends to look past me as she takes

hurried glances at where my ear should be. I tug my bandana tighter so she can't see there's no left ear left, just a canal hole and a lobe remnant whose survival defies explanation.

I tilt my head back to restrain the building tears. Thanks to the contracting of my cheek scars, my bottom eyelids are more like busted levies, barely able to hold back the slightest moisture.

But I will not cry. Not here.

I try to calm my racing heart as I continue down the hallway, reminding myself that I don't need these people any more than they need me. I force my head higher, but what I really want is to crawl into one of these lockers to escape all the eyes. Their stares tell me I'm different, sure, but they reveal an even deeper truth: I'm less.

Something to be looked at, not talked to.

This is why I don't need mirrors; I can see my reflection in the eyes of everyone around me.

My face always finds me.

I pretend not to notice the group of boys elbowing each other or the fact that everyone else squishes together on the other side of the hallway. Without my headphones to soundproof me, I act like I don't hear the whispers behind cupped hands.

Through the din of lockers and feet and chatter, my good ear picks up the words I'm not meant to hear:

Burned.

Fire.

New.

Gross.

Zombie.

A white-hot pain shoots to the tips of my fingers, and I realize I've been death-gripping the strap of my bag with my good hand. I stretch my palm, flexing my stiff skin.

I make it to my first class, exhaling the air I've been storing since I left the office. One hallway down!

Only ten days to go.

I slink to a seat in the back row. This is my plan: Stay in the shadows. Get through today.

The earth science teacher is a large man with an even larger bushy black beard. He strides into the room and drops a pile of books on the front table. When he scans the room, he does a double take at me. So much for Big D's warnings.

He starts talking, but the damage is done. His brief pause in my direction gives my classmates permission to turn and look. I sink lower in my seat.

When I was a little kid, I could summon an invisibility cloak by closing my eyes. My parents would play along as I yelled, "You can't see me!" Mom would walk right next to me, saying, "Where's Ava?" and Dad would bump into me, crying, "Oh no! We've lost her forever."

I could use those toddler superpowers today.

I remind myself that today is the worst day—it has to be, right? Everyone has to see me for the first time. And in two weeks, it will be over. Cora can check off my good-faith recovery effort in her binder, and I can retreat to the solace of a bedroom without mirrors or prying eyes to remind me what I am.

The bearded teacher scrawls the word *life* on a whiteboard.

"Today, we start a new unit." He underlines the word emphatically. "Together, we will plumb the depths of what it means to be alive. We will study the living world around us and the world within us."

He tells us we're having an assessment quiz and gives a boy in the front row a bunch of papers to hand out to the class. When the boy gets close to me, he hesitates, holding the sheets tentatively, like he's offering a bunny carcass to a rabid dog.

A squeaking, strangulated sound escapes from his throat when I reach out my left hand without thinking. His eyes lock on my fused flipper fingers and my prominent "thumb," which dwarfs the rest of my hand because it belongs on my foot and not here in the open, freaking out the villagers.

I quickly flop my Frankenhand back to my lap, horrified. The boy half chucks a quiz at me, recoiling quickly.

He speeds back to his desk, and I pick up the paper from the floor, trying to ignore his wide-eyed glances that make me feel distinctly subhuman.

Perhaps I should make a public service announcement? DON'T WORRY, FOLKS! UGLY'S NOT CATCHING TODAY!

That's when I notice another boy next to me, staring with reckless abandon at the disproportionately huge toe-thumb in my lap. I push my hand into my pocket and train my eyes back on my desk. He screeches his desk closer to mine.

"Is that your toe?" he whispers.

I ignore him.

"Hey!" he says a little louder. "Is it?"

I thrust my shoulder forward so he knows my hearing isn't the problem. If talking to other people was part of my survival plan, I would tell him to go away.

Instead, I pretend this assessment is one thousand times more interesting than it actually is and seriously consider rescuing my headphones from my bag so this kid will stop trying to strike up a convo. My fingers move upward in a habit I can't seem to break, searching for my hair to twist around my finger.

"Good talk, good talk," he says.

I shrink further into my paper. He hesitates for a second before inching back to his row.

I sneak a sideways glance in his direction. His eyes are on his paper now, allowing me to see he's a small kid with warm brown skin. The black curtain of his hair flips up, and his dark eyes meet mine before I can turn away. He gives me a thumbs-up, and I'm not sure if he means it as a cruel joke or some outdated symbol of camaraderie.

I flick my eyes away.

I tick through the normal reactions: Shameless staring? Not really. Not in a gawking, don't-tap-on-the-glass kind of way. He's borderline frantic friendliness with his excitement over my toe-hand, but that's still not it. Not pity. *Definitely* not like I'm invisible.

I scribble in the corner of my notebook, trying to label this boy's reaction.

~~Nosy~~
~~Curious~~

Clueless curiosity

The boy waves at me like we're old friends when the bell rings, so I shoot him my best "What's your problem?" stare. He smiles back. Clueless it is.

This kid has no clue how he's supposed to act around me. Because no matter what reaction people have, there is always one common thread:

1. Everyone looks at me.
2. Then everyone looks away.

Until now.

5

I employ my best covert-ops tactics to make it through the rest of the day. I skulk along locker walls, looking down at my phone, pretending to be super interested in the texts Cora sends every thirty minutes to make sure I'm okay. In each class, I retreat to the back row and basically try to dissolve into Crossroads High.

When I walk past the gym and see the girls in shorts, I'm extra grateful Cora negotiated my way out of phys ed so a coach with a whistle and the power to make my life miserable can't make me "suit up." My compression garments don't really make me a candidate for running/jumping/throwing, plus there's the whole my-sweat-glands-burned-off thing. But mostly, there is absolutely no way I'm going to disrobe in a locker room full of high school girls whose big body-image issues include whether their boobs and thigh dimples are the right size.

Luckily, even though it's the middle of the semester, I'm not too lost in my classes since I've been working at least a year ahead online.

But after each class, I face the hallway again. A group of girls walk by, all talking at the same time, reminding me of the friends I left behind. Like a flock, the five of us would fall into formation—Emma walking backward, gesturing wildly, regaling us with a story about the latest senior boy in her chem class who she was 100 percent positive brushed her hand on purpose. Stacy always text-walked next to her, head bent over her phone, thumbs flying, while Blake came a few steps behind with her nose buried in flash cards, stressing about a test or a Spanish oral. Chloe and I walked in the middle, Chloe's huge hair and even bigger laugh filling the space around us.

We belonged to each other.

We had a pattern.

I had a place.

At lunchtime, I take one look at the hordes of hungry students barreling into the cafeteria and head the other way. Even with a normal face, walking into a high school cafeteria is like infiltrating a lion's den.

No place for an already-wounded straggler.

I consider going full-throttle pathetic and eating in a bathroom stall, but a sign with an arrow to the auditorium changes my mind. At the end of a long hallway, I poke my head through a pair of double doors into a silent, darkened theater with rows and rows of cushioned seats and a stage curtain drawn tight.

Down the next hall, I find a smaller, second door leading

backstage. A maze of thick curtains leads me past a costume closet and a single mirrored vanity until I find a dark corner concealed by black fabric.

I tuck myself against the wall. I peek under the gap below the curtains and see three pairs of combat boots huddled together on the far side of the stage. Judging by the draft and the odor, they belong to some students taking a lunchtime vape break by an open backstage door. But thanks to the thick curtains, they have no idea I'm here.

Invisible at last.

I balance my paper bag on my legs, inhaling my turkey sandwich along with the burned popcorn vapor from my backstage-hideout compadres.

Cradled in the corner of the stage, I feel safer than I have all day. In a former life, Chloe and the rest of my flock would be here, too, laughing about Emma's latest crush and taking turns running lines for our next musical.

No matter what, we had the stage—and each other.

I take out my phone to read the latest text from Cora.

All OK?

I send her a GIF of a Viking giving a thumbs-up.

Then I put on my headphones, dial my own number, and listen to the message I've heard a thousand times. Mom's voice cuts through the loneliness—just slightly, but enough.

"I'm at the store, honey, and I can't remember if you like the deodorant with the pink flowers or the cucumbers. Call me back. Love you."

Okay, so it's not some deep, existential message from beyond the grave or anything, but I'll take it. The only other remnant I have of my parents is a half-burned chunk of metal that used to be one of my mom's handbells.

I listen to the message again, relishing this moment alone. Only nine and a half more days.

I rest my head back on the wall and stretch my tired legs out straight under the black curtain in front of me.

But my solitude is short-lived, as a gaggle of girls files in. Instinctively, I scrunch my feet back so they won't know I'm here.

Through the slit between the curtains, I spy three girls huddling around the backstage vanity, all trying to see themselves at once. Another girl opens the costume closet, digging through a pile of brightly colored fabrics.

Afraid they'll spot me, I pull my knees into my chest, wincing as the skin stretches tight. A month ago, Dr. Sharp cut Zorro-style slices in my knees to help them move better, but the skin still feels like someone shrank it two sizes in the dryer. I ignore the pain and hug my legs tighter.

The mirror trio lay out the contents of a pink makeup bag on the small table below the glass. An arsenal of eyeliner and concealer stands ready to jump into action, as if the girls are about to perform open-heart surgery with blush and lipstick.

The girl in the middle brushes her long, black hair. Her voice echoes around the stage.

"Did you see it?"

"Be nice, Kenzie," a girl calls out from the costume closet. "It's a *she*, by the way, not an *it*."

"I know it's a girl, dummy. I meant have you seen *it*—her face? I caught a glimpse, just for a second, but believe me, it was more than enough."

"Is it really *that* bad?" She slams the closet shut, so I can't hear the answer, only the last two words.

". . . Freddy Krueger."

The girl who said it pauses to blot her hot-pink lips.

"I'm not being mean, you guys. It was shocking. Not like I'd say it to her face or anything, but can you imagine going to high school looking like *that*?"

Another girl swirls a brush of powder around her forehead.

"I skipped school two days last week for a zit. If I looked like that, I'd crawl into a hole and never come out."

The girls nod as they pack their tools back into their bag. Through the curtain gap, I watch them give themselves a final, affirming glance in the glass.

Smooth hair: check. Quick glance at their butts: check. Lean in for spinach-in-the-teeth investigation: check. Girls like that never have dental meal remnants. Karma is too kind.

They're on their way offstage when my phone vibrates loudly with another Cora text. The girl who called me Freddy Krueger stops and turns, and for a split second, her eyes catch mine through the slit. I tug my legs closer as she whips her long black hair around, with her finger pressed to her lips.

37

"Guys." She points in my direction as she whispers. "We're not alone."

My knees protest as I pull them all the way to my chest, praying she leaves. This can't be how they find me, the weirdo going all *Phantom of the Opera* on my first "normal" day.

The "it" hiding backstage.

The girl's black hair fills my line of vision through the gap as she walks toward me.

"Hey, who's back there? It's not nice to eavesdrop."

I bite my lip as my knee splits open. Blood soaks through my pants.

Please. Not like this.

"Let it go, Kenz. It's probably some terrified freshman."

Yes. Let it go. Let *me* go.

Her footsteps stop right in front of me, her shoes nearly touching mine beneath the black divide. She grips the curtain, sending ripples across my fabric shield, and I watch helplessly as she yanks it away.

6

The girl pulls the curtain all the way back, revealing me, my legs pulled tight against my chest, my face no doubt as surprised as hers.

"Oh," she says, covering her mouth. "We didn't know it was you."

I continue to hold my legs, mostly because I don't know what else to do. Walk out like it's totally normal that I was back here, desperately trying to disappear into the wall?

I look away from her, tilting my head too late. A few tears burst the bounds of my droopy eyes, making this pathetic moment even more hideous.

The girl with black hair lets the curtain fall back between us. I hear them confer with each other, half whispering, half giggling in a choppy, nervous way.

"You say it," one girl whispers, prompting another one to yell, "Sorry. Welcome to Crossroads High!"

They scurry off the stage like it's on fire. I wait until their laughter and footsteps fade before lowering my legs.

My right knee screams at me as I pull back my compression garments. Blood outlines the baby-pink square of skin covering my joint. Dr. Sharp will not be happy I busted up his handiwork.

The bell rings, but I stay put, soaking up the blood with my brown paper sack. I wait until halfway through the next class period to emerge from my hole. When I do, I peek around the curtain first before venturing out. I pick up a stick of forgotten lip gloss on the vanity, a shiny pink shade just like one I used to wear.

In the mirror, my reflection gawks back. My tightened skin tugs down my bottom eyelids, revealing so much pink moistness that my eyes look like they're threatening to turn inside out. Cora says it gives me an endearing puppy-dog look. I think it makes me look like an extra on *The Walking Dead*.

I push up my drooping eyelids with my fingers.

Those girls have no idea that I used to be a normal girl with friends, and eyeliner in a pencil bag, who reapplied lip gloss between classes and covered my sun-induced freckles with foundation. They mocked me without even meeting me.

If my life were a Greek tragedy, I would have been a major mean girl in my life before the fire. At least then I'd learn some poetic lesson about kindness in a classic cosmic twist.

But I wasn't a mean girl. I was a normal fifteen-year-old who went to football games on weekends and spent way too much time rehearsing for the spring musical. I was a daughter. A friend. A brunette. A singer.

I was a million things.

I release my eyes and fade back into the scars.

Now, I'm only one thing—the Burned Girl.

And between this backstage diva blitz and back-row Captain Clueless in science, I may have seriously miscalculated my ability to disappear.

———

By the time Uncle Glenn picks me up at the end of the day, my body aches from my full day of "being normal." My beleaguered muscles scream at me as I climb into his truck.

"So how was it?" he asks, chipper to the max. Aunt Cora probably coached him on how to keep upbeat about my foray into normalcy.

"Fine."

"Make any friends?"

"Loads. I'll probably have to hold auditions."

Glenn smiles and puts his hand on my arm. "That bad, huh?"

I slouch in my seat as we drive past a row of jocks flirting with field hockey skirts. Glenn and I both pretend not to see them turn to look as we pass.

"It's whatever." I shrug. "It's high school. I'm just ready to go home."

I use the term loosely, of course. My real home would be a place I could retreat after a day like today. I'd turn the corner onto our street and enter my own little refuge. Just Dad and Mom and me, and the calming assurance that I don't have to be anything or anyone else.

"I'm sure you are," Glenn says. "I hate to remind you, but the support group is today."

Groan. I forgot about that little stipulation Cora sneaked in as part of my return-to-life extravaganza.

"Are you really making me do that?"

"Cora feels strongly about it. Says you need support during your reintegration."

The word sounds foreign coming from Glenn, who generally steers clear of therapy talk. He's a member of the Committee on Ava's Life and all, but Cora holds most of the executive power while Glenn mostly represents the actual bloodline.

"Whoa, someone's been learning the lingo," I say. "Cora giving you extra credit for reading the recovery binder?"

Glenn's hearty laugh fills the cab of his truck.

"I know Cora can be a little much—"

"A little?"

"Okay, a lot much, but you have to understand she couldn't—" His voice breaks for a split second. I look out the window, pushing down the guilt. "She couldn't save Sara. So she'll be damned if she lets anything happen to you."

Snow flurries flit by outside. A single white seagull circles aimlessly like it missed the migration memo, the pure white peaks of the Wasatch Range towering behind it.

Glenn pats my leg as we roll to a stop at the light.

"Whaddya say, kiddo? Give it a chance?" He looks at me so earnestly, my mom's nose making me wish I were driving home with her, heading to my regular life, where reintegration and headshrinkers didn't exist. "You know Dr. Layne only wants to help."

Dr. Layne also holds a seat on the committee as my psychologist during the sixty days I spent at the regional burn unit. Sixty days for 60 percent of my body covered in burns, not counting the almost two months I spent comafied, sleeping while doctors salvaged what was left of me.

Dr. Layne has tried to coax me back to her support group ever since I left the unit eight months ago. I've avoided it mostly because I didn't want to disappoint her again. Everyone was always barfing up their childhood sadness, having these emotional breakthroughs and breakdowns, but I couldn't seem to reach any sort of epiphany.

Plus, the whole point of therapy is to pinpoint the pain, dissect it and stick it under a microscope.

Why would I want to feel the hurt more clearly?

Forgetting is no accident—it's survival.

"It happened. It's over," I say. "Swapping woe-is-me stories with a bunch of other weirdos won't undo the past."

"You're not a weirdo." Glenn glances at me sideways as he drives. "You know the most basic cowboy rule? If you get thrown from a horse—"

I complete the well-worn adage often used in our family: "You get back on."

Glenn nods. "Unless you land in a cactus. Then you have to roll around and scream in pain for a bit. I hope you know, kiddo, that's okay, too."

Right. Like my having a total breakdown wouldn't disrupt the unspoken truce Glenn, Cora, and I have developed over the past year. Cora cries behind closed doors. Glenn buries himself in work. I tiptoe in Sara's shadow.

We're constantly fine-tuning the arrangement, but it boils down to this: we all have grief—no need to share.

When the light turns green, Glenn turns left, which means he's headed to the community center. The committee has spoken.

"Where is Cora, anyway?" I ask.

It's not like Cora to miss a big "recovery moment." I would've expected her to meet me at curbside pickup with pom-poms and a cheer about getting psyched for psychotherapy! Rah-rah, sis-boom-bah.

"She wanted to be here, but she got that second interview at Smith's," Glenn says, his voice artificially happy about the possibility of Cora managing a grocery store. I sink into my seat.

"Oh."

Glenn's fingers grip the steering well, his nail beds stained oil black from the auto body shop he owns. He's been coming home later and later, and now Cora's super pumped about this grocery gig because she says she "needs a new project." I'm not buying it. Before I got here, Cora never worked and they still had plenty of money for vacations and dance camps and anything Sara wanted.

But nineteen surgeries put an end to that. A bunch of people from my old town even ran a big fund-raiser after the fire, but it's clearly not enough. Through their closed bedroom door, they talk in low voices about depleted life insurance policies, and Cora argues on the phone about copays and deductibles.

Tragedy isn't cheap.

Glenn puts his right hand in his lap when he catches me staring at his overworked nail beds.

"Oh, Cora says to tell you there's a girl in the group from your school. Your age and everything."

Classic Cora. As if finding a friend can make all my problems disappear. I agreed to move to this stupid town because I don't want friends. I saw the way my old friends looked at me in the hospital, like they didn't even know who I was. I kept waiting for Chloe's deep belly laugh, or for Emma to gush about a new boy. But they all just kept staring at me, trying not to cry. I knew right then that our familiar flock would never be the same. I was too different, from them and from who I used to be.

They tried to contact me after I moved, Chloe especially, but I never responded. No one needed me around making them uncomfortable. It's better this way—they don't have to deal with me, and I don't have to watch them try.

So I'm not in the market for replacement friends or a replacement life.

Besides, Sara was my cousin—my closest lifelong friend—and she's gone.

I lived. She died.

End of story.

"I don't need friends. How many times do I have to say it? I don't need anyone."

Glenn pats me on the knee again and reassures me that this group may be exactly what I need. He smiles that crooked smile, hopeful this support group will heal me—body and soul.

I just hope they have refreshments.

7

The instant I walk into the community center rec room, Dr. Layne wraps me in a hug.

"I'm so glad you came," she says.

"Cora and Glenn made me," I say, trying to keep her expectations low.

Guilt needles me for wasting her time—again. Of all the headshrinkers who tried to fix me with their clickity-clack pens and legal pads, Dr. Layne actually seemed to care about me beyond our thirty-minute sessions. Maybe because she's lived it. She's a makeup wizard, though, so the burned side of her face looks like nothing more than a rough swath of skin. Her scars pull her mouth a little tight in one corner and crisscross down her arms, but other than that, she looks and acts normal. Two kids. Husband. Career.

I'm sure Cora hopes Dr. Layne will sprinkle some of her magical recovery dust on me.

I pick a spot in a circle of chairs in the middle of the room, which is an overwhelmingly vast space with a noncommittal vibe that works as well for a group of burn victims as it does for senior bingo night. Only two other kids populate the therapy ring of awkwardness. A boy who looks like he might be a senior sits with his arms folded across his chest—one arm appears normal, and one with wrinkled burn scars culminates in a club for a hand. A girl on the opposite end picks at her dress. If she has any scars, I can't see them.

After four months in a burn unit, I've become quite the skin reader. I can't tell anything about the scarless girl, but I'm guessing the boy was holding some sort of explosive device, since his face and right arm have the worst scars, and because his hand no longer exists.

The girl and boy try to read the story of my scars, their eyes widening. Winner! I'm the freakiest freak of them all.

My scar story goes like this: The ceiling collapsed before my dad pushed me out the window, so my face, scalp, arms, and upper back got the brunt of it. My legs are a mixed bag: knees and calves are burned, thighs are not, thanks to the shorts I was wearing, and my Ugg slippers saved my feet. My pajama top also kept the middle of me—stomach, boobs, lower back—relatively unscathed.

Of course, harvesting skin for grafts mucked up my unburned areas, and then we plucked off my big toe for my hand, so now there's really no part of me the fire didn't claim. (By the way, *harvesting* is not *my* word, it's a doctor's word that makes me feel like

I was abducted and probed by aliens. Like I need to feel any more extraterrestrial.)

Sometimes I fantasize about Dr. Sharp *actually* fixing me one day. I've even collected pictures and articles about surgeries like eyebrow implants and ear prosthetics and water balloons beneath the scalp to stretch the non-bald skin.

Of course, my drooping eyes are first on my to-do list of fantasy surgeries that will never actually happen. Insurance companies aren't too fond of coughing up cash for co$metic $urgery. Plus, after my toe-to-hand transfer, we decided to take a surgery hiatus. Give my body and Glenn's bank account a breather.

Honestly, I've enjoyed the respite from the never-ending cycle of surgeries and skin grafts and waking up mummified every few weeks, always believing when we peeled off the thin white gauze, I'd be me again.

Hope is exhausting.

Dr. Layne stands in the middle of the circle, appropriately dressed in the psychologist uniform of a pencil skirt and a capped-sleeve blouse I wouldn't dream of wearing with the way it showcases her scars. She's halfway through a formal welcome when the double doors swing open and a girl in a wheelchair maneuvers through.

"Pardon the interruption!" Her voice echoes through the vast room.

Her brown hair swishes from a high ponytail, revealing some serious burnage on her neck. The deep-purple discoloration reaches toward her face, stopping just shy of her chin. A hot-pink-striped sleeve covers her right arm, and it takes me a beat to realize it's her compression garments.

The stripes continue down her right leg. A cast—also hot pink and signature-free—encases her left. She's like the love child of a zebra and a psychedelic clown.

She wheels herself into the circle.

"Wait a second." She looks around at each of us. "I'm beginning to think this *isn't* the cross-country tryouts."

I try to turn my chuckle into a cough when I notice no one else finds this funny. The girl smiles at me, though, while Dr. Layne smiles patiently at her.

"We were just about to do introductions. Piper, why don't you start us off."

The girl straightens up in her wheelchair.

"I'm Piper. Car accident six weeks ago, on New Year's Eve. Mostly deep second-degree on my right side. All sorts of bones in my leg shattered." She taps the pink cast. "Have a touch of spinal injury, so the wheelchair is temporary, knock on wood. Scars are here to stay.

"What else, what else?" She strokes her chin. "Oh, I like long wheelchair rides on the beach, and I'm a Taurus."

The boy goes next but can't finish because he starts crying. Something about a campfire and an exploding gas can. Called it.

The girl with no burns talks for a full ten minutes about her invisible injuries from a propane-leak flash fire when she was a baby. What could she still have to talk about?

Hearing everyone swap burn stories morphs me back to the

unit, where patients wear percentages and burn degrees like badges of honor.

I'm 60 percent mostly third-degree burns, which are the nasty buggers that devour every layer of skin, taking everything along the way—hair follicles, sweat glands, fat cells, and nerves. My hands achieved fourth-degree status when the flames reached all the way to my bones. I had a bunch of second-degree wounds, too, but those are kind of a joke among burn circles. They're red and oozy and impressive, but they mostly only eat away the top layer of skin.

The funny thing is those shallow burns hurt like a mother when they're fresh, but the deeper ones you don't even feel. Nothing left to feel with no nerve endings. For these burns, the real pain doesn't start until later, with the skin grafts and the cleanings and the nurses ripping off gauzy skin with tweezers.

When a wound's that deep, it's the healing that hurts.

I realize everyone in the circle is looking at me.

"What am I supposed to say, again?"

"Something about yourself. It's up to you how much and what to share," Dr. Layne reminds me.

Heat prickles up my neck. All the eyes in the circle wait to hear the details of my scartastic tapestry.

"My name is Ava. I moved here recently from central Utah. I guess I'm a student at Crossroads High now, and I'm a junior."

They wait for more, and when I deliver only silence, all eyes turn to Dr. Layne. Pink Zebra Girl speaks first.

"Ummm . . . aren't you going to tell us about your scars?"

Dr. Layne interjects.

"Piper. We've talked about this before."

"I think she knows she's burned, Dr. L." She turns to me with her hand over her mouth in mock surprise. "Oh my gosh . . . did I totally just let the cat out of the bag?"

"Piper! Enough!" Dr. Layne says sharply, smacking her hand on her clipboard. "Over the next few months, you are going to all share as much or as little about your stories as you are comfortable with telling. There will be no right amount, and no right answers."

Her gaze lingers on the girl in the wheelchair, who smiles back innocently. Dr. Layne proceeds to tell us how we will focus each week on a new element of empowerment.

"Today, let's briefly discuss the power of words," she says. "Words have power because we give them meaning. *Hate. Love. Hope. Anger.*" She turns to us. "Let's start with some of the words that describe you. Which ones stick out?"

Crickets chirp as she scans the circle. Even scar-free Chatty McChatterson is quiet.

Dr. Layne seems pleasantly surprised when I raise my hand.

"A girl called me Freddy Krueger today," I say.

Piper chuckles next to me. "Oooh . . . good burn."

Dr. Layne narrows her eyes at Piper but directs her words to me.

"Names are indeed a type of word, but today let's discuss the words we use to describe ourselves."

She turns to the whiteboard behind her and writes the word *VICTIM.*

"How does this word make you feel?"

"Hurt," the girl with no scars says.

The boy adds: "Hopeless."

Dr. Layne writes again: *SURVIVOR.*

"How about this one?"

The boy volunteers: "Hopeful."

"This week, pay attention to how you talk about yourself. Use words that give you power rather than strip it away."

She writes some other examples on the board for us to ponder—*ugly, disabled, burned, beautiful, weak, strong, healing*—then gives us each a marbled composition notebook.

"Write about anything you don't feel like sharing out loud. The most important thing is *you* are in control. You can't change what happened to you, but you can take control of your story. Your lives have changed. My goal is to help you find a new normal."

Dr. Layne releases us to the refreshment table after more details about support-group etiquette. How this is a safe place. Why talking about our trauma is so important. The usual mumbo jumbo.

Piper scoots her wheelchair up to me at the refreshment table.

"First group?"

I shake my head. "Nah, wrong room. Thought this was the modeling callbacks."

Piper's laugh fills the empty space.

"Uh-oh. Don't let Laynie hear you cracking jokes." She slaps on a somber face. "This is serious business. This is burn-survivor therapy, or as I like to call it, BS therapy."

Piper fills a plate in her lap with cookies.

"So I take it you've done this before?" I ask.

"Yep, bona fide support groupie. My parents are happy as long as they think I'm 'making progress.'" She puts air quotes around the last two words.

She reaches for a cup but can't grab it from her chair. I hand it to her, and when my fingers touch hers, she doesn't flinch.

"Thanks. So, fellow Crossroader, huh?" she says. It hits me that this is the girl Glenn mentioned, the one Cora thinks will be my insta-BFF.

"Sort of. First day today."

"Oh man, with that mug, I can only imagine. How rough was it?"

I think of the looks, the whispers, the boy throwing a pencil at me like he'd seen a ghost.

"Brutal."

Piper pops a cookie in her mouth and talks while chewing.

"Yeah, we're not too good with outsiders. You've seen the mascot, right? The xenophobic Viking with anger issues?"

I nod. "He's hard to miss. But I won't be there long. Kind of a temporary trial run on life situation. After two weeks, everyone can forget I even exist."

Piper cocks her head sideways, her lips stuck out in a mock pout.

"Well, that's about the most pathetic thing I've ever heard." She pulls out her phone—hot pink like her stripes. "Okay, since *I* know you exist now, what's your handle?"

"Don't have one."

"I'm sorry, what kind of person isn't on social media?"

"Hate to bring attention to the charbroiled elephant in the room, but—" I point to my face. "The kind of person who has no business plastering pics online."

Piper puts her phone in her lap and folds her arms, looking me up and down.

"I'd like to revise my earlier statement. *That* is the most pathetic thing I've ever heard."

"Hey, this is therapy. No judging the depths of my patheticness," I say.

Piper smiles. "Touché. Well, your lack of social media savvy aside, I, for one, am glad you graced us with your pathetic presence today, Ava."

She crumples her napkin into a ball, tosses it into the air, then smacks it midfall with a quick flick of her wrist, sending it sailing through the air into a trash barrel.

"Ace!" She turns to me. "So, you free after group?"

"For what?"

"To hang out," she says, as if we've already synced our calendars.

I search her face for an explanation.

"Did Dr. Layne tell you to be my friend?" I say.

That's exactly the kind of thing the committee would do. Cora and Dr. Layne probably had a powwow about my social status, and this wild-eyed girl in her hot-pink compression garments is the best they could come up with.

Piper holds up her hands.

"Wow, defensive much? No, she did not, and I wouldn't have

done it even if she did," Piper says. "Jump all over me for trying to be burn buddies."

"I don't need buddies," I say. "I'm only here for two weeks."

Piper considers this for a second and then leans toward me.

"I don't care if it's two weeks or four years, no one survives high school alone."

The late-afternoon sun streams through the rec room in slanted polygons, bouncing off Piper's bright garments and a small, golden bird charm around her neck. I recognize it immediately—a phoenix, the mythical bird that rises from the ashes of the fire unblemished.

"You swear this isn't some rigged charity mission? Because I do *not* need it."

Piper puts one hand over her heart and holds up her other hand with four fingers separated in the middle to make the *Star Trek* Vulcan salute.

"Scout's honor—"

I think about today, those girls finding me alone backstage, the hallways parting before me like a leprotic modern-day Moses, that clueless kid staring at my toe-thumb.

Maybe a friend isn't the committee's worst idea.

"Yeah," I say. "I'm free."

Piper smiles and raises her fruit punch cup high in the air toward me.

"To finding a new normal!" She taps her cup to mine. "Whatever the hell that means."

8

Cora practically wets herself when she hears I'm bringing home a friend. She tries to cram in a few minutes of bonding/interrogation time before Piper's mom drops her off.

"I want to hear everything," she says, patting the sofa cushion next to her.

She wants me to plunk down and tell her all about my new life, but I'm too drained from a full day of pretending to be stronger than I feel to dish out a play-by-play. If she were my mom, I'd plop next to her, inhale her vanilla-bean scent as she stroked my hair, and tell her every detail. Sara probably would have done the same.

"Come on," Cora prods. "About school. Group. Everything."

"All fine," I say.

"I've been dying all day to hear what happened."

"Let's see. Principal is a jock. Most of the kids are jerks. And I am a joke."

Cora frowns. "I'm sure they weren't *all* jerks. What about this girl who's coming over? She had a car accident, right?"

"Yeah."

"Well, is she nice?"

"She's weird."

"Nice weird?"

"Weird weird."

Cora studies me from the couch, her aggressive optimism rippling out in irritatingly hopeful waves. I duck into the kitchen to avoid exposure.

She talks louder. "So do you think you'll stay?"

"Too early to know."

"When will you know?"

"If it stops sucking, I'll know."

Cora intercepts me on my way back to my room and wraps me in a soft hug. When she steps back, her eyes glisten.

"You are an inspiration, Ava. A survivor, through and through."

A knock on the door announces Piper, and I extricate myself from Cora's embrace.

"So everyone keeps telling me."

———

Glenn helps Piper's wheelchair over the front step. Inside, he stops, evaluating the long staircase up to my bedroom.

Piper shifts in her chair with a weak smile. "No worries. I'm a first-floor kind of person anyway."

Glenn's eyebrows inch together as he shakes his head.

"Oh, I'll get you there." He studies the stairs and then Piper again. "Okay if I lift you?"

She nods, and he reaches out his arms to hoist Piper out of her chair, her hot-pink cast dangling in the air. He carries her up, one arm under her knees and one around her back like he used to do with me at first, when those stairs might as well have been Mount Everest.

I carry Piper's chair up behind them, and Glenn places her back in it inside my room.

"What in the name of Ken and Barbie?" Piper says before Glenn even shuts the door all the way. Sara's insanely large doll collection looms in front of us in tall, glass-front cases.

"They belong to my cousin," I say.

Piper tries to pry open one of the cabinets, but it's locked tight.

"Why doesn't your cousin keep them in her room?"

"This *is* Sara's room. Was Sara's room. She died in the fire."

Piper stops trying to infiltrate the doll display. She picks up a pointe shoe.

"Is *all* this stuff hers?"

Sara's old things fill the room: the quilt with bright yellow daisies, the corner shelf with pictures of her dance troupes, the box of pointe shoes.

"A lot of it is." I grab the shoe and put it back on the shrine. "It's fine. All my stuff burned up anyway."

Piper picks at a strip of faded butterfly wallpaper trim that runs through the middle of the wall.

"You should at least repaint or something. Otherwise, you're just living in a dead girl's room."

I shrug. Most of the time, I don't mind living in a makeshift mausoleum because my own room is gone and this one holds the memories the fire didn't take. The bed we squeezed into for our monthly cousin sleepovers. The desk where Sara tried in vain to teach me makeup contouring. The butterfly wallpaper where we wrote our initials teeny-tiny beneath a purple wing.

Piper points to a frame with a picture of Sara in a dance skirt, her hands lifted gracefully over her head.

"This her?"

"Yeah."

"Pretty."

In the picture, Sara's long blond hair sweeps over her petite, Cora-esque body. She was the kind of girl who was so pretty you wanted to hate her but was so nice you couldn't. We were different as Country Barbie and City Barbie (as Glenn used to call us), but we were bound by one thing: our love of performing. As kids, every summer, I'd fumble through dance camp with her; she'd tolerate drama camp for me. I'd always be in the front row at her ballets, and she'd be the first one on her feet on my opening nights.

Piper points to a wall-size poster of *Hairspray* Cora found at a garage sale.

"Yours or hers?"

"Mine. I guess. I used to be into singing and musicals and all that."

I say this like it's no big deal, like my parents weren't grade A theater junkies who raised me on a steady diet of Broadway.

But that was another lifetime, one where spontaneous choreographed dances and happy endings seemed not only plausible but likely.

At some point, you realize life is *not* a musical.

"Yours or hers?" Piper says, picking up the charred handbell I keep on my dresser. The once-shiny surface is all greenish black on one side, but it was the only thing at "the site" worth salvaging, according to Glenn. I'm all too happy to take his word for it, since seeing my house in ashes is pretty low on my to-do list.

"My mom's," I say. "So yeah, mine now."

Piper puts it down to pick up a picture. Mom has her arms around me on the stage in my lopsided Rizzo wig and Pink Ladies jacket, while Dad gives a dorky thumbs-up trying to act like one of the leather-clad cool kids from our production of *Grease*.

"Your parents died, too?" Piper says.

She looks at me expectantly. I never know what people want me to say. That being an orphan sucks? That no one will ever love me like my parents did, without limits or fine print? That they left me adrift—untethered, unanchored? I cross my legs on the bed, with my pillow bunched up on my lap.

"I really don't want to talk about it."

Piper puts down the picture among all the other framed memories I'm trying to forget.

"Noted," Piper says. "Kind of picked up that vibe at group. I have to warn you, though, Layne has ways of getting you to talk."

She strums her fingers together like an evil genius. "Let us help you, Ava. Let us heal you."

She picks up the therapy notebook on my desk.

"Trust me: the best way to get through these survivor powwows it is to play nice, say the right things, and look like you're having some major breakthrough every few weeks." She flaps the notebook at me. "And fill this up with all sorts of gobbledygook about your inner feelings or Layne's gonna make you do one-on-ones."

"What do I write about?"

"Anything. I write lots of lists and poetry because they take up more pages, not to mention I get bonus therapy points because Layne thinks I'm using art to 'process' what happened."

"What *did* happen?"

"Drunk driving. Well, technically, drunk passengering."

"Who was driving?"

"Someone else." Piper picks up another frame and spins around toward me.

"Were you at Regional? Me too!"

A chorus line of nurses and doctors and Cora and Glenn stand with me in the hospital on the day I left the burn unit.

"Terry the Torturer!" Piper shouts. "That guy was a total sadist."

Terry (who is technically a physical therapist) has his arm around me in the picture. He used to come in with all his medieval torture devices to make sure I didn't heal like a human Shrinky Dink. He'd strap my arms into "the airplane," splaying me out like a taxidermied pheasant in flight.

"PT: pure torture," I say.

Piper tosses the frame into my lap. "Well, you look pretty happy here."

In the picture, I'm smiling huge. I was leaving after more than four months of imprisonment. No more dressing changes in "the tank," where nurses pried off my dead skin. No more screams in the hallways. No more Nickelodeon on loop. No more poking and prodding. I was going home.

Turned out home was as unrecognizable as my face.

"I was an idiot," I say.

I hold up both pictures—the one of me encircled by my parents, and the one of me surrounded by professionals trained to keep me alive.

"Ava Before the Fire, and Ava After the Fire." I look at me on the stage as a normal teenager. "I don't even know this girl anymore."

Piper nods.

"One second you're loving life, and then you cross a little yellow line on the road and *bam!*" Piper slams her palms together. "Goodbye, walking."

"Or an electrician puts a faulty wire in your wall before you're born and sixteen years later, your life burns down."

I lie back on my pillow and swat at the Native American dream catcher I hung above my bed a few months back.

Piper nods to the round web of string and feathers tasked with catching all my nightmares. "Bad dreams?"

"Yeah."

"Me too. Dumb stuff like crashing on my bike. Layne says it's my brain's way of working out trauma in a familiar context, or some psychobabble."

"Yeah, I get those." I fail to mention that I also dream I'm facing down the flames again. I feel the heat. Taste the smoke. See my dad rushing through the fire.

Then there's the dream where I'm me Before, jumping on the trampoline with Sara, or helping my mom weed the garden. No face full of scars. No flipper hand. No missing ear.

I don't know which is worse. When I wake from the nightmares, relief washes over me because the fire isn't real.

But with the dreams of Before, the nightmare starts when I open my eyes.

Piper takes the lid off a shoebox jammed to the brim with cards, opens the top one, and reads out loud:

"'We have been so touched by your bravery and wish you a speedy recovery.'"

She sticks her finger in her mouth, making a gagging noise as she holds the box over my trash can.

"May I?"

I grab the box before she can chuck it.

"Cora thinks they inspire me."

"Inspire you?" Piper scoffs. "They're total junk. Everyone's on the front steps with balloons at first, but where are they when you're sitting on the toilet having your mom wipe you because your shoulders won't stretch?"

I toss the box back on my desk.

"Wait—they don't make a Hallmark card for a successful tooshie wipe?" I say. "That seems like a serious oversight in the product line."

Piper laughs. "Like 'Congratulations on your first bowel movement after surgery! Hope everything comes out okay!'"

"Or 'That graft looks way less pus-filled! Here's to an infection-free New Year.'"

"Or how about this?" Piper leans back in her chair, her arms folded with a serious, deadpan face. "A card with Zac Efron smoldering off the page, saying, 'Girl, those compression garments hug you in *all* the right places. Keep it tight.'"

I laugh. "I would definitely buy that one. At least it's funny."

"Right?" Piper says. "Like today, when Layne was trying to be all serious and you bust out your Freddy Krueger comment. I almost died. Who said it, anyway?"

"I don't know. Some girl in the theater. Keira or Kenzie or something."

Piper's face scrunches up tight.

"Kenzie King?"

"I don't know."

"Long black hair? Face looks like the wind changed right when she was on the verge of a massive snart? Like she's always right on the cusp of sneezing and farting simultaneously?"

I try to remember the girl's face. I was so worried about her seeing me that I didn't get a good look at her or the degree of snartiness on her face.

"Maybe?"

"Well, that's not a surprise. Kenzie is the worst. The. Worst. Whatever you do, stay so far away from her that when she does finally snart, you're nowhere near the splash zone."

I laugh. "Gross."

"Yes, she is. In fact, now that I know she was the one who said it, I no longer think it was hilarious."

I send the dream catcher spinning with my claw-hand.

"One time, a girl at the checkout line scream-whispered to her mom that my face looked like melted crayons. I was only like a foot away from her. I'm burned, people, not brain-dead."

Piper laughs. "I've heard that this one senior boy calls me 'Meals on Wheels' because I'm lightly toasted," she says. "Gotta give him credit. That one's got some nuance to it. You wouldn't believe some of the dumb things people call me."

"I guarantee I've heard worse," I say, mildly insulted that Piper thinks she could compete with me, the face that launched a thousand quips.

"Like what?"

"I don't know if you can handle it, Wheelie," I say.

Piper leans back in her chair, a sly grin on her face. "All right, then I'll start with an oldie but a goodie: roadkill."

"Not bad," I counter. "And I'll go with bacon face."

"Quadriplegic zombie."

I kneel on the bed, shouting through my laughter. "Scarface!"

Piper screams back, trying hard to stay in her wheelchair as she leans forward to bellow another one. "Snakeskin!"

"Crusty crab!"

65

"Crispy cripple!"

"Mutant mouth!"

"Pig face!" Piper clasps her hand over her mouth, realizing she called me a name instead of one of her own. This strikes both of us as hilarious, and I collapse onto the bed, holding my stomach. Piper doubles over in her wheelchair just as Cora bursts through the door.

"Girls!"

Piper sucks in her lips, trying not to laugh. Cora looks from me to Piper, her face red.

"That. Is. Enough."

When she closes the door again, Piper and I both exhale giggles. She wheels to the side of the bed and motions for me to scooch as she hoists herself out of the chair and then inches backward onto the mattress, flopping her limp legs next to mine.

"So who wins?" Piper says.

"I'm pretty sure we both lose."

Piper's breath slows.

"The names don't even bother me. Rubber and glue and all that," she says. She points to the box of cards on my desk. "Those are the offensive ones." She puts her hand to her chest and does a high fake voice. " 'Inspiration!' 'Your story is so inspiring!' 'You've inspired me to live to the fullest!' Well, great, I'm glad my terrible personal tragedy could help you get your crap together."

"And 'miracle,' like there's some higher reason I'm alive," I say. "My dad pushed me out a window. I lived. He died. That's not a miracle; it's gravity."

"People are the worst," Piper says quietly.

"Totally."

"Except you. You don't totally suck."

"You should definitely write Hallmark cards."

Piper laughs. "No, really. You don't make me want to get a lobotomy, and that's saying something."

Piper's zebra-striped arm presses against my own compression garments. She doesn't jerk away or seem to notice she's touching me. She's not even a nurse or an aunt or a counselor who has to be close to me.

"You know what I mean, though, right? It's hard to put into words," she says.

"So don't," I say. "Words are overrated."

Side by side, we watch the dream catcher dangle above our heads.

And for the first time in a long time, I'm not facing the nightmare alone.

Ava Lee
BS Therapy Journal
Feb. 26

Words I hate
(in ascending order of loathing)

gross
toasty
crab-hand
the penguin
scarface
pizzaface
zombie
well-done
crispy critter
freddy krueger
brave
inspiration
miracle
lucky
survivor
survivor
survivor

What do you call someone who didn't mean to
    survive?
Who sometimes wishes she hadn't?

9

If the high school hallway is the gauntlet, then the cafeteria is the guillotine.

When the bell rings for lunch the next day, I scan the crowd for Piper's wheelchair, determined not to walk in alone. I wouldn't even be considering it if she hadn't texted me after first period.

Claimed a lunch spot yet?

Keeping my options open

Hit me up by the vending machines

I'll think about it

Don't be a hero

My combat-boot lunch pals from the stage yesterday file past me toward the auditorium. I consider retreating to the anonymity of the curtains as well when Piper texts me again.

Are you coming or what? No one survives solo

While I weigh my options, I notice a poster outside the bathroom, advertising the spring musical. In my old life, I would have auditioned with my friends, would have been part of a group to call mine. Now, I *am* a solo act.

But maybe Piper's right: the only way to get through these two weeks is to belong—somewhere.

The clatter from the lunchroom spills into the hallway along with the aroma of Tater Tots and teen sweat.

I push the doors open despite the itch spreading down my arms.

A table of girls closest to me turn in unison. I pretend not to notice how they bunch their heads together over their cell phones, their texting thumbs and eyebrows flying in rapid-fire girlspeak.

I scratch my arm outside my compression garments as the itch intensifies. Where is Piper? I must look lost or confused, probably confirming everyone's suspicions that my mind is as messed up as the rest of me. The roar of the cafeteria crescendos around me, making me wish I had my headphones, and I'm just about to turn tail and run back to the stage when—

"Ava!"

I've never been so relieved to hear my name. Piper waves from a table in the back corner, the hot-pink stripes of her compression garments now visible above the crowd.

"Welcome to the Island of Misfit Toys!" she says when I make my way to her.

The other kids at Piper's table don't seem to share her enthusiasm. They briefly scrutinize my face and return to their lunches.

One boy tinkers with a clarinet, wiping the reed on his shirt before wedging it back into the mouthpiece. A girl pores over a math textbook, and another keeps her eyes glued to her phone while she chews a sandwich.

Piper pats the seat next to her.

"Okay, for real, though, I don't even know what these guys do after two-thirty every day," she whispers. "But my regular squad kind of disintegrated recently, and like I said, you need a pack to survive."

Even though I can feel people looking at me, eating lunch at a table is way better than hiding backstage, and with Piper chatting about BS therapy and all the people and teachers I should avoid at Crossroads, the lunch period is almost over before I know it.

As Piper talks, a boy walks toward us. It isn't until he gives me a thumbs-up that I recognize him as the kid with no boundaries and zero ability to pick up on my serious "leave me alone" vibes yesterday.

Suddenly hyperaware of my body, I rearrange my arms twice, finally leaning against Piper's wheelchair handle, trying to act casual. My face heats up, and for once I'm grateful my scarred face doesn't blush anymore.

"The girl with the space-age hand!" he yells to me above the din of the cafeteria. "We didn't scare you off, then?"

He squats between Piper and me. I tug my bandana closer across my absent ear, which I am suddenly supremely aware of as well.

"Almost," I say.

"She speaks!" he says.

Piper looks at us, her eyebrows cocked upward as she chews.

"You know each other?"

"We have earth science together," he says. "But we haven't been formally introduced."

Piper digs in her sack lunch, doing the honors without looking at us.

"Asad, Ava. Ava, Asad."

The boy grips my hand so tight that I wince. He stands and, with a flourish of his wrist, bows. *In the middle of the cafeteria.* His black hair flops in front of him as he smiles at me, dimples raging.

"Asad Ebrahim, at your service."

Piper rolls her eyes.

"Ignore him. He thinks the world's a stage."

"And we mere players," Asad says, beaming.

I try to swallow my own smile, but I know I'm failing at that about as hard as I am at looking casual. I recheck that my bandana is covering my earhole.

"Shakespeare in the lunchroom?" I say. "Bold."

Piper guffaws.

"Right? He's like a very old, very cheesy man trapped in a barely pubescent body. It's the worst of both worlds, really."

"I will not apologize for my knowledge of the classics." Asad smirks down at Piper. "Excuse me if I think there are more interesting things than *The Real Housewives of Atlanta.*"

"I do *not* watch that," Piper says, throwing her balled-up paper bag at Asad. "I watch *The Real Housewives of New Jersey.* Besides, I've seen some Bollywood, so your taste is definitely suspect."

Asad throws the bag right back at her.

"If you're going to be racist, at least be accurately racist. My family is from Pakistan, not India."

"Same diff," Piper says.

"Actually, not. But I will forgive your ignorance, as there has not yet been a *Real Housewives of Lahore*." Asad bows at the waist toward Piper. "I accept your humble apology."

Piper shakes her head.

"Drama kids."

"Speaking of which—" Asad straightens up. "That's what I need to talk to you about."

My chest deflates a little. Of course—he's here to talk to her.

"There's a vicious rumor going around that you're not auditioning."

"Not a rumor, my friend. Truth," Piper says.

His smile falls along with his shoulders.

"You're going to drop us, just like that? Where's the loyalty?"

Piper backs up her chair, turning it abruptly to face him. She pops a clementine section in her mouth, chewing while she talks.

"Good question. If you find any shred of loyalty in that group, I want to be the first to know. Until then, I'm out."

Asad starts saying something, but Piper cuts him off.

"I'm out!"

"All right, all right. Message received." He holds up his hands and backs away slowly, stopping only to deliver another bow to me. "Ava. So glad to have a name to go with the face."

For the second time with this kid, I can't tell if he means his words as a subtle dig or he's the poster child for social awkwardness.

73

Before I can decide, the bell rings and Asad disappears into the wave of reenergized students barreling toward the door.

"What a doofus," Piper says.

"He seems nice," I say.

"This is high school. Nice is a death sentence."

Piper's eyes shoot across the crowd to a girl standing by the recycling bin, staring at me.

"Can we help you?"

The girl shakes her head quickly and rushes out the doors, still holding her lunch tray. A few other girls nearby giggle. My face heats up again, my neck itching like wildfire.

"Well, that's not going to help us fade into the background," I say.

Piper yanks backward on her wheels, grinding to a stop before we reach the door. She looks up at me quizzically.

"Who said anything about fading away?"

10

For the next two weeks, Piper and I walk/roll the gauntlet to-gether. At first I think we'll double the spectacle—two burned girls, one in a wheelchair with striped neon skin and one with no hair, no ear, and no hand—but our partnership seems to lessen the stare factor. Maybe people are used to seeing Piper?

Or maybe everyone has had their initial gander at the Burned Girl, and soon, some other weirdo will get top billing. They won't even see me anymore.

Or maybe it's because Piper is straight-up ruthless.

When a scrawny-looking boy shamelessly points at me one afternoon of my second and final week, Piper runs her wheelchair over his foot.

"Picture for your spank bank?" she says, one hand behind her head like she's in a pinup calendar. He practically nose-dives into the crowded hallway to escape her.

Whatever the reason, the halls of Crossroads High are a lot

less daunting with Piper by my side, and I fall back into a familiar rhythm of school—reading and textbooks and long lectures punctuated by short bursts of hallway chaos. I breeze through most of my homework, and before I know it, my sentence is up.

Saturday morning, the day after my official "reintegration" period has ended, Piper sits on my front porch, a can of paint in one hand and her cell phone in the other.

"I'm here to fix your room. Well, your walls, anyway." She flips the phone to me. "Oh, and I made a playlist for you."

I read the name of the album.

"Fire Mix?"

"Yep. All the best combustion songs."

She reaches out to turn up the volume on her phone as I bump her wheelchair up the front step.

"Really? You're playing *this* song for me," I say as Alicia Keys blares into the living room singing "Girl on Fire."

"Fight fire with fire, right?" She grabs a paintbrush from her backpack and belts the chorus into her makeshift mic. " 'This girl is on firrrrrrrrrrrrre!' "

She holds the last note until her face turns red and then takes a small bow in her wheelchair while I slow-clap. She turns the volume down as Billy Joel ticks through the decades of "We Didn't Start the Fire."

"I had to get that out of my system." She produces two more paint rollers out of her backpack and holds up a can of paint the same hot pink as her compression garments. "Let's do this."

"I should ask Cora and Glenn first," I say.

"It's your room, isn't it?"

"Technically, yes. But still, I should ask."

Glenn carries Piper upstairs and I almost abort the whole mission when I show them the paint and Cora's bottom lip trembles. Glenn leans against the doorframe, Cora leaning into him, looking no bigger than one of Sara's dolls next to his Paul Bunyan–esque frame. Her mind seems like it's floated elsewhere. She lightly touches the wall.

"Robin's-egg blue. Sara must have taken a hundred samples from that paint store before she picked this one."

I run my own fingers across the butterfly wallpaper runner, the backdrop for our many two-person plays and ballets. Part of me wants to preserve this room forever.

Another part—the one I try to ignore—wants to rip it down to the studs.

"We don't have to paint it. I like the blue," I say.

"No, no. It's your room now." Cora smiles, but it's missing her usual "everything's going to be okay" assurance. "Probably should have done this a long time ago."

Quietly, Cora gathers up the pointe shoes from the shelf in the corner but can't hide her shock as Piper smears the first long streak down the wall.

"Pink?" she asks, looking from the paint to Glenn like she's about to shut down this whole operation.

"I love it," I jump in, even though I'm not sure that's entirely true. The hot-pink paint is loud and wild, and it wouldn't have been my first color choice, but it's different—and that, I like.

Cora starts to say something but stops, clutching Sara's shoes to her chest as she walks out. The lock on her door clicks softly as Glenn goes to gather some old blankets and tarps from the garage.

He throws them over the carpet and furniture while Piper and I take down the Broadway posters. Glenn shows me how to use a putty knife to scrape off the butterfly wallpaper runner and tells us to only paint up the wall halfway since he doesn't want me on a ladder and Piper can only reach so high from her wheelchair.

Piper transfers her Fire Mix to my phone and we paint for a solid hour to the sounds of every fire song ever, from Adele's "Set Fire to the Rain" to "Great Balls of Fire." When we reach a song that starts with way too much synthesizer, Piper stops painting to sing along, belting out lyrics about a girl who flies, wearing her scars like wings.

"What song is this?" I yell over her singing.

"Called 'Phoenix in a Flame' by some band called Atticus. This is basically my anthem now. Even set it as my ringtone."

Piper sings while I turn sideways to try to get the right angle on the butterflies with my only good hand wielding the putty knife. I can use my toe-hand as a makeshift pincer, but even after months of PT with Terry the Torturer, it's still too weak to grip and scrape at the same time.

Her anthem finished, Piper's having her own struggles, trying to reach the wall without ramming her wheelchair into it. She finally gives up and slides to the ground, scooting backward along the tarp while she paints.

"So, Monday's the big day, huh? Back to pajamas and days without seeing the sun?" she says.

"It's not quite that pathetic."

I finally loosen a section of wallpaper with the scraper and tug it away from the wall. The paper rips down the middle, slicing the butterflies in half.

Piper dabs paint into the corner.

"If the sad sack fits, my friend. But tell me this: Is school so bad?"

I look down at her while inching the next butterfly off the wall, trying to keep at least a portion of it intact.

"I ate lunch alone, hiding behind stage curtains, on the first day."

"Ouch." She sucks in air between her teeth. "That *is* rough."

"That's what I'm saying. Life is just easier without constantly being reminded of what I am."

"*Who* you are."

"Same thing."

Piper hoists herself back into her wheelchair and scrapes at a half-torn wallpaper remnant with her fingernail.

"So why did you even come back at all?"

I check the door to make sure no one's eavesdropping. "Guilt, I guess. Cora's on a one-woman quest to make me a normal teenager again. She's probably only letting me paint this room because she has a magazine clipping somewhere titled 'Redecorate Your Way to Healing.'"

"Okay, pop quiz," Piper says. "In the last two weeks, did you battle with inadequacy and self-loathing?"

"Check."

"Did you feel like everyone in the school was talking about you and staring at you?"

"Check."

"And did you compare yourself to others and always come up short?"

"Check."

Piper raises her hands high above her head, her fists pumping with the paintbrush still in one, so little flecks of pink paint splatter everywhere.

"Congratulations! You're a normal teenager."

I roll my eyes. Across the room, I catch my reflection in Sara's curio cabinet. The plastic sheeting distorts me even worse in the glass.

"It's not the same, and you know it."

She wheels herself backward to admire our paint job.

"Well, that looks just terrible." The paint is drying a little less shockingly bright, but the overall effect is that an erratic Easter Bunny couldn't decide between marshmallow-Peeps pink and robin's-egg blue.

When I ask Glenn if Cora wants to see, he says she's already gone to bed, so I tuck the single remnant of butterfly trim I managed to save into my desk drawer.

Glenn carries Piper back downstairs, where we nuke popcorn and brave the cold to escape the paint fumes. Piper wheels her chair to the edge of the in-ground trampoline and lowers herself down to the black surface. I try not to bounce too much as I lie down, the familiar sway beneath me. I've never been out here without Sara next to me. Sun in our faces in the summer. Snow angels in winter. Trading secrets, making plans.

Funny how when your secret keeper is gone, all those dreams and conversations vanish, too.

I block the light from the house with my hand so I can find the familiar configurations in the sky above me. I point out the North Star, and the dipper part of the Big Dipper, just like I used to with Sara when we'd camp out on the tramp.

"I learned in middle school that the stars we see are already dead," Piper says, munching popcorn. "Which is depressingly awesome."

Dad and I used to stare up at the sky just like this in our backyard. The stars were easier to see back then from our remote spot of the world.

"It's more like we're seeing the stars the way they once were," I say. "Like, if a star is one hundred light-years away, we're seeing the glow from a century ago."

"So it's like we're seeing into the past?"

"Sort of. My dad used to say, 'The past is all around us.' He also used to make up this story about how stars are peepholes to heaven so our loved ones can check in on us."

Piper almost chokes on her popcorn.

"How very Lion King of him."

I laugh, and my breath spirals away from me. Piper and I stare up at the sky, the trampoline swaying slightly beneath us. The night air nips at me, but I can barely feel it through my second skin.

Piper props herself on her elbow.

"What if he's right? What if your parents are up there, watching your life?"

My eyes focus on the black nothingness between the stars.

"I sure hope not."

Piper gives me a rough shove in the arm.

"Then stay," she says. "Ditch the quarantined Quasimodo act and give normal an actual chance."

"No way. I put in my two weeks as the Crossroads sideshow and now I'm free," I say. I've served my time. Why would I subject myself to more? Still, Piper looks at me so hopefully, for a second I feel bad she'll have to cruise the hallways alone on Monday. "Don't worry. You'll be fine without me."

Piper scoffs. "Always am. It's *you* I'm worried about. Two weeks ago, you showed me a picture of a girl in a truly hideous Rizzo wig who you clearly miss. I highly doubt you're going to find her sitting in a dead girl's room, pretending you died in that fire, too."

"Exactly. Because *that* me is gone."

Piper sits up on the trampoline, the whites of her eyes barely visible in the dark.

"Then let's find her." She pulls a sheet of paper out of her back pocket and smooths it out on the trampoline between us. "Auditions are on Friday."

"'Crossroads High Clubs,'" I read out loud. "Spring Musical" is circled in black marker. "You've got to be kidding me."

"Hear me out." Her voice is quick and excited. "The first step is to do something you used to do. Reclaim that part of yourself."

I imagine myself before the fire, standing on the stage of my old high school. My mom holds up her cell phone, and my dad claps loudly, doing that embarrassingly loud whistle with two fingers. But stages belong with singing and ponytails and bathing suits and makeup on the growing list of Things I Lost in the Fire.

"This face does not belong under a spotlight, unless the goal is to scare small children."

Piper laughs. "Yeah, you definitely have a face for radio."

"I have a face for living under a rock. Is there a club for that?"

Piper gasps and points to an item halfway down the list.

"Right here! The antisocial club. We eat lunch behind curtains and collaborate on ways to evaporate. We hope to one day merge permanently with the walls."

"Sign me up!"

"Oh, wait"—she deflates—"it looks like you're already the president of that one."

I chuck a handful of popcorn at her. Piper catches some kernels midair and stuffs them into her mouth.

"What about you?" I ask.

"What *about* me?"

"Why aren't *you* in drama anymore? I heard that Asad kid asking you about it."

Piper shrugs.

"Eh . . . I used to be friends with some of those drama girls, but they turned into total divas. I can't stand them."

"But I can?"

"You're new. They have no reason to hate you."

Lying back on the trampoline, I stare up into the night sky. My breath evaporates in smoky wisps.

I think of Dad telling eight-year-old me that my life was as limitless as the galaxies. "Shoot for the highest stars, Ava, and you're bound to hit something. But first, you have to shoot."

What would Dad think of me now, hiding in my bedroom, staring at posters rather than shooting for something—anything—of my own? Even if my two-week trial is technically up, he'd tell me to get back on the stage.

He'd tell me to shoot.

The trampoline bounces wildly as I sit up and snatch the sheet of activities from Piper.

"If I stay at school—" Before I can finish, Piper throws her hands up in celebration. I hold up the sheet. "*If* I stay, then it's on one condition: you are doing this with me."

Piper lowers her hands and scrunches up her face. "Drama? No way."

"Then something else. What's something you used to do before the accident?"

"Volleyball." Piper jerks her head toward her wheelchair on the grass. "But that's obviously out."

"No way. If I'm going to sign up for the drama club with *this* face, you can find some way to get on the court with *those* legs."

Piper looks from me to her chair, her eyes narrowed.

"And then you'll stay?" she asks.

"I'll stay."

A smile spreads across her face so bright that it cuts through the darkness. She shakes my hand hard.

"Deal."

March 9

I don't remember much.
Just heat.
And smoke.
Everywhere.
Eating me up.

And then, it vanishes.
Not gone.
Just moved.
Inside me.

Each breath
burns white-hot.
I try to scream.
No voice,
only pain.
I swallowed the fire.

I land on my back.
I remember a smell.
Me.
Burning.

My brain screams.
Move!
My body won't listen.

Only my arm obeys,
moving slowly,
like the air is wet concrete.
Where is my hand?
Only
flaps of skin
and
bone
where fingers should be.
What's wrong with me?

Then,
pain.
Waves
crushing me.
Until
                    there is nothing left
                                        but hurt.

"Stay with me."
A voice.
A face.
My neighbor
rocks my body

back
and
forth

rocks me

       rocks me

             rocks me

She
Puts
Me
Out.

Her lips say,
"You're going to be okay."
Her eyes say something else

Blackness

      closes in

          like a telescope.

               Quiet.

                   Easy.

"Hold on," she says.
To what?
      To

          pain

              heat

                 panic?

The blackness beckons.

I feel myself letting go
     of
          pain
              heat
                 panic.

"Hold on. For your parents."
Mom.
Dad.
They need me
to stay.

I open my eyes.
Through the blackness—
stars.

Untouched by
smoke
and
hurt.

I cling
to the stars
as sirens near,
heavy footsteps
fall.
Voices shout.

From a million miles away,
tiny lights
anchor me
to the earth.

Hands on my back.
Lifting me.

No.

No.

No.

Don't take the lights.
Leave me
here.

Where the stars
can hold me
together.

II

Our plan is simple: I will sign up for some small, back-of-the-stage part—like a tree or another glorified stage prop—in the spring play, and Piper will see if her old coach will let her be a water girl or something else wheelchair-appropriate. It's not going to be glamorous, but by the way Cora disintegrates, you'd think I'd won an Academy Award and Piper was going to the Olympics.

"I just can't believe it," she says through tears on Sunday night when I tell her I'll be a Crossroads Viking for at least a week longer. "It's like a miracle."

"Miracles don't exist." I pack my math textbook into my bag. "This was all Piper."

———

When the final bell rings Friday afternoon, Crossroads High transforms from a normal educational facility to the land of after-schoolers. Before I head to the auditorium for the drama club's first meeting, I drop Piper off by the locker rooms so she can talk to the athletic coordinator.

I wedge Piper's wheelchair through the throng of uniform-clad athletes drinking protein shakes and spraying Febreze on football pads that have no chance of ever not smelling like teenage-boy sweat again.

"Break a leg," Piper shouts over the din. "But not a spine!"

Heading toward the auditorium, a shoeless boy and girl leap arm in arm through the hallway, narrowly skipping over the proof pages of this month's *Crossroads Crier* sprawled on the floor. As I get closer to the end of the hall, the sound of tuning instruments wafts from the orchestra room.

Everyone has their group in this extracurricular menagerie.

The auditorium buzzes with voices as I sneak in the side door and into the first available velvet seat. Other kids are sitting, too, but most are scattered across the room—belting out a mash-up of show tunes, sitting on the edge of the stage with their legs dangling, or talking loudly in the aisles.

I used to be one of them—a stage-adrenaline junkie. The thrill of opening night, the energy of the theater coursing through me as I took my mark. The lights in my face. The blackness of the audience in front of me. I knew my parents were there, Mom probably cursing her phone for not having enough storage space and Dad uncontrollably saying my lines with me.

The stage was my second home. A place I felt safe. Alive. Confident.

A girl prances across the stage barefoot, and I instantly

recognize her as the girl who called me Freddy Krueger. Piper's right; she does look like she's about to sneeze-fart.

She leaps across the stage (nowhere near as gracefully as Sara would have) and takes a bow in front of a boy, who gives a fake clap. She tousles his hair and, as she stands up straight, catches me watching her before I can turn away. She whispers to the boy, who turns to look at me, too.

The news of my attendance spreads quickly, judging by the not-so-covert head turns rolling like a wave through the crowd: *Alert! Alert! Drama crisis! The Burned Girl is here. In* our *theater.*

I scrunch farther down into the velvet seat, trying to shake a feeling that I've never associated with the sanctity of a theater before.

Fear.

How am I going to get on that stage if just sitting here makes my skin crawl?

I guess the fire claimed both my homes.

As the seats fill, except—noticeably—the ones by me, I hug my bag as I fish out my headphones. I'm about to put them on when a boy actually scoots into the row, and I look up into dark eyes and hazelnut skin.

"Asad, right?"

He points behind us to the hallway.

"Out there, I'm just Asad. In here, I'm Asad Ebrahim, stage-lighting manager extraordinaire!" He punctuates his sentence with some over-the-top jazz hands. His arm brushes mine on the armrest and—perhaps even more alarming—he doesn't recoil in horror.

"What about you? Cast or backstage crew?" he says.

Backstage? Piper and I decided I was going to try out for a part, but I hadn't even considered the crew option. Backstage totally still counts.

"Crew," I decide quickly. I put the headphones back in my bag. "Definitely crew."

"Cool. Me too." He points behind us at a small boothlike room with large, round lights facing the stage. "I handle all the lights, so I'm usually trapped up there."

He looks around me and his smile fades for a millisecond.

"So Piper really didn't come, huh? Aren't you two attached at the hip?"

"She's not doing drama anymore."

"Bummer," he says. "She was the only one of the drama queens who ever bothered to learn my name. I think some of them actually think it's 'More spotlight!' "

I laugh despite myself, which clearly only encourages him.

"So you *can* smile!" he says triumphantly. "Okay, name that musical: 'You're Never Fully Dressed Without a Smile.' "

"*Annie.*"

Asad sits back in his chair with a grin.

"I'm impressed. My repertoire of Broadway lines usually goes unnoticed—and most certainly unappreciated—by the high school masses. We need more people like you around here."

I sink into my seat.

"People like me?"

Asad keeps talking nonchalantly, like he doesn't realize I'm waiting for some gut-wrenching definition of exactly what kind of "people" he means.

"You know, people who actually appreciate the theater."

I allow myself to unclench when I realize his comment had nothing to do with my face.

"Well, sometimes *Real Housewives* is a repeat," I say.

Asad smiles.

"I'm glad you're here, Ava."

I glance at the empty seats stretching out on the other side of me.

"Well, that makes exactly one of you. Besides Piper, you're basically the first person in this whole school to talk to me, unless talking *about* me counts. Which, FYI, it doesn't."

"You do give off a pretty intense 'don't talk to me' vibe. Even in the hall with Piper, your eyes are always on the floor."

I force myself to look at him, suddenly aware that I have, in fact, been staring at my shoes. Asad's shocking, almost-black irises are so dark I can see myself in them.

"That is *so* not true."

He smirks. "Okay, do you remember when I tried to talk to you on your first day?"

"Yeah."

"You totally ignored me."

"I thought you were just being nice. Throwing a pity conversation to the new, burned girl."

Asad rolls his eyes. "I *was* being nice. And you shut me down."

Clueless. That's what I called him. A hastily scribbled description in the corner of a lined page. The flip-flop of my stomach tells me I may not be able to write him off as easily I did in that notebook.

"I'm just saying maybe look up once in a while," he says. "Who knows what you're missing."

I stammer for words. I'd think Asad was a total jerk if he weren't sitting there with a smile on his face, totally free of malice as he tells me I'm to blame for having only one friend in this whole place.

I'd probably be more offended if that smile didn't make me feel like this boy with no filter might be number two.

A lanky boy dressed in black strides onto stage barefoot and claps, scattering the actor and actress wannabes to their seats. Asad snaps to attention as the boy in black paces on the stage, his chin cradled in his palm thoughtfully, as if he's about to deliver a Hamlet-worthy soliloquy.

"If you're here to get class credit or use this as an extracurricular for your college applications, you're in the wrong place. No room for impostors here."

He pauses, surveying the crowd, his impressive height commanding immediate authority on the stage. Judging by his manicured goatee and short ponytail of dark hair gathered at his neck, the boy in black has spent ample time reading *How to Look Like a Broadway Director,* and I'd bet good money he's got a picture of Lin-Manuel Miranda on his bedroom wall.

"In the immortal words of Polonius, 'To thine own self be true.' So make your choice. Are you in or out?"

Through the hush in the vast auditorium, a rustling draws everyone's attention to a freshman-looking boy in the back who gathers up his stuff and scurries out the door, followed by every set of eyes in the room.

"For those who remain, this will not be like any other club. Theater is a way of life. Theater *is* life."

He turns dramatically, pointing to a girl in the front row.

"You will find yourself on this stage. The lights can reveal you, if you let them."

Yeah, this was definitely a bad idea. I would flee after that other poor impostor if I weren't glued to my seat with fear of interrupting this guy's grand monologue.

"This year, we will be bringing the stage to life with . . ."

He pauses for dramatic effect, soaking in the anticipation as every head leans forward. I worry Asad may literally fall out of his seat.

"*The Wizard of Oz!*"

A gasp ripples through the rows, followed by a chorus of chatter.

"Like Dorothy, we will wend our way down the yellow brick road. We will head into the dark forest. We will emerge triumphant—transformed."

He points a finger again toward the girl in the audience.

"Are you ready for the journey?"

He offers her his hand and in one fluid movement lifts her onto the stage. Row by row, everyone leaves their seats to climb up, too. Asad stands and turns to me.

"You coming?"

I grip my bag tighter against me.

"Wait, we have to do that? Even if we're crew?" I hope there's been some serious miscommunication and the backstage folks like us get to slink unseen behind black curtains.

"Yup. Drama club tradition. Follow me," he says.

I shake my head.

"I—I think this was a mistake."

He looks at me for a second and then at the row of people behind us like he's noticed for the first time that they're whispering, watching to see if the scar-faced girl will take the stage.

His dark eyes capture mine.

"'Fortune Favors the Brave,'" he says.

I think for a second.

"*Les Mis*? No, wait, *Aida*. Definitely *Aida*. Final answer."

He smiles wide.

"Oh, you *so* belong here. Face it, these melodramatic thespians are your people." He holds out his hand, palm up, toward me. "We'll do it together."

The assurance in his dark eyes calms my buzzing skin. I slip my hand into his and try to ignore the voices around me as I make my way to the front. When we get to the stage, Asad talks up to the boy in black.

"This is Ava. She's new."

When the boy reaches out his hand for me, I make sure to reach only my right hand back, keeping my flipper hidden at my side. He hesitates for a split second when he sees my compression garments, but before I can explain, he grabs me and pulls me forcefully onto the stage.

"Hello, new Ava. Welcome to Oz."

March 16

I wake to beeping.

And a balloon.

"Get Well Soon."

Someone is sick.

Who?

Beep.

Beep.

Beep.

A woman in blue scrubs.

"You're in a hospital."

Why?

I can almost remember.

Something happened. Something bad.

Car accident?

"We've been waiting for you."

Where have I been?

Why is it so hard to breathe?

Something hard blocks my voice.

I'm mute.

Something white covers my face.

I'm mummified.

Why can't I move?

Little white footballs where my hands should be.

"You've been in a fire," a nurse says.

Sixty percent of me burned up.

Sixty percent?

What's left?

Cora by my bed

crying

always crying.

Pain

always pain.

Then sleep

beautiful sleep.

You were in a fire.

You've been asleep

for two months.

Reality flits away like a butterfly.

Only pieces appear:

Fire

Smoke

Flesh

Dad pushes me.

The stars save me.

Through the fog, I understand one thing:

Life has changed—

Forever.

12

For the first time since the fire, I wake up excited.

The house is quiet, just like last night after Glenn drove me home from school. Cora had gone to bed while it was still light out, and I never had the chance to tell her I'm officially a member of the Crossroads High drama club.

Another first: I actually *want* to tell Cora about being back in the theater. I want someone to know I'm shooting for a star, even if it's a small one.

I find Glenn on the front porch swing, eyes trained on the snowy peaks in the distance, rocking himself slowly heel to toe, heel to toe.

"You're burning daylight," he says when I plop next to him. "We've already been out and back to the cemetery. Thought it'd be a nice way to commemorate the day."

I'm about to ask what we're celebrating when it hits me: March 17. Sara's birthday.

"I'm so sorry, I forgot—" I start, mentally kicking myself for being so wrapped up in drama club that I completely missed it. Not that I would have gone anyway. I don't visit cemeteries for the same reason I don't visit burned-down houses: I already know what I lost.

"I know cemeteries aren't your thing," he says. "But just wanted to give you a heads-up. Cora's taking it pretty hard."

"Where is she?" I ask.

Glenn nods toward the house.

"Remember last year? Didn't surface all day."

"I wasn't here last year."

He pauses for a second and stares at the mountains, some memory rolling through his mind. I was still in the hospital at this time last year, lost in a coma, somewhere deep inside myself.

From my hospital bed, I could see the same mountains—the Wasatch Range. The jagged peaks reach so much higher than the foothills around our house in Utah's farm country, where I grew up memorizing the rise and fall of the land outside my bedroom window. The mountains here are different, but their presence is comforting—a geologic North Star—standing steady and reliable to the east, connecting me to home.

"Do me a favor?" Glenn asks.

"Anything."

"See how she's doing in there. I hate for her to be alone, but this morning just about wore me out."

I leave Glenn on the swing, where he lays his head back, eyes closed, an unshaved jawline darkening his face. I drag myself to Cora's bedroom door, unsure whether I should disturb her. Cora handles "down days" behind closed doors, her grief locked up tight. A rustling movement when I knock tells me she's gathering up tissues.

"Come in," she says. When I open the door, she wears a weary smile. Without makeup, her eyes seem slightly sunken and age spots dot her cheeks. A picture of Sara sits wonky on her nightstand, her pointe shoes next to Cora on the bed.

Cora wipes the corners of her eyes with a balled-up tissue, forces a huge smile, and pats the bed next to her.

"Tell me all about drama club!"

I want to tell her, about *The Wizard of Oz* and the over-the-top director and the boy who helped me get back onstage, but I can't make today about me.

Today is not *my* day.

"You don't have to do that," I say.

Cora deflates like I've poked her with a pin. "I'm sorry. I've been in here wallowing, haven't I?"

"You're allowed to wallow."

She picks up Sara's picture off the dresser.

"It's just so strange having your child's birthday without your child. Like this day should somehow not exist anymore. But here it is, the annual reminder of the day I became her mother."

Cora picks at the edge of her blue paisley comforter. I feel like I should put my arm around her, but I'm afraid I'm the last thing Cora needs today.

The reminder of what she lost.

"You're still her mother."

Cora sighs.

"It's been more than a year, Ava. Twelve months without her and I still wake up sometimes in the morning and forget. And when I remember, it's like I lose her all over again and—"

She cuts herself off for a second.

"I'm tired of losing her. I'm just—tired."

She laughs weakly.

"I shouldn't be telling you this."

I shake my head. I want to tell her I get it, that I wake up sometimes from a bad dream and make it halfway down the hallway, heading for the warmth and safety of my mom's bed, before reality hits: I live in a world where my parents don't exist. Without fail, the weight crushes me every time like it's the first time.

I want to tell Cora that, but I can't quite get the words to go. Like if I say it out loud, I'll never be able to stuff it back in again. Instead, I give her an awkward side hug along with the same empty words people used to offer me: "I'm here if you need anything."

I reclose her door behind me.

I take out my math textbook on my bed and try to concentrate on the figures on the page rather than on Sara's dolls, which I swear are staring at me more aggressively than usual. I listen to Mom's deodorant message, my eyes shut tight, savoring the singsongy way she says "Call me ba-ack." But even that doesn't settle me the way it usually does.

After the third time listening to it in my pink/blue room, trying to ignore Barbie's stink eye, I can't sit anymore. So I head to the kitchen and line up eggs and oil and a nearly expired Funfetti cake mix Sara and I kept stashed in the back of the pantry for sleepover bake-a-thons, although we'd always end up just eating the batter on spatulas until we got sick.

I make an enormous mess in the process, thanks to my clumsy left hand, but I manage to make a decent cake, and only clatter a mixing bowl on the floor once. When it's done, I ice the cake with rainbow-chip frosting just like Sara would have, lick a spatula in her honor, and then stick in sixteen candles.

As I plunge the last one into the cake, it hits me.

The candles represent years.

Years lived.

I've just made the most depressing cake in the history of baked goods.

I yank out the candles and shove the whole thing into the garbage disposal, letting the blades abolish any evidence of my deluded idea that Funfetti could fix a family.

Unable to take away the hurt, I stand helpless in the hallway in front of Cora's closed door.

An insurmountable wall of wood and pain between us.

13

"Please tell me you're kidding," Piper says as I fill her in on drama club on our way to class Monday morning. "You're a backstage crewpie?"

I stop at the door to Piper's math class.

"Crewpie?"

"The curtain dwellers who don't have the guts to try out."

"Wow, you really are a drama diva."

"Was. *Was* a drama diva. And I'm just saying stage crew is not what we agreed to, and you know it."

I shift my weight from side to side as other kids file past us into the room. Nobody says anything, but a few of them smile faintly as they step around Piper's chair, which she's parked smack in the middle of the doorway.

"Technically, backstage is still on the stage. I think I'm going to like it." It's been me, myself, and I for so long I nearly forgot how good it feels to be part of something bigger, to be part of a crew. "And one of the guys—"

"A boy!" Piper leans forward dramatically, resting her chin on her hands and batting her eyelashes. "I want to hear Every. Last. Detail."

"No details to tell." Based on Piper's overreaction, I decide immediately not to mention Asad's name. "He was nice. That's all."

Piper swats playfully at me.

"Oh, stop. This X-rated talk is making me blush!"

I sling my satchel over my shoulder and start to leave, but Piper grabs my arm.

"For real, I want all the juicy gossip at group tomorrow."

I sweep my hand toward my face, showcasing my scars.

"This face gets no juice."

"Well, if there's a boy involved, then I guess crew is better than resuming your post as dungeon master. It's not like I'm going to be spiking volleyballs between filling water jugs." Piper smiles up at me as the bell rings. "Look at us being normal teenagers. I'm on a team again, you're in love—"

"I'm not in love."

"Pretty soon we'll be going to football games and loitering at the mall. Dr. Layne will be so proud."

"Let's not get ahead of ourselves," I say. "Besides, it's *new* normal, so it hardly even counts."

"Ava!" she yells after me as I start to walk down the hallway. "My new normal sucked before you got here."

"News flash: it still sucks," I say just loud enough so she can hear me over the loud pack of football players walking between us. "But yeah, mine too."

After school, Asad waves for me to join him on the stage when I walk into the auditorium. I take the stairs around the back rather than try to climb up with my compression garments and scars holding my knee joints together like superglue.

A bunch of other people are already standing in a circle on the stage when I slide in next to Asad.

"What's this?" I say.

"The circle of trust," he whispers, like he's uttered sacred words. "We do it every day before practice. Tony says it helps us bond."

"Tony?"

"The student director. The 'Welcome to Oz' guy? Looks like Lin-Manuel Miranda's taller and more dramatic brother? Anyway, he makes us hold hands, and we all say one thing about someone in the group."

I roll my eyes, trying to look more annoyed than terrified. I've inadvertently walked into a total nightmare.

Tony strides into the middle of the circle, a good foot taller than anyone else, with his arms outstretched as he completes a 360-degree turn. He's wearing all black again, and I wonder if he changes after the final bell or if his drama-demigod status is an all-day thing.

"The circle of trust," he says solemnly. "Let us begin."

He grabs the hand of a girl next to him. She grabs the boy's next to her, and so on around the circle. I watch the hand-holding wave push toward me, expecting full well that when it hits, the wave will crest, break, and drag me under.

When it reaches me, Asad grabs my right hand quickly,

whispers something, and nods for me to hold out my left hand to the boy on the other side of me. So I do.

Only it's not a hand.

It's my flipper. My claw. My penguin Frankenhand with my big fat toe sticking out and my fused fingers all clumped together like a flesh-colored oven mitt.

The boy next to me already has his hand out midway when he sees it. When everybody sees it. His fingers hang in the air between us like someone pressed the pause button on my life. Oh, how I wish they would. Maybe some rewind action while we're at it.

He grabs the hand of the girl on the other side of him instead, who—because fate is just that unkind—happens to be Kenzie, the girl Piper warned me about. She directs her pinch-faced snartiness right at me and my unheld fingers.

"You *have* to hold it," she says. "It's bad luck if you don't."

The boy's eyes flick from me to Kenzie to Tony, then back to my hand again. My skin buzzes up the back of my neck, and I scratch it even though I'm not supposed to, partly to ease the itch, partly to do something with the claw of shame hanging by my side.

"It's okay," I say. "It's kind of painful anyway."

I slide my mutant appendage into the pocket of my jeans. The boy, breathing out a heavy gasp of relief, drops his hand.

I look at the floor as the wave pushes away from me around the circle.

"Close your eyes," Asad whispers to me.

I squint out of one eye as the boy in black leads the circle, which centers on a Polly Pocket–size girl I know little about other than that she often skips through the halls, arm in arm with Kenzie. I mumble a comment about her cute pixie haircut when it's my turn.

But I'm not thinking about her hair. I'm not even thinking about the painfully obvious break in the circle of trust on my left where the boy wouldn't touch me.

I'm thinking about the boy on my right with hazelnut skin, who did.

14

I silently curse Piper.

She put this idea in my head with all her juicy-details talk. This is exactly why I didn't tell her Asad is the nice boy on crew. She'd make this into a whole thing when there is absolutely no way this could *ever* be a thing.

Boys clearly belong on the list of Things I Lost in the Fire.

My sophomore-year boyfriend was the last boy for me. Josh and I shared lingering embraces in the hallway, long, late-night phone conversations, and even a post-football-game kiss once below the bleachers. It was mostly tongue mingled with Juicy Fruit and awkwardness, but it was my first and final kiss, so my mind graciously remembers it as romantic and lovely and full of just the right amount of sexual tension, autumn chill, and body contact.

When Josh came to visit me in the hospital, I refused to see him. Mostly, I couldn't bear to see him see me. I wanted to remember the way he looked at me Before, that night beneath the bleachers when I hid my nervous smile behind my hair, and he brushed it away, his eyes fuzzy as he leaned in.

The fire could at least spare me a memory—one fading snapshot of when a boy looked at me like a girl he could love.

But that's all it is—a memory. Boys don't think of me like that anymore.

And neither do I.

Still, I peek at Asad's fingers interlaced with the wrinkled ones protruding from my compression garments. When we open our eyes, he lets go. I look away, hoping no one caught me staring like a weirdo at our briefly intertwined digits.

Tony breaks us into cast and crew, and I sit cross-legged next to Asad on the wooden stage, awaiting orientation on how to be the Best Darn Stagehand in the History of High School Theater! Asad leans back on his arms, his legs outstretched in front of him.

"So, Ava Lee, Piper tells me you did drama at your old school."

"Well, not like this." I want to ask why he and Piper were talking about me, but instead I nod toward the cast members who huddle around a freshly posted cast list. "I was one of *them*."

Kenzie jumps up and down, hugging the pixie-haired girl, squealing loud enough for everyone to hear that she got the lead role of Dorothy. A twinge of jealousy hits me: that used to be me with my friends.

"Why'd you cross over?" Asad says.

I laugh. "You're kidding, right?"

Asad's eyebrows stitch together, so I point to my face to spell it out for him.

He pushes himself up and scoots closer. To my right, two girls elbow each other and nod toward the boy who is blatantly gawking at the Burned Girl.

"So how did they happen, anyway?"

"My scars?"

"Yeah."

The way the girls stare, waiting to see what I say, makes me channel Piper, who wouldn't care at all that some girls are looking at her or that some stupid kid didn't hold her hand in the circle of shame. She would say something shocking and hilarious that makes everyone forget her wheelchair and her burned skin. I lean forward with the creepiest smile I can muster and whisper, " 'You wanna know how I got these scars?' "

Asad's eyes widen as a smile spreads across his face.

"You did *not* just quote *The Dark Knight* to me."

"Technically, I quoted the Joker."

"Well, then technically, you may be the coolest girl I know."

I stare at the stage, trying to ignore the flip of my stomach. Fortunately, the boy in black appears from behind the curtain and everyone snaps to attention, making Asad momentarily forget his question, which I have zero intention of answering with these girls lurking close, waiting to turn my personal tragedy into lunchtime gossip.

"So you want to be on crew?" the boy says. "I warn you now. You won't get roses or applause."

He pauses, scanning our faces.

"But without you, the show stops. You are the invisible hands behind the scenes." He holds a black T-shirt high in the air. "In

117

fact, your sole purpose is to disappear into the stage itself. Can you do that?"

I nod. Yeah, *that* I can do.

Everyone passes around the black T-shirts, putting them on over their clothes. I slip mine over my head, hoping I can get myself dressed like a big girl. But of course, my life is the cosmic joke that just won't quit, and I somehow insert my head into an armhole. I silently panic in the 100 percent cotton-polyester darkness as I try to get my elbow to bend enough to get me out.

Through his laughter, Asad asks if he can help. I give up and let my arms hang limp at my side as I nod from within the shirt.

He tugs on the collar, straightening out the holes for me, and as my head wriggles through—because the universe is nothing if not thorough in its humiliation quest—my bandana slides off.

Asad's eyes reach my scalp before my fingers can, and for a split second, his eyes go wide. Instead of the long, stick-straight brown hair I had Before the Fire, my scalp now boasts little bald spots where the doctors cut out skin to graft onto my face. Some of the follicles burned off completely, and the hair that did survive is growing back coarse and frizzy. Dr. Sharp says this spriggy regrowth is temporary, but I'm not holding my breath for shampoo-commercial locks.

My patchy scalp only contributes to my crypt-keeper vibe, but instead of running off screaming, Asad reaches out to adjust my bandana. "Congratulations! You've officially crossed to the dark side of drama." He slips his own T-shirt over his head. "Soon you'll be like me, classically trained in fading into the background."

I tug the bandana tight around my earhole just to make sure. "I can only dream."

Tony leads us on a tour of the inner sanctum of the stage. Single file, we weave through the black curtain maze as he points out sound booms and lighting rigs and secret storage closets.

Asad leans closer to me to whisper when Tony turns around to explain how the curtain pulley system works. A piece of his black hair tickles my forehead.

"Want to see where the real magic happens?"

When the group goes off toward the dressing rooms, Asad leads me the other way to the back of the auditorium. The skin on my knees pulls painfully tight as I follow him up a dark, winding staircase, to a room that looks like the control station of a spaceship. He sits in a rolling chair and glides backward, his arms wide, gesturing to the rows and rows of switches and buttons.

"Welcome to my lair," he says. "It's humble, I know, but chicks dig it."

I fold my arms across my chest and lean against one of the panels, trying to ignore the throbbing in my knees, afraid if I rub them or collapse on the floor like I want to, he'll suddenly wonder why he's hanging out with the bizarro Burned Girl.

"How many chicks, exactly, have you had in here?"

Asad hits a button and turns off all the lights in the auditorium, which stretches out below us through a large window. He hits another and just the center-stage spotlight blinks on.

"Quantity is not the key when it comes to chicks," he says.

Asad brings the lights back up in the auditorium. The floor

seems a million miles away as I peer over, sending my stomach churning. My mind darts back to a memory of me leaning out my bedroom window. My dad yells, "Jump," but my feet won't listen. He pushes me, and I fall, watching the ground zoom toward me.

I step back quickly from the glass before the memory burrows too deep. As I do, a group of girls walk onto the stage, Kenzie at the helm, her tight-pinched face even snartier than usual.

"That girl really thinks she's something, huh?" I say.

"Kenzie King? She owns this place."

Asad points to the sign at the back of the theater, which I can barely make out by squinting. THE KING FAMILY THEATER.

"As in, she literally owns it. Her family donates buttloads of money every year to the drama department, so Kenzie naturally thinks she runs it—and everyone in it."

He rubs his palms together in excitement. "Shall we listen in?"

He cranks up a dial on the panel in front of him, and the sound of the girls' footsteps fills the room.

"Umm . . . creepy voyeur much?" I say.

Asad laughs and turns the dial louder.

Kenzie's voice wafts through the speakers on the walls, already in the middle of a sentence.

"It's *her* I'm worried about. That whole circle-of-trust disaster was so embarrassing, although who can blame that kid for not wanting to touch that . . . *thing*. And I honestly think she has no idea that she smells like a walking old-folks home."

My muscles tense as I inch away from Asad, hoping he won't

take a whiff to confirm. Instead, he flicks a switch, silencing the conversation.

"I'm sorry, I didn't know—"

I shrug. "I'm used to it."

"You shouldn't be." Asad's face contorts as he taps a switch back and forth, flickering a small light at the back of the stage on and off. I step farther back from the glass, less afraid now of the height and more of Kenzie noticing the light and looking up to see me watching her like a stalker. "We should say something to her. *You* should say something."

I lean against the control panel, trying to be casual even though all I really want to do is get out of this small space that has suddenly filled with the hospital-drenched scent of my lotion.

"Right, because people like me can just walk up to people like her and say, 'Please like me. Pretty please'? Girls like that are just one of the irrefutable laws of high school—like gravity. No matter what I do, they'll always be there."

Kenzie and her entourage file out of the auditorium, their mouths still moving even though Asad has momentarily silenced their mockery.

"Besides," I add, "if I stood up to every injustice, when would I find time to watch *The Real Housewives*?"

"It's still not right," he says with a weak smile. "Even if you *are* friends with Piper."

I stand straight, not sure I heard him right.

"What does Piper have to do with anything?"

"You know . . ." Asad pauses and swallows hard. "Everything that happened on New Year's."

Asad waits like I'm supposed to understand what he's talking about. I stare blankly back.

"How she and Kenzie were best friends and then they weren't anymore and then you showed up and took her place, and from what I understand about girls—which I warn you is pathetically little—that's like a big no-no."

I put my hand out to stop him.

"Piper and Kenzie were friends? In what world?"

Asad lets out a long, low whistle as he shakes his head.

"Piper hasn't told you any of this?"

"No. We have a pretty strict don't-ask-don't-tell policy."

Asad blankets the auditorium in darkness by flipping all the switches with his palm. "It's probably time to ask."

15

That night, I do some reconnaissance on my phone. My first stop: the online profile I've avoided looking at since the fire.

I wasn't technically lying to Piper about not being on social media—I'm not. At least, not this version of me.

In the small, circular selfie in the corner of the page, Ava Before the Fire grins in front of the enormous maple tree in our old yard. I don't open my profile page. I made that mistake once in the hospital—took me an hour to scroll through all the aggressive commands to *Get well soon!* and the *You're a hero/inspiration/ survivor* comments. I never responded to any of them. What was there to say?

Besides, I kind of like that the old me still exists out there, untouched by fire and death and reality. Ava Before the Fire with her flawless skin and happy smile. That's how I want her to stay, frozen in the amber of the interwebz.

So I don't tap on my name or the red 153 in the corner

announcing the backlog of messages from my old friends. I guess I want them to remember the old me, too.

A picture of Chloe pops up first on my feed. She's straightened her wild hair and lost so much weight that I almost don't recognize her sitting on the edge of our school's theater, Emma and Stacy flanking her.

And then I'm down the rabbit hole. Pictures of all my old friends, still hanging out, going to Tommy's Burgers & Shakes, hiking up the canyon, taking a bow on my stage.

My life, my friends, moving on without me.

I pause when I get to a picture of Josh, standing in the high school parking lot, arm around some girl with long, beach-wavy hair.

I x out of the photo quickly. This is exactly why I don't look. This recon mission isn't about *my* past, anyway.

I type Piper's name and spot her easily by the neon-striped compression garments radiating from her profile pic. The rest of her photos are classic Piper—oddly angled black-and-whites of her wheelchair spokes, close-ups of her burns, angsty poems about scars and endless tattoo variations of phoenix wings. But her photos only go back to mid-January, nothing about the crash on New Year's Eve, nothing about Kenzie.

I try "Kenzie King" and tap on a close-up of a windblown, beach-in-the-background girl.

Bingo.

Her account is private, but through some sleuthing, I sift through her friends' accounts, finding photos of her and Piper wearing massive New Year's Eve glasses and top hats, grinning into the camera. Before that, more pictures of them with the girl with the pixie haircut huddled under blankets at football games, in sequined dresses for homecoming, and standing arm in arm on the lip of the stage.

In what bizarro universe were Piper and Kenzie friends?

I scroll through the pictures of the past that Piper has clearly tried to delete. And if I'm going to survive in Kenzie King's theater, I need to know why.

———

The next afternoon, Dr. Layne goes on forever at support group about the power of fear, but all I can think about is getting a minute alone with Piper.

Piper rolls her eyes as the crying boy—I think his name is Braden—talks about how he's afraid he'll never play the piano again because of the whole one-hand thing, and then he launches into how his girlfriend wants to get freaky, but he's scared she'll be grossed out by his scars.

"Thank you for sharing," Dr. Layne says over Braden's muffled sobs. "I want you all to think about the greatest fear in your life right now. How can you take back control? Grab a partner and discuss."

Piper turns to me and nods toward Braden, who continues to wipe his face with a tissue.

"Forget the scars, he's gonna blow his first time by crying the whole way through it. Blubbering is not hot." She props her head on her hands and grins wildly. "Speaking of which, time to dish on your backstage Romeo."

"Nothing to tell. He's on stage crew and didn't recoil at the sight of me."

Piper nods, eyes blazing like I've just read her a page out of a smutty adult novel.

"Hot. It's just a matter of time before you're making out behind the curtain."

Heat rushes to my face, and I look over at Braden, talking through tears, terrified his girlfriend will run screaming once she sees him in all his fleshy splendor.

"Yeah, right. Boys are off the table for me."

Piper cocks her eyebrow.

"So Dr. Sharp will be the last man to ever see you naked? I hope it was as good for him as it was for you."

"Okay, now you're just being disgusting."

"Hey, a girl could do a lot worse than Dr. Sharp and his bangworthy dimples," Piper says. "I'm simply suggesting you shouldn't shut the door on boys so quickly."

"And I'm just saying that door has already been shut."

I don't even know why we're talking about this, especially when we need to be talking about why Piper let me walk blindly into a theater run by her newly minted archnemesis.

Piper pretends to write on her palm with an imaginary pencil, her face mockingly somber.

"Now would you say that living a life of virginal celibacy is your biggest fear?" She says this last word extra loud. Dr. Layne smiles, satisfied we're discussing our deepest, darkest terrors.

"Right now? My biggest fear is Kenzie King, your ex–best friend."

Piper drops her hands along with her smile.

"Who told you?"

"Asad." I don't mention my social media stalking.

"That kid should mind his own business."

"Is it true?

"Yes."

"How is that even possible?"

Piper shrugs, and for the first time since I've known her, she avoids meeting my eye.

"I don't really want to talk about this. We were friends. Now we're not. End of story."

"Yes, but *why* are you not friends? She clearly hates me because I'm friends with you. You can't send me into a mean-girl massacre without at least some intel."

Piper's nostrils flare as she points her finger at me.

"Being friends doesn't give you the right to snoop around in my past."

Her voice rises as the conversations around us stall and all eyes shift to Piper, frantically trying to wheel her chair away from me. She rams another chair, a sharp, metallic sound piercing the circle as the chair's legs intertwine with her spokes.

"Piper, why are you freaking out?"

She wrestles her wheels free and answers without looking at me.

"Because I don't want to talk about it. Because I don't want to think about it. Of all people, *you* should understand that."

By this point, Dr. Layne is walking toward us.

"Girls, is there a problem?"

"Everything's fine!" Piper says, finally detangling the chair from her own wheelchair. She half throws it out of her way and abruptly backs away from Layne and out of the circle.

"It's therapy—everything's always fine, right?" Piper says.

"Now, Piper, I just—"

"I know, I know, you want to know my biggest fear so you can fix me. Well, get your clipboard ready, because here it is: I'm sixteen and I have to start my life over because of a split-second error on the highway. But every time I get close to actually enjoying my new life, you all dig into the past and make me relive it. I just want to move on. And my biggest fear, Dr. Fix-It, is that I never will."

Turning her back on the group, Piper pumps herself furiously toward the exit, the heavy door banging shut behind her.

16

I find her by the community-center roundabout, streaky mascara dried on her cheeks and the front wheels of her chair teetering precariously over the curb. I slow-clap as I plop down next to her.

"Wow. You will do *anything* to win therapy points. You should see Dr. Layne in there scribbling furiously on her clipboard."

The corner of Piper's lips lift reluctantly, but her eyes stay trained on the ground as she rocks her wheels over the curb until they're just about to fall, and then snaps them backward.

"Don't you have things you're tired of talking about?" she asks.

Across the parking lot, Cora watches us from the driver's seat of Glenn's truck, probably trying to figure out why I'm sitting on the curb with a tearstained Piper instead of "recovering."

"I just can't believe you were ever friends with Snartface McGee."

Piper wipes her face with the back of her zebra compression garments.

"Since fourth grade." Piper turns to me, her eyes almost as pink as her sleeves. "But now she's erased me, along with the memory of what she did."

"What did she do?"

Piper continues to stare at the mountains now bathed in pink-hued shadows as the sun goes down behind us. Sitting at the base of her wheelchair, I can see the burns on her neck more clearly, the way they wave upward toward her face like a plume of smoke from a candle.

"This," she says, pointing to her leg. "Well, technically, the streetlight she hit broke my leg."

"Kenzie was the one driving?"

Piper nods. "Yeah. Crossed the median. Plowed into a pole."

She tells me how she and Kenzie used to be inseparable, and how Kenzie had a few too many drinks on New Year's Eve and crashed driving home. She didn't visit Piper in the hospital, and when Piper went back to school, Kenzie turned their friends against her and looked right through her in the halls.

"She full-on ghosted me," she says.

I shake my head in confusion.

"Wait, so if it was her fault, why does *she* hate *you*?"

"Who knows? Guilt? I became this constant reminder she didn't want around anymore."

The guilt of the healthy. The first time my old friends visited me in the unit, I felt it.

I was burned.

They were not.

A river of guilt between us.

I flick a jagged rock in the street with the big toe on my left hand.

"Trust me. I get it."

"I should have known she'd take it out on you," Piper says. "It probably kills her that I'm not alone anymore." She holds out the golden bird charm dangling from a black rope around her neck, outlining the bird's wings with her thumb.

"It's cheesy, I know, but I wear this phoenix to remind myself that I can rise above all this. Just like in that song I played you, I can soar above everything—this chair, these burns, my friends cutting me out." Piper rubs the phoenix between her fingers, her eyes still locked on the mountains. "I want to move on and never look back."

I follow her gaze. Is it possible to move on so easily, forging ahead unhindered by yesterday's scars? I stretch out my fingers in front of me, the tight tissue resisting.

What if you can't escape the scars?

"You know what I think?" she says, suddenly sitting up straighter in her wheelchair. "I think we need to focus on the new part of Laynie's new normal."

I pick at the cuff of my compression garments where my fingers stick out, nervously waiting to hear the rest of her idea. The last time Piper got that "I've got a great plan" look in her eyes, I ended up on a stage, playing the starring role of leper in a circle of trust.

"Like what?"

Piper tilts her head back, thinking, her tongue clicking on the roof of her mouth. She turns to me decisively.

"Yearbook photos are next week. Are you thinking what I'm thinking?"

"Umm . . . if you're thinking that there is absolutely a zero percent chance I'm getting in front of a camera, then yes."

Piper rocks back and forth on the wheels of her chair, dismissing my protest.

"You *have* to have a yearbook picture. And I'm going to help you." She claps excitedly. "That's right—a makeover!"

Everything in me wants to tell Piper no. Why in the world would I want to commemorate this year with a yearbook photo just begging to be defaced with zombie blood dripping from my mouth or a Freddy Krueger fedora? God took a permanent marker and already went to town.

But the prospect of a picture-day makeover has eclipsed Piper's anger, and I can't bring myself to say no when she motions for me to kneel by her chair. She turns my head left, then right, studying my face.

"Lost cause, right?" I say.

"Not at all, dahling," she says in a mock Southern drawl. "I don't believe in lost causes, but I do believe in makeup."

I shake my head. "No way. No makeup. Unless you're going for an escaped-killer-clown vibe."

Piper squinches up her face and clasps her fingers together, begging. "Not even mascara?"

I point to my eyes. "No eyelashes."

Piper sighs heavily and yanks the bandana off before I can stop her.

"Then our first task is this mess you call hair."

My right hand hides my head while I grab for my bandana with my toe-hand. Piper's eyes land on the spot where my ear should be but says nothing about my missing pieces.

"Well, you can't be photographed like this." She shakes the bandana at me. "Or wearing this fashion faux pas."

I snatch again at the bandana in vain.

"Exactly. Now you see the beauty of my no-photographs policy."

"Not so fast."

She nods toward Cora, who is doing a super-duper clandestine job of acting like she's not watching us. She's even killed her engine and rolled down her window to aid her eavesdropping.

"Will your aunt take us somewhere?"

Cora pulls up to the curb when I wave her over. Envelopes and hospital bills with big red FINAL NOTICE declarations screaming from the top of the page cover the passenger seat.

"You girls okay?"

"We need a ride," Piper says.

"Where to?" Cora asks, gathering up all the paperwork.

Piper grins mischievously at me.

"To get Ava some new hair."

17

"I must look like an undead hooker."

I whisper because we are the only people in the creepiest store in the history of strip malls. A lady with wide eyeliner circles and innumerable piercings pretends to brush out a frizzy brown wig behind the counter, but she's watching us through the rows of faceless dummy heads.

Piper directs me to a full-length mirror on the wall.

"See for yourself."

I force myself to look in the glass to see the monstrosity of a wig Piper has placed on my head. It's hot pink—of course—with short bangs tickling my forehead and a bob cut coming just below my chin.

"It's exactly what you need," she declares.

The curl of the bob does cover my earlessness perfectly, and the bangs draw attention to my eyes rather than the wrinkled skin around them.

I lean closer to the mirror.

"Don't you think it's kind of . . . desperate?"

Piper laughs as she smooths out a long blond wig with straight strands reaching down to her lap, like a Coachella flower child.

"Desperate times, my friend. Desperate times."

I step back from the mirror and put my hand on my hips, trying to look normal. Oh hey, just here being super casual in my clown wig and scarred-up body.

"Maybe something a little more subdued. Like light brown? This feels like I'm trying too hard."

Piper deflates and looks up at the ceiling like she's praying for patience.

"Ava, a brown wig is just sad. If you show up in this, you're making a statement." She stretches out her zebra-striped arm next to my beige one. "Like our compression garments. No one thinks those dullsville nude ones are your real skin anyway. Why not have some fun with it?"

The Goth lady behind the counter watches us as Piper's voice gets louder. She spins her wheelchair in a circle, sending the blond hair flowing behind her.

"It's like the universe dealt us this horrible hand in life and it's our duty to scream back: 'Well played, craptastic cosmos, but you haven't met *me* yet.'"

"So zebra stripes and pink wigs are like your big middle finger to the universe?"

Piper smiles and wiggles her eyebrows at me through the glass.

"I also have my eye on a sweet tattoo, and if you'd hurry up and buy that amazeballs wig, we might have time to stop by the shop next door before your aunt gets back."

The pink hair tickles my face as I whip around to Piper. "A tattoo? Are you kidding me?"

She nods, eyes wide. "You should get one, too!"

"More than half of me is scar tissue. Why in the world would I intentionally add to that morbid statistic? Why would you?"

Piper reaches up to bop me on the nose and says in a sing-songy voice: "'Every party has a pooper, that's why we invited you.' Ava Lee. Party pooper."

I turn back to my reflection.

"One ridiculous cliché at a time. Let's start with this zombie streetwalker wig, and *then* we'll talk tattoos, okay?"

Piper squeezes in next to me so the glass captures both of us, me giving the wig one last shake. "So you're getting it?"

"People are going to look at me."

Piper rolls her eyes at me in the glass.

"Right. Might as well give them something to see."

Before I can stop her, she grabs my phone, presses her cheek against mine, yells, "Cheese!" and clicks.

"See, that wasn't so bad was it?" she says.

I stuff my bandana in the bag Goth lady gives me and wear my new hair all the way home.

———

"What in the blazes is on your head?" Glenn says before he even has his boots off that night.

"You like?" I shake my head so the bobbed strands shimmy in front of my eyes. In my peripheral vision, I see Cora giving Glenn a "cut it out" sign, as if I don't know I'm sporting hot-pink hair and the best thing to do is ignore it like she did all the way home in the car, her eyes never veering from the road.

"Do *you*?" he asks.

"It's different," I say, shrugging.

"Good different?"

"Different. Piper thinks it's time for a change."

We sit to a cooking-channel-worthy spread for dinner, which means Cora has hauled herself out of her "down day" on Sara's birthday and is now spiraling headfirst into an "everything's-going-to-be-fine! recovery week," aka competing for Chef of the Year. At home, meals were simple affairs, usually eaten off paper plates. But on days like this, we eat on china plates with small yellow birds on them, and every seat has a full place setting of silverware, except for Sara's, of course. No one ever sits there, like we're just waiting for her to dance in and claim her rightful spot.

Glenn passes me the mashed potatoes in a porcelain serving dish, not even trying to keep his eyes off the wig.

"That Piper's a real spitfire, isn't she?"

"She sure is," Cora says, though not in quite the same innocuous, upbeat tone.

"What's that supposed to mean?" I ask.

"Oh, nothing. She's just unique, that's all. But if you like her—" Cora says.

"Yeah, I like her," I say.

"Well, good then." Glenn dings his fork like a gavel on the table.

Cora chews quietly, her eyes down.

"I was reading an article," she starts. Here we go. "About these camps they do every year where you can go and spend time with other survivors."

Cora produces a magazine from her lap and places it on the table next to me. On the cover, a black girl with a melted face like mine swings from a rope over a pond. "You might find friends who are serious about recovery."

I put my fork down, the tines pinging against the china.

"My life is already *dead* serious. But if you want to say something about Piper, just say it."

Cora fidgets like she can't get comfortable, her eyes flitting from me to Glenn to her plate.

"It's just. You know. The whole thing—this wig. Those terrible things she was saying that day in your room."

"I was saying them, too."

"That's my point. Maybe she's not the best influence—"

I push my chair back from the table.

"You were the one who made me go to group. You told me to make friends. Now they're not the right friends? You're giving me whiplash."

"It's just, Glenn is right: Piper has a big personality," Cora says, her eyes drifting over my pink hair reluctantly. "I don't want you to lose yourself in it."

"It's just a wig, Cora. It's still me under here. Trust me—there's no escaping that."

Glenn and Cora look at each other across the table, a silent conversation taking place about what to say next. I get tired of waiting.

"May I be excused?"

Glenn nods. I leave the magazine next to my half-eaten dinner.

In my room, I pull out the folder of plastic surgery ideas I keep in my desk. Close-ups and clippings of reconstructed eyes and ears and lips, cutout fantasies from the people in Cora's *Burn Survivor Quarterly* who are lucky enough to get real plastic surgery. I arrange all the "after" pictures on my bed into a bizarro face collage. On top of a dainty, perfectly constructed nose, I place a pair of eyes the same blue as mine.

In the glass of the curio cabinet, I examine myself. Beneath the hair, the edges of each skin graft chop my face into harsh sections, the bright white of my forehead contrasting with the pinkish hue of my chin and neck.

My nose is new, too. It's more bulbous than my real one, but that one went the way of my ear. My lips puff out below my new nose, seeping beyond their bounds like I applied permanent bright pink lipstick while driving on a gravelly road.

And while my eyes are mine—the only thing that looks exactly like before the fire—my eye sockets sag into my cheeks.

I tug up the corners of my drooping eyes. Under the wig, my face isn't as horrific. It's like when I used to put on my costume before a play, like the clothes and makeup and hair gave me permission to be someone else.

Someone better.

I let my eyes fall again and smooth out the hot-pink strands of the wig. I'm not delusional. I know this wig won't fix my face. But at least it's real, not pipe dreams hidden in a drawer.

In the glass, my eyes are extra blue against the pink.

It's dumb. It's loud. It's completely not me.

Piper's right: it's exactly what I need.

18

I wait until picture day the next week to debut the new me.

My hot-pink hair causes a definite uptick in the stare factor. A girl in my Spanish class tells me she "loves the look." A group of boys whistle and whisper-laugh as I walk by in the hallway. Piper "accidentally" rams her wheelchair into one of them.

"I should just take it off," I say. I pull a bandana from my backpack, which Piper promptly grabs and throws into a trash can.

"No way. You look amazing."

I fidget with my new hair in the back of science class and try not to smile too big when Asad tells me he "digs the wig." What world have I allowed Piper to pull me into, where I get worked up over a boy and wear punk-rock wigs from stores with mannequins sporting fishnet stockings?

When Mr. Bernard tells us to partner up, Asad grabs my sleeve.

"Dibs," he says.

"Did you just dibs me?" I say.

"Totes."

"I'm not sure if I'm more distressed by your use of the word *totes* or by the fact that you think I'm dibs-able."

"You're stage crew now. We stick together."

Side by side, we lay out the materials for today's lab, which involves mealworms and petri dishes. Mr. Bernard spent the first half of class regaling us about the insights into human nature we will gain from watching these squirmy little dudes for the next few weeks. I have my doubts, considering I can't even tell which end is the head and which end is, well, the end.

"Each group of organisms create a community, and these simple mealworms are no exception," Mr. Bernard says. "In life, community is key, whether you're an arthropod or a *Homo sapiens.*"

A snicker waves through the back table, where three hulking boy-men in varsity football jackets repeat the word *homo.*

"*Homo sapiens* are humans," Mr. Bernard says.

"Whatever floats your boat, buddy," the tallest meathead says. Mr. Bernard looks at him for a minute and tries one more time.

"No, literally, *Homo sapiens* is a classification of people. It follows *Homo erectus.*"

This only ignites another round of laughter, whereupon Mr. Bernard sits in his chair and begins to read rather than attempt to enlighten these modern-day knuckle draggers.

While we prep our luxury plastic habitat for our segmented charges, Asad talks about set design and his lighting concept, which is apparently going to "blow my mind."

"I think of lighting as its own character, you know? Like how I illuminate the stage tells a part of the story," he says.

I fill our petri dish with wood shavings as he talks, which is basically nonstop, telling me how he wishes we were doing *Wicked* instead of the original *Wizard of Oz* because it's his favorite musical of all time and he's been lobbying to do it since freshman year.

"It changed my life." He looks straight into my eyes when he says this, as if he's revealing a part of himself. All I know is his coffee-black eyes reveal *me* in their glassy darkness so clearly that I look away.

"I've never seen it. It came to Salt Lake once when I was little, but we couldn't go," I say.

"But you know the songs, right? *Everybody* knows the songs."

I shake my head.

"Nope. Personal rule: no music until I see the play. Don't want to spoil it. But isn't *Wicked* just like *The Wizard of Oz* on acid?"

Asad puts down the handful of wood shavings he was making into a small mealworm bed, props his elbows on the counter, and drops his head into his hands like I've betrayed him.

"It is *nothing* like *The Wizard of Oz*. It is like taking the yellow brick road and twisting it until it snaps in half and then you look inside and there's a whole other world in that road that's dark and deep and soul-exposing." Asad's face is solemn. "That's it. We have to go."

"You and me, we?" I'm surprised I can even get my sentence out when the only word bouncing in my head is *we, we, we, we*.

Asad nods matter-of-factly.

"Yes, you and me. It's coming to Salt Lake in a few weeks." A sheen of urgency covers his face. "I don't want to oversell this, but after this play, you will never. Be. The. Same."

He picks up our petri dish habitat and walks to the front of the room. On his way back, he holds out the dish, where three small and squiggly worms roll around on top of each other.

"Congratulations. Triplets!"

Before he reaches our station, one of the back-row football boys shoves Asad's arm so hard that the petri dish flies toward me. I reach out for it, but not fast enough, and it hits the ground, the mealworms ejected into the air and onto the ground like small segmented stuntmen.

"Drama queer," the boy says, just loud enough for us to hear. "Shouldn't *you* be the one in the drag queen wig?"

Asad bends down to pick up the worms and the chips like he doesn't hear the boy towering above him.

"Uh-oh," the other jersey boy says. "You touched him and now he's getting *Homo erectus.*"

Football boy high-fives another kid in a Viking jersey in the back of the room. Asad plunks the dish on the counter in front of me.

"I know, I know. What kind of parent drops their babies, right?"

"What was *that* about?" I ask.

Asad rearranges the mealworm in the dish without looking up.

"Oh, that? Nothing."

"It didn't look like nothing."

"It's just part of this little game we play where he makes my life hell, and in return, I let him."

I grab the mealworm dish so Asad has to look up at me.

"Aren't you the guy who told me to stick up for myself? And you're letting those jock straps push you around?"

Asad shrugs. "Ava, I'm one of a handful of brown kids at a school whose mascot makes Attila the Hun look like Mother Teresa."

"And I'm what? Running for prom queen?"

"That's why we stick together outside the safety of our stage—survival," he says. He holds up the petri dish so I can see the mealworms burrowing deep into the wood chips, their bodies pressed up against the plastic. "Now. What shall we name these little guys?"

We decide on Magical Mr. Mistoffelees, Rum Tum Tugger, and Macavity.

"Now, that's a community that would make Andrew Lloyd Webber proud," Asad says, then pauses. "It's stuff like that, isn't it? That makes them think I'm"—he looks around and whispers—"a *Homo sapien*."

I laugh. "And maybe the jazz hands?"

"What? A guy can't do spirit fingers without having his sexuality questioned anymore? See, this is exactly why I do stage crew instead of cast."

I nod toward the back.

"To avoid that guy's ridicule?"

"And my father's." Asad wags a finger at me and in a thick Pakistani accent says, "Theater is for girls, Asad. Men go to medical school."

I sigh. "'It's the Hard-Knock Life,' my friend."

"Too easy—*Annie*," he says, then quickly, "I'm not, by the way."

"Not what?"

"Homo sapien."

"I didn't ask."

"Okay, just wanted you to know."

My pink hair falls slightly in front of my face, just in time to hide my smile.

———

Piper tries to escort me to the auditorium for my photo, but Vice Principal Lynch busts her for not having a hall pass.

"No special treatment, girls," he says.

I don't know why this guy hates me so much. Maybe I remind him of a more scarrific version of his own loser teenage self. Maybe he's just a jerk whose perpetually tight collar has cut off the oxygen to his frontal lobe. He points for Piper to head back to class. She mock salutes him.

"Ja, Kapitän!" She yells over him to me, "Don't forget to say cheese!"

"Thanks, *Mom*!" I holler back. I'm sure I look as surprised as Piper to hear my voice ringing through the hallway.

"The power of the pink!" Piper yells after me with a triumphant smile.

I walk alone, but armed with my wig, I keep my eyes up instead of studying the speckles on the linoleum. In the auditorium, about a dozen students wait for their turn in front of a velvety purple backdrop on the stage with a barstool facing a tripod. I join the throng and await my turn, adjusting my wig the whole time. Picture day was terrible Before, but now, my skin itches beneath my compression garments, spreading little fiery twitches up my arms.

As if being a teenager isn't harrowing enough, we commemorate it with wallet-size mementos of awkwardness. In middle school, we used to trade our photos like baseball cards. I'd sign mine with my name like I was a celebrity, turning the *v* into a heart. Back then, how many school photos you collected directly correlated with your cool factor.

I'll be lucky if even Piper wants this year's edition.

When my turn comes, I muster a smile that I know looks like I'm either eating rancid fish or trying not to soil myself. I can tell it doesn't look good by the way the photographer smiles nervously and fiddles with the camera.

I think he may be having some sort of mini meltdown. He tinkers with his flash for a solid five minutes, even though with everyone else he snapped two rapid-fire shots and voilà, high school memory complete. He wipes beads of sweat from his forehead with the back of his shirtsleeve.

"Let me try one more thing," he says, starting another round of button pressing.

"I'm sure it's fine," I say. We both know the equipment isn't the problem here. "You can just take it."

He resumes his position behind the camera. "Okay, on three. One, two . . ."

147

I swear he winces when he pulls the trigger. As I get up to leave, he waves me over behind the tripod.

"I have an idea."

He pulls up my digital picture on a laptop next to him. My pink hair fills the top half of the frame.

"So, this is totally up to you, but we do offer an editing package," he says. He moves the mouse over my image, hovering it above my nose. "Just watch."

As he moves the cursor around my face on the screen, my skin blurs beneath it. The smudging effect erases the lines separating my skin grafts and washes out the wrinkles of my scars. He does one entire side of my face, which is now a little out of focus but still—better.

He grabs another tool with his curser.

"And this can just kind of fill in some . . . problem areas," he says. He clicks around my eyes, filling in the skin beneath my eyelids. Then, he shapes the lines around my mouth so the pink of my lips doesn't bleed into my face.

He turns to me, smiling. "What do you think?"

"I think that's amazing."

"So do you want it?

"Want what?"

My old face? How much?

"The editing package. This picture would go in the yearbook instead."

I stare at the girl on the screen. Ava Before the Fire. A little blurry, but still—there she is.

"People really do this?" I say.

He nods. "Oh yeah. All the time—wrinkles, scars, unsightly moles. It all comes down to how you want people to remember you."

The girl on the screen tempts me. I want people to remember her, not the thing they see in the hallways. I want them all just to forget about that girl. Photoshop her into oblivion.

"But it's not really me," I say.

The photographer smiles like we're coconspirators.

"Yeah, that's kind of the point—it's better."

A hushed whispering behind me makes me turn, instantly aware that all the other students in line are also staring at the fantasy me on the screen. Their eyes shift from the photoshopped version to reality and then back again.

Next to this smooth-faced girl on the computer, I feel more hideous than ever. Hot hatred for her rises in my chest.

"Just erase it," I say under my breath.

The photographer leans his head toward me like he doesn't understand.

I repeat myself. "I don't want it."

"Oh, okay," he says, obviously confused. "So just the regular photo, then?"

I gather up my backpack hurriedly. This was so stupid.

"No, just delete everything. I don't want a picture."

"Are you sure? I—"

"Erase it!" My voice echoes through the auditorium. I turn to him and lower my voice. "Please."

He drags the file to the trash icon on his screen.

"I was just trying to help."

Tears threaten to spill out. I choke them back as I grab my bag and head for the door.

"I don't need your help. I don't need anyone."

19

I'd rip the wig right off if Piper hadn't trashed my only backup bandana, and there's no way I'm going to drama club totally exposed.

I hang out in a bathroom stall, kicking the door. I'm so stupid—a wig and Photoshop can't change reality.

I linger in the stall, partly to conveniently miss the circle of trust, but also to give the photo guy enough time to clear out. When I finally go to drama club, Asad is already painting the yellow brick road we started earlier this week, and next to him, Piper paints green skyscrapers in the Emerald City. She's been rehearsal-crashing all week while the volleyball team is on the road.

"Hey hey! How'd the glamour shot go?" she asks.

I pick up a paintbrush and kneel next to Asad, channeling all my focus into the yellow brick lines up and down the backdrop.

"Imagine the worst scenario possible, and then make it ten times crappier, and you might be getting close."

"It couldn't be that—" Piper starts.

"He photoshopped me." I say it quietly, hoping not to make this a big scene in front of Asad.

Piper pauses, her green-tipped paintbrush in midair.

"Who did what, now?"

I tell her about the nervous photographer and his airbrush-editing package. "I think he was just trying to be nice."

Piper looks at Asad, who shrugs, and then back at me, her voice high and shrill, echoing across the empty stage.

"Ava! You have to tell people where they can stick their nice." She shakes me by my shoulders, flicking paint on me in the process. "If we don't tell them, who will?"

"Tell them what exactly?" I say.

"That you don't need Photoshop. That his definition of beauty is archaic and ignorant."

"See, this is why you should have been with me."

"I can't fight your battles for you, Ava."

"Yeah, well, apparently I can't, either." I run my fingers through the strands of my new pink hair. "I thought this wig was like some new beginning for me, facing my fears and all that. But I totally crumbled."

Before Piper can affirm that yes, I am a huge coward, Kenzie walks across the stage toward us, her eyes glued to Piper.

"What are you doing here?" she says.

Piper doesn't look up, almost like she's waiting on one of us to defend her presence. She glares at Asad, who stares intently at the canvas. Piper mutters under her breath before turning to Kenzie.

"Free country," she says. "I'm here with Ava."

Kenzie's eyes shift from me to Piper and back again.

"So when you said you didn't want to do drama anymore, you meant you didn't want to do it with *me*?"

"Yeah, something like that," Piper says.

"Can we at least talk abo—"

"Nothing to talk about," Piper says. "Don't worry, I won't rock your world by rolling back into your precious drama troupe. You can continue to forget the whole thing ever happened."

Kenzie stares down at Piper, her face softening slightly.

"That's not fair, Piper," she says quietly, blinking away the tears in her eyes before they escape.

Piper half laughs and mock applauds. "Bravo! Two thumbs way up for this award-winning performance. Encore! Encore!"

And just like that, Kenzie's momentary softness vanishes, replaced by her usual tightly pinched scowl. She folds her arms across her chest and huffs past me to prop open the backstage door with a classroom chair.

"It smells like a morgue back here." She looks right at me when she says this, then adds, pointing to my wig, "Don't let her fool you, Ava. When she's done playing dress-up, Piper will only look out for one person. Fair warning: it won't be you."

She turns on her heel, kicking the extra paintbrushes as she goes.

"Save the drama for the stage, right?" Piper says after she's gone.

I nod. "Seriously. She's the one who wanted you gone in the first place."

Piper turns back to her green skyscrapers.

153

"Technically speaking, I quit. I am not about to spend my time where I'm not wanted, and trust me, she did *not* want me. No one wants the sad cripple around bumming everyone out."

Asad finally looks up from his painting. "Nobody said you weren't wanted."

Piper gasps and raises her hands heavenward.

"It's a miracle! Your selective mutism has passed! Funny how you never shut up when you're with us, but someone a few rungs higher on the social ladder appears and suddenly you're at a loss for words." She turns to me, gesturing her paintbrush toward my wig. "And you. I don't care if you wear that thing or not, you know. I was just trying to help."

I straighten the hair on my head, which has crept down my forehead while I was painting.

"I might be beyond help."

I pull my headphones out of my bag and put them on over the wig, trying to block out today. We paint together for the rest of the hour, mostly in silence, me mulling over today's photo disaster, Piper no doubt fuming at her Kenzie run-in, and Asad trying not to get mocked again. I brush up and down the canvas, finishing the final curves of the yellow brick road.

Follow the path. Click the shoes. Go home.

If only life were so scripted.

———

When we're the last three in the auditorium, Asad and I lug the canvases to the back wall, and when we return, Piper is sitting on the edge of the stage, her legs dangling, staring into the dark auditorium with her empty wheelchair behind her.

"So you wanted to face a fear today, huh?" she says, her lips half smiling but her eyes in full blaze.

"Yeah. And I failed."

Piper gestures toward the empty auditorium.

"We got a stage."

"And?"

"And screw the yearbook photo. Face an even bigger fear."

"What? Sing?"

Piper nods. Asad jumps up and pulls the curtains all the way open, his usual smile returning.

"No. Way," I say.

Asad strides to the end of the stage.

"Here, I'll go first. Warm the place up a little."

He faces the empty auditorium, hands outstretched toward the invisible audience, face contorted with artistic anguish as he sings an off-key (okay, not even key-adjacent) version of "Circle of Life" from *The Lion King* complete with an earsplitting vibrato that makes Piper grimace. When he finishes, he takes an over-the-top bow, his black shock of hair falling dramatically over his eyes.

"Well, *that* I can follow," I say.

"A dying cat could follow that," Piper says. "Pun intended."

"Haters gonna hate." Asad grabs my hand and pulls me to my feet, half dragging me to the front of the stage.

Piper waves me forward, rolling her eyes. "It's just us, Ava. One of us who loves you to pieces, and one who is clearly tone-deaf."

Asad scowls at her. "Rude."

Facing the darkness of the theater, I tighten my hoodie around my waist. The last time I sang on a stage, Sara was in the audience with Mom and Dad. My people—unseen but buoying me up from the darkness.

Now, only empty seats look back, and I'm definitely not the same girl looking out.

"Just sing the audition song," he says. "You know it, right?"

I nod. After years of singing along with my mother as she brushed her fingertips up and down my arm at bedtime, I know it by heart.

But that was before I traded lullabies for lotion and spotlights for stage crew.

I'm not even sure I *can* sing anymore.

I stand at the lip of the stage and sing the first word, which comes out shaky and uncertain.

" 'Somewhere—' " Halfway through the word, my unfamiliar voice cracks, falling short of the high note.

I touch the spot just below my voice box where my skin puckers around my tracheotomy scar. I clear my throat, fearing the smoke and tubes and flames changed more than my skin.

"It's been too long," I whisper.

"I have an idea!" Asad says. "An old theater trick for stage fright."

"I am *not* imagining you in your underwear."

"Only if you want to, sicko," he says with a wink. "But that's not part of the exercise. For real. Close your eyes."

I blink out the light.

"Now, imagine you're anywhere you want. Alone. At Abravanel Hall. On Broadway—"

"Hiding behind stage curtains," Piper adds.

"You be quiet over there," I say in the direction of her voice.

With my eyes closed, I go somewhere else in my mind.

Somewhere without photoshopped scars and wigs and empty seats around the dinner table.

Somewhere safe.

A place where a song scares away nightmares.

I'm in my bed, tucked in tight, while my mom sings about blue skies and rainbows, her voice soft and sure.

Quiet and unsteady, my own is barely recognizable.

Somewhere over the rainbow—

I peek down at Piper, who motions for me to keep going. I shut my eyes tight and force my voice to swell as I sing about blue skies and wishing on stars.

My bedroom floor rumbles as the garage door opens. Dad's home. Mom's voice lulls me to sleep as Dad locks the front door behind him.

My voice crescendos in the space, filling my head, my ears, my memory with words about a place where troubles melt and blue-birds soar. Air fills my lungs. Tingles snap across my skin.

Waking me up.

For a time-bending second, I'm me again.

I fall asleep, safely wrapped up in my family in our corner of the world. We're home, together—what harm could ever reach us here?

My voice whispers.

157

Birds fly over the rainbow
Why, then,
Oh, why
Can't I?

Salt on my lips tells me I'm crying, but I don't open my eyes. Not yet. I soak in this moment.

The feeling of the stage and the music and the electricity in my skin.

The sound of a forgotten voice.

The memory of home.

When I open my eyes, Piper holds up her unburned arm. "Goose bumps. And if I had hair on my other arm, it would be standing, too."

Asad stares at me, his mouth slightly agape, eyebrows furrowed in thought.

"Explain to me why you are on crew again?"

I point to my face, but he keeps shaking his head.

"No, seriously, Ava. You are better than most of those cast girls. You should try out."

I gather up the paintbrushes, my shaking hands clinking the wooden handles together.

"Well, even if I wanted to—which I absolutely do not—tryouts are over."

Asad wags his finger at me.

"Not so fast. Cynthia Chang just found out she got mono for Valentine's Day, so they're holding last-minute reauditions for Glinda."

"As in Glinda the Good Witch. The beautiful, angelic fairy? You're kidding, right?"

Asad shakes his head while we gather painting supplies, but Piper stares at me.

"Not everyone has a voice like yours, Ava," she says.

"Or a face," I say.

"We're not talking about your face."

Asad closes the curtains, eclipsing the make-believe audience.

" 'Everyone deserves the chance to fly,' " he says quietly, almost to himself, before he realizes Piper and I are both staring at him. "My favorite line from *Wicked*. Gah, how have you not seen that?"

A few of the paintbrushes slip through the gap between my toe-thumb and my fused fingers. They hit the ground like pickup sticks as I try to get Asad and Piper to see this idea is a nonstarter, no matter how good it felt to sing again.

"Life is not a musical, okay?" I say. "I can barely look in the mirror, and you're saying I should get up on a stage in front of the whole school?"

Piper reaches out and picks up the paintbrushes for me.

"I'm saying the same thing I was about that bonehead photographer," she says. "The fire didn't take your voice. So use it."

March 27

Nobody tells me my parents are dead for two weeks.
Buried while I slept.
"We needed you to fight," a nurse says. "We were
afraid you'd give up if you knew."
She's right.
I do.

                                    I fade away.
                              Away from the truth.
                               Away from a world
                                 with no parents.

Cora chatters by my bed.
Nurses ask me questions.
I talk only when I have to.
They want me to look at my face.

                                            Not yet.

They want me to walk.

                                      I'm not ready.

They want me to say where it hurts.

                                          Everywhere.

Nurses change me
wash me
manage me.

But I'm already gone,
tucked deep inside my broken body.
A dying star
collapsing.

My voice feels broken, too.
It's not.

I just can't find the words.

20

Piper and Asad take turns all week pointing out the audition list hanging outside the auditorium door.

On the last day of sign-ups, Piper does her best chicken impression with her hands tucked into her armpits to make wings. "Bok, bok, bok."

"Nice," I say. "I don't see you trying out."

She puts away her wings.

"That's different."

"How?"

"It just is."

"So it's not because you think it'll bug Kenzie to have me in her play and you're using me as a pawn in your feud?"

Piper stops in the middle of the hallway, eliciting a dirty look from a boy who nearly trips over her wheelchair. She flips him off.

"I want you to do it because you can. I can't walk. That crying kid at group can't play the piano. You can't look in the mirror. But you *can* sing."

During drama, Asad not-so-subtly mentions the sign-ups while we sort through the disheveled costume closets backstage. He pulls a ginormous Pepto-Bismol-pink hoop dress from the back and holds it up to me.

"I really think you could get it."

"Getting it and actually doing it are two totally different things." I push aside the layers upon layers of satiny fabric. "And this dress? Are you trying to get me to audition or run away screaming?"

He stuffs the dress back in and puts a Tin Man's hat on his head, locks his arms at ninety-degree angles, and does an inde-scribably bad robot dance. I put on a pointy black witch hat as he swaps out the tin hat for a lion's mask with a matted mane.

"'Courage cannot erase our fears.'" He strikes a nowhere-near-ferocious pose. "'Courage is when we face our fears.'"

"*Newsies*. Too easy." I pull off his mask. "And too easy to say for someone hiding up in his lighting booth."

"Touché, my friend. Touché." He reaches deep into the closet, pulls out a pair of ruby-red shoes, and places them in my hands.

I click the heels together. Three clicks—*POOF!*—you're home. Dorothy had it so good.

The sound of someone else's feet entering the stage makes us both look up, and I chuck the shoes back into the closet. Asad presses one finger to his lips as Kenzie's unmistakable voice reaches us.

"I *know* Piper put her up to this," she says.

"It's not even a big role," says a high-pitched voice that I think belongs to Kenzie's sidekick with the pixie cut.

"That's not the point," Kenzie snaps. "This is all some twisted revenge plot. Piper blames me for the crash, so she's throwing her new friend in my face."

Asad holds up the dress as if to ask if I've signed up for auditions. I shake my head decidedly.

"Maybe she won't even get the part," Pixie Cut says.

Kenzie scoffs.

"Of course she will; what kind of monster could say no to *her*?"

"You," Pixie Cut says, making me almost like her.

"*I* am not the monster here," Kenzie half shouts. "I'm legit worried about her. She doesn't even know she's a laughingstock, walking around with that wig like Piper's little dress-up Troll doll. Letting her on this stage is just cruel."

She lowers her voice, but it still reaches us through the curtains.

"Unless it's the part of the witch who gets smashed by a house. *That* part she can have."

They keep talking, but I'm distracted by Asad, who has slowly started pulling down a ladder attached to the wall next to us, one hand over the other to keep the squeaking quiet.

"What are you doing?" I whisper.

"What I should have done last time."

The ladder down, Asad climbs up, pausing when the bottom rung makes a loud creak. We both look to the stage curtain, but it stays closed, and the girls keep talking. He climbs up the ladder until he's a full person above me and reaches out to the support beams that hold up the heavy grand curtain. Smiling down at me, he holds up his fingers, counting silently—one, two—

"Three!" he says, snapping a metal clasp wide-open, and as he does, the thick, velvet grand curtain plummets to the stage, completely covering both girls and prompting an outburst of squeals.

Asad hurries off the ladder.

"Let's go," he says, running down the backstage steps, and I follow him at a full sprint through the aisle, my hand on my wig to keep it from falling off.

We open the auditorium door and are almost home free when—

"Ava!"

Kenzie stands in the middle of the stage, hands perched on her hips and her hair sticking out at inexplicable angles.

Asad pulls me through the door, rescuing me from my paralysis. In the hallway, he pumps his fist in the air as I bend to catch my breath. My heartbeat pounds in every part of my body, threatening to leap from my throat. I haven't run that fast since Before.

"Who's hiding in their lighting booth now, baby!" Asad yells down the empty hallway. "Now you *have* to audition just to stick it up her I'd-like-to-thank-the-Academy butt."

"How's that logic again?" I say between winded breaths.

"Kenzie knows you were listening, so if you back down, she wins."

I shake my head, my heartbeat slowing to a trot from a racing gallop.

"She wins, okay? There is no scenario where she doesn't win. Besides, I can't back down because I never signed up. All *you* did was paint a huge target on my back."

Asad scrunches up his face as he looks behind me and then turns me around by my shoulders.

"I think that target was already there."

There, on the last line of the sign-ups, two words reignite my pulse: *Ava Lee.*

21

No hablo inglés

I know it was you

Doing what?

I'm not doing it.

I know nothing

You KNOW what!

Thank you

You're impossible

At least think about it. You owe yourself that much

Like I can stop thinking about it. I think about it the whole time Dr. Sharp works his fingertips across my scars at my monthly frisking.

I think about how good it felt to sing again, and how much I've missed that part of me. I think about sticking it to Kenzie, waging my own war for backstage crewpies and Piper and girls with bandanas instead of hair.

Mostly, I think about being someone other than the Burned Girl.

But then I think about what it would feel like to stand on a stage again, all those eyes staring at me, inspecting me. Might as well dream of soaring over rainbows. I can't face an audience. Not with *this* face.

Dr. Sharp makes some computer notes as my brain wanders off the stage and back into this sterile exam room.

"You're healing nicely," he says.

Always healing, never healed.

"And how is reintegration going?" he says.

"Well, Doctor, the native species have accepted me into their ranks. I'd say the infiltration is a success."

Dr. Sharp smiles and shakes his head. Cora puts her hand on my shoulder.

"She's doing wonderfully. She's even made a friend at support group."

"Piper, right?" he says.

I nod, unsettled that Cora has clearly already given him—and probably the whole Committee on Ava's Life—this update.

"She's a live wire, that one. When she was in the unit, I had to keep reminding the nurses that there were other patients. She just kind of took over—everything."

"That's Piper," Cora says from her usual position at my side, my recovery binder open on the desk. "But she did convince Ava to join the drama club."

Dr. Sharp looks up from his computer screen. "Theater?"

"Stage crew," I clarify quickly. "It's not like I'm in the play or anything."

Dr. Sharp searches my face in a way that's different from his usual scar scan. Like he's seeing past my skin.

"Do you feel your physical appearance is holding you back?"

"It is what it is." I lift my thighs off the paper, and it crinkles beneath my shifting weight. Dr. Sharp scoots backward on his little doctor stool, folding his arms across his chest as he studies me.

"What if it wasn't?"

Cora's face tells me she's as surprised by this question as I am. We both know I'll have surgeries for the rest of my life to fix and remix my scars as they heal, but we were taking a break from the blade. The committee decided.

Dr. Sharp taps a pencil to his chin and screeches his stool toward me.

"It may be time to consider some more specific reconstruction."

"Like plastic surgery?" I say, my mind jumping immediately to the collection of eyes and ears and "after" photos in my room.

Cora tenses, but Dr. Sharp looks only at me, like I'm finally part of the committee. Like I *am* the committee.

"Like reconstructive surgery," he says.

I start talking quickly, barely able to catch my breath.

"I have so many ideas. I have a folder—oh, I should have brought it—I didn't know we'd be talking about this. Okay, so definitely my eyes first—right? And then there's this really cool thing I read about where you take donor hair for eyebrow transplants, and it doesn't look like a *real* eyebrow exactly, but it's amazing, and I don't even know—"

Dr. Sharp holds up his hand.

"Whoa, whoa, slow down, there. Let's start small."

He pulls the sagging skin below my left eye up slightly, closing the gap between my bottom eyelids and my eyeballs.

"I'm thinking something like this."

He hands me a mirror, and I feel like I'm back on picture day, watching time reverse, revealing the old me. I think of all the times I've lifted my drooping eyes, a momentary dalliance to make sure I'm still in there.

"It would be like that permanently?" I ask.

"Yes. It would be a fairly simple procedure. We'd graft a small strip of skin from behind your ear to patch this area. You'd be looking at about a week back in the unit, and you'd have your eyes sewn shut like before."

The last time Dr. Sharp sealed my eyes, I was in a postcoma morphine haze. I remember nurses globbing gel onto my eyes so I wouldn't go blind. I remember being able to blink after the surgery because I had eyelids again.

Most of all, I remember the impenetrable darkness.

"I could do it again," I say.

To look more like me, I could do anything.

Dr. Sharp shines a light into my eyes, telling me to look up, down, sideways. Then he calls in a nurse to hold an optometry board for me to read the capital letters. I make it almost to the bottom.

Dr. Sharp turns to Cora now.

"The good news is her eyes are stable. No corneal ulcers. No waning sight. The bad news is, that means a surgery at this stage might be considered an optional procedure, so you'll need to talk about it."

"We'll think about it," Cora says, her voice tight and quick, so unlike the usual friendly banter she exchanges with anyone with a name badge in the unit.

"Of course," Dr. Sharp says.

Cora tells me to give her a minute to check out, but from the waiting room I see her talking heatedly with Dr. Sharp, who just went up like a thousand points in my book for going rogue without the express permission of the committee.

I turn my attention to a series of black-and-white photos on the walls from former burn-unit patients, each one rock climbing or swimming or something equally awesome, and each one has a one-word moniker: *COURAGE* for the ziplining girl with swirling scars up and down her leg. *SURVIVOR* for the burned boy playing baseball with one arm.

My nurse asked to take my picture before I left the unit. Said she was going to label it *FIGHTER*. I said no. I didn't belong on the wall of inspiration. The people in these pictures have earned their titles, earned their triumphant "after" photoshoot. A man with one leg crosses a finish line under the word *ENDURANCE*.

I look past him at my own reflection in the glass, holding the skin taut around my eyes.

It's a small change, maybe not even noticeable to anyone else. But it's a step.

Toward the old me.

To finally earning my after.

22

Neither Cora nor I mention the surgery all the way home.

A new message beeps on my phone. The drama demigod with my audition time, Friday at three-fifteen.

I don't write back. Not yet. Two hours ago I would have said absolutely no way. But then Dr. Sharp lifted my eyes and offered me a glimpse of the girl I used to know. A girl who wouldn't let anything keep her off that stage.

But first, I need Cora and Glenn to agree to the surgery. I at least need to wait for Glenn to try my luck. Sara could give him a hug and an "I love you, Daddy," and he would give her a kidney without batting an eye.

Unfortunately, Cora ushers Glenn into their bedroom and shuts the door before I even have a chance. When they emerge, the conversation is already off to a bad start.

"Hey, kiddo, want to help me touch up some paint in your bedroom?" Glenn asks.

I recognize a consolation prize when I see it.

So even though it's late and I have a math test I haven't studied for, I agree, hoping I haven't missed my chance to make my case. While we paint, I conjure every therapy buzzword I know, laying out my plan on how the surgery could help with my *reintegration* and my *self-perception,* and I remind him how he and Cora were the ones who said I should try to make a new life for myself.

When I'm done, I notice Cora standing silently in the doorway.

"You've been through so much this year. Your body needs time to heal. Now is not the time for elective surgeries," Glenn says, dabbing his brush into the seam where wall meets ceiling.

"Yes, now," I say. "I need the surgery *now.*"

"Why?" Cora asks. She supervises our painting but can't seem to bring herself to pink over Sara's blue. "There's no rush, and you're already doing so well at school."

I pick at a fleck of pink paint that's hardened on Mom's charred handbell.

"There's a spot in the spring musical. But I can't do it like this."

Glenn stops painting midstroke.

"Who says you can't?"

"*I* say."

I'm losing the argument. Losing the surgery. I know I could get on that stage right now without most people noticing or caring about the state of my eyelids.

But I care. In all my dreams of getting back on the stage, I look like Ava Before the Fire, the girl who sings in spotlights. And this surgery would bring me that much closer to finding her again.

Glenn balances the paintbrush on a can of paint on the top rung and steps down the ladder, toward me. He leans against it, his hands together in front of him like he's about to say a prayer.

"Ava. The surgery is optional."

There's that word again.

"Yes. I opt to do it," I say, but I know that's not what he means. Optional equals expensive.

Optional means no.

Glenn runs his hand through his hair, his eyes on the ground.

"We just can't afford it right now."

Silence settles on the three of us. The Smith's Manager tag on Cora's shirt glares at me. Glenn is hardly home anymore, and even though they try to hide it, the collectors call at all hours now.

"What about the money from the fund-raiser?"

Cora shakes her head.

"No, not for this," she says. "Who knows how many surgeries you'll need in the future—surgeries you *have* to get, not elective ones. You need to save that."

"I'll get a job," I say, starting to feel desperate. "I can work after school and weekends. I could pay you back in no time."

Glenn shakes his head, reaching out his hand for mine. Deeply entrenched oil stains outline each fingernail. Every night, he washes his calloused hands, trying to scrape off the overtime.

For me.

"It won't be enough," he says. "It's just out of our reach right now, Ava. That's all there is to it. If it's not a surgery you absolutely need, we'll have to wait."

I lay my hand in his and feel the tears dribbling out of my sagging eyes. Yesterday, this surgery wasn't even in my realm of possibility. But now that it's here, a small but real fix, the pain of it slipping away crushes me.

"I *do* need this surgery. I wouldn't ask if I didn't."

My head feels woozy from the paint. I sink onto my bed, tossing my schoolbag onto the floor. The bag Cora was convinced could make me normal. Spoiler alert: it didn't.

"We'd do it if we could," Glenn says, his voice tight until it breaks.

"In a heartbeat," Cora says.

I know it's the truth. They've done their best. But standing here in this half-painted room that's not even mine, something ugly rises in me. Another truth I keep pushed down deep where it can't get me: I'm an orphan.

The only two people in the world who loved me unconditionally, who would do anything for me, are gone.

I am no one's.

So even though I know I shouldn't, I ask the question anyway.

"Would you do it if I were Sara?"

Glenn straightens up, meeting my eyes.

"We'd do it if we had the money. That's all it is. There's just not enough."

"You mean *I'm* not enough," I say.

"No, that's not what—" Cora begins.

"It's fine," I say.

But it's not. Nothing's fine. I want to tell them I'm sorry I'm asking for this. I'm sorry she died and I lived. I'm sorry they got stuck with me.

But guess what. I got stuck with me, too.

Instead, I tell them I want to go to bed.

Glenn opens my window before hauling his ladder out of the half-pink room. Alone, I put my lotion on haphazardly. A petite pair of slippered feet blocks the light under my door for a second, but no knock ever comes.

I shouldn't have asked. I should just be grateful. They took me in. They sat by my hospital bed all those months, ever-positive Cora trying to distract me from the fact that I was lying there like a charred Tater Tot.

They've done enough.

On Sara's bed, I open my laptop and stare at the profile pic I've avoided so long. I force myself to click on Ava Before the Fire, filling the screen with square, digital time capsules of who I used to be.

Me standing with my drama girls, arms around each other, leaning against our lockers.

#dramagang

Dad handing me flowers after the spring play.

#mybiggestfan

Josh with his arm hugging me around the waist almost as tightly as the green satin dress I'm wearing.

#lookingspiffy

In the final post, Sara's frozen in midlaugh. I'm making a wannabe-sexy face next to her, showing off the smoky eye makeup we were trying to master.

#bestcousinsforlife

Smooth skin. Wide smile. Absolutely no idea that by morning, both of us would be gone.

As I stare at the old me, my reflection comes into shape on the screen. My face pulled in all the wrong directions. The scars are all I see.

I slam the laptop shut.

A familiar darkness creeps into my chest. The same insidious ache as when I learned my parents were dead. The same tempting nothingness from when I lay on the grass, clinging to the stars.

The blackness never actually left; I just keep it at bay.

So it won't drag me under.

The darkness is easy.

Quiet.

Numb.

If I stay too long, I'll never leave.

But as the dream of a better face, a stage, maybe even a boy slips away, the darkness tiptoes in.

From across the room, my reflection assaults me again from the glass of Sara's doll cabinet, where Barbies with perfect skin and anatomically impossible waistlines mock me.

I rip off my wig and throw it at the mangled girl in the glass.

Looking at her now, I feel the same way I did the first time we met: Who could ever look at a face like that?

Who could ever love it?

March 30

I knew my face was bad.
How could I not know?
The way people looked at me.
The purply-pink swirls on my body.

I knew.

So I didn't look.
For a month.
Until Cora and the doctors say it's time.

In the mirror,
a stranger.

A stitched-together face.
Some nightmarish Tim Burton character.
Scabby and raw
and unrecognizable.

White patches,
Pink patches,
Wrinkled patches like a melting candle,
frozen in time.
Skin tugged tight here,

Loose there—
A skeleton/zombie hybrid.

Like a fun-house mirror,
Everything is slightly off—too big, too small,

too not me.

Fat, puffy pink caterpillars for lips.
Pointy, upturned nostrils with a whisper of
cartilage clinging for dear life.
No eyelids to hide the wet pink innards.

No eyelashes.
No eyebrows.
No ear.

"That's not me."
"Look in your eyes," Cora says.

Trapped deep within the monster,
                    a familiar blue stares back.

23

Piper isn't at school Monday to commiserate. I text her while walking the hallway alone.

> **Where are you?**

Home

> **Sick?**

Bad day

> **Understatement of the century. Every day is a bad day**

Talk at group

> **Minus two friend points**

Put it on my tab

I squeak by on the math test I didn't study for and eat lunch without Piper, her weird lunch partners staring at their phones the whole time. Asad waves to me from his table of crew buddies, all laughing and talking like normal people. I skip drama club, partly because I don't want to face Kenzie's wrath about Asad's chivalrous curtain-bombing, but mostly because I know Tony will ask me about the audition. I'm definitely not doing it, but I can't seem to bring myself to say no, either.

Piper doesn't show up to group, leaving me to suffer alone through Dr. Layne's lecture on the power of pain. When she asks us to think of our most painful moment, my mind shoots straight to "the tank," aka the torture chamber. It's not really a tank but a sterile room in the burn unit where nurses hose down patients and peel dead pieces of skin from tender, charred flesh. The technical term is *debridement.*

The layman's term is *hell.*

Muffled cries from the tank often filled the burn unit, so even when it wasn't my turn, I could never forget the threat of it down the hall. The nurses hopped me up on morphine and let me pick the background music, as if finding the right soundtrack could make scouring off skin any less hellish. The only way to survive was to go somewhere else in my head, to separate from my body.

Olivia, the talkative girl with no scars, prattles about the pain in her past.

"We have to be stronger than the hurt," she concludes. "Or we miss the whole point."

Maybe it's the memories of the tank, or the more recent pain of yesterday watching my new normal slip through my grotesque fingers, but something inside me snaps.

"What could *you* possibly know about pain?"

Olivia purses her lips, folds her arms across her chest, and looks to Dr. Layne.

"Ava, this is Olivia's pain, not yours," Dr. Layne says.

I hold my arms out so my toe-hand is pointed toward Olivia.

"*This* is pain." My voice bounces off the nothingness of the room. I point to my face. "This is real. You don't even have any scars."

Olivia's cheeks flush red.

"I have scars." She stands and starts to roll up the bottom of her shirt, but Dr. Layne jumps up.

"No." She lays her hand on Olivia's. "Nobody has to prove anything. Not here."

Olivia lets her shirt fall back over her perfect skin and sits while Dr. Layne beckons me out into the hallway.

"What's going on, Ava?"

"Nothing."

"It's okay to be mad," she says. "But hidden scars hurt, too, and Olivia gets to choose how much or how little she reveals about them."

I kick the toe of my shoe into the wall softly, keeping my eyes away from Dr. Layne's.

"That's just it. *She* gets a choice. I can't hide my scars. I can't choose."

I didn't choose any of this, actually. My dad pushed me out a window. Doctors saved me without my consent.

"I get it." Dr. Layne points to the rough side of her face, where her scars pull her lips downward slightly. "Trust me, I've been there. It took me a long time to accept this. To accept myself. But I got there. It just takes time."

"I don't have time."

"Cora told me about the surgery," she says. "And the play."

"It's not about the stupid play."

Dr. Layne takes a step back, holding me at arm's length.

"Ava. You don't need that surgery to do the play, if that's what you want to do."

"You don't get it. I look in the mirror and I don't even know that girl. I'm not naive—I know the surgery won't fix me. But it could make me a little more *me* again. Maybe just enough to get back on that stage."

Dr. Layne sighs heavily. "How about this. Maybe today it would be more helpful if you could share a positive, happy memory."

I scoff. "I'm all out of warm and fuzzy moments."

Dr. Layne looks at me, somewhat sterner this time, and I realize I'm not getting off without penance today.

"Dig deeper." She points to my chest. "It's in there."

I mutter a half-genuine apology to Olivia when I return to the circle. She smiles weakly.

Dr. Layne directs the group: "Let's switch gears now to the power of positive thinking. Ava has offered to start us off with a memory."

Olivia and Braden turn to me. I wish Piper were here making some joke about how stupid this all is. Because it is. All this talking and sharing and feeling. I breathe deeply and try to summon my best therapy-appropriate psychoanalysis.

"So we used to have a big, bushy sunset maple tree in our front yard that had all these leaves that would turn yellow and red and orange in the fall. Dad called it our burning bush. Anyway, when Dad would get home from work, I would run outside and he would scoop me up in his arms beneath that huge tree.

" 'Ready to fly?' he'd say. Then he'd toss me up high into the air, so high that I got that roller-coaster stomach-drop feeling. It felt like the earth and my dad were a million miles away. For a split second at the top, I'd panic. But then I'd see my dad's face and his arms outstretched to catch me. He'd fold me back into his chest and whisper, 'I'll always catch you.' "

Dr. Layne scribbles in her notepad.

"That's beautiful, Ava. Thank you."

Gold star for therapy today—an outburst *and* a breakthrough. She tells us to take a few minutes and write a good memory in our notebooks.

But Layne doesn't realize my story is not a good memory.

Dads *don't* always catch their little girls.

As I fell from my enflamed bedroom window, I waited for his hands.

I waited.

And waited.

Until I hit the ground.

He didn't catch me.

He shoved me headfirst into a life where he couldn't protect me from pain.

The memory is a lie.

Just like everything else.

Like my toe is a finger and my hair is hot pink. Like Glenn and Cora are my parents.

Like a boy could ever see me as a girl, or I wouldn't be a laughingstock on that stage.

Like silly songs can chase away nightmares.

April 2

A memory?
How about this one?

A chance encounter
in aisle 5.
Josh.
My Josh.
No longer mine.

He clutched a box of Corn Pops
like it could save him
from this moment
from the girl
he once knew.
A girl
without a face.

His cheeks drained white.
Lips I once kissed,
hung open.

Eyes, once adoring,
now wide,
like he'd seen a ghost.

We both had.
A hollow specter of what used to be.
A boy looking at a girl.

But the Fire made it ugly.
Like everything it touches—
even the memories went up in smoke.

24

Glenn picks me up from group, a jacket and hiking boots on the passenger seat.

"Up for a stroll?" he asks.

I put on the boots while he drives, unsure why I need such footwear for a "stroll." He steers his truck farther and farther up the canyon, cutting through the Wasatch Mountains. This is no little saunter he has in mind.

When he pulls off at a small, unpaved parking lot on the side of the winding canyon road, he points to a steep trail disappearing into the still-naked trees. As the mountain rises away from us, the snowpack deepens.

"I don't think I can do that," I say. It's been more than a year since I've worked out more than the pathetic knee bends and arm lifts with two-pound weights that Terry the Torturer forced on me.

Glenn hops out of the truck, pulling on his work jacket.

"You can."

He climbs ahead of me, leading me through a trail that I have serious doubts about being an actual trail because we have to step over boulders and under low-hanging branches every few paces. The trail gradually steepens, the snow slowly thickening on the ground, my compression garments squeezing my knees.

I catch my breath against the skinny white trunk of a quaking aspen. When Glenn doesn't stop, I follow in his footsteps, sunk deep into the snow now, making every forward movement an exhausting routine of step, sink, pull out, repeat.

I'm beginning to think this is some style of corporal punishment for my mini temper tantrum last night, when Glenn finally stops. He waves me to a row of boulders overlooking the valley. I sit and exhale heavy white puffs into the thin air.

Glenn and I look out over the valley spread below us. Ant cars creep along the highway, and even though snow still blankets the mountains, the grass in the valley is gearing up for spring. A massive flock of seagulls rises from the valley like an avian tornado, twisting and turning north as one until the white specks fall in line to soar home.

To the south, I can almost convince myself I can see my own home beyond where the cookie-cutter subdivisions give way to verdant fields. I lean over the edge, trying to catch a glimpse. Glenn puts his arm across me exactly the way Mom used to in the car, making a human seat belt when she'd slam the brakes.

"Sara and I used to hike up here," Glenn says, gazing out. "Funny how I thought of it as our spot. Like we owned it. Now she's gone, and these hills are still here."

He reaches into his pocket and pulls out a small black hunk. I recognize the shape of it immediately.

"Joining a handbell choir?" I say.

Glenn transfers Mom's bell slowly to me with two hands like it could crumble to dust if we breathe wrong. The metal is cold like it always was, but the surface is a dusky black instead of shiny bronze.

The clacker thuds against the inside when I shake it. The sound is different from before—deeper—but I'm always surprised it still chimes at all.

"Do you know how this handbell survived?" Glenn says.

"If you're gonna say a miracle, I'm walking down this mountain alone."

Glenn takes the bell back.

"It survived because copper has a high melting point." He turns the bell over, tracing the pad of his finger along the blackened, bowed side. "The tin isn't immune to fire, though, so it looks a little different."

I bristle.

"I get it. I'm the bell. I'm ugly but still here. Yay, survival!" I fist-pump into the air.

Glenn rests the charbroiled chunk of my mother's memory on his flattened palm, totally ignoring my sarcasm.

"You're not ugly," he says, still examining the bell. "And you are not your body."

Glenn means well, but he sounds like he's reading directly from *The Big Book of Lies to Tell Burned People*. I am every bit my body. We're kind of a package deal. Okay, maybe more like a hostage situation, but still—inseparable.

"Why do you keep this bell on your dresser if you think it's so hideous?" he asks.

The bell is so small in Glenn's hand. It doesn't look like it could produce the rich tones I remember reverberating through the church at Christmastime when Mom performed with the handbell choir.

"It was Mom's," I say, surprised by the lump in my throat. "It's all I have of her."

Glenn smiles, holding it up in the slanted evening light. "I can still picture your mother in those ridiculous white gloves up there in that church ringing these damned bells she loved so much."

Glenn pauses like he's searching for words.

"Just think how much more she loved *you*." He holds the blackened bell between us. "You are the part of her that survived. And now, you're part of us."

My guilt from yesterday rises, spreading through my chest and up my throat, making me wish I could go back in time and swallow all my vain requests, all my harsh words.

"Glenn, you don't have to—"

"Yes, I do. I want you to hear this. The truth is, you'll never replace Sara, and we'll never replace your parents. We wouldn't want to. But sometimes I don't know how we would have survived this last year without you."

Glenn clears his throats as he straightens up. He places the bell on the rock between us, his hefty hand engulfing what's left of mine.

"And we realize this surgery is important to you."

"It's fine—"

"No, it's not. You don't ask for much. Never have. In the hospital, nurses would find you biting your lip rather than asking for help. Probably because you've got your mother's genes—tougher than a trotline. Too tough for your own good, sometimes," he says. "So Cora and I know you wouldn't ask unless it mattered."

I hold my breath, afraid even the slightest wind may knock the universe off-kilter and stop whatever is happening here.

Glenn's eyes meet mine.

"So you're gonna get your surgery."

I throw my arms around Glenn's bulky shoulders before he can say anything else.

"Thank you," I whisper. I want to say more, but words don't seem to do this moment justice.

"You understand your scars will still be there, right? It's just your eyes?"

"Yes, yes, just my eyes." I pull back slightly. "But the money—"

"We talked to the insurance, and they'll cover part of it."

"And the other part?"

"You know your aunt Cora. If there's a solution, she'll find it. She's been on eBay all day, selling stuff we don't need anymore to people with way too much money." Glenn forces a laugh but then smiles genuinely as he takes my hand.

"We just want to make you happy," he says. "Are you? Happy?"

"I can't remember the last time I felt like this," I say, hugging him again so tight his five-o'clock shadow scratches my cheek.

We hike back down, hand in hand, Glenn walking sideways to help me with my weak knees threatening to buckle.

I smile uncontrollably all the way home. Cora meets us at the doorway, already crying. She hugs me tight, and I let her.

"I scheduled it for four weeks from today," she says.

I hug her one more time, which seems to surprise her so much that she lets out an audible gasp. She sniffles in my ear as she hugs me back.

"I hope you know, Ava, surgery or no surgery, you're enough."

She tells me to go check out my room, where I find perfect pink paint reaching all the way to the ceiling. I write on my calendar on April 30 in big red letters: SURGERY!

Before I can finish, the sight of the empty curio cabinet stops me short.

The dolls are gone.

No longer locked, the glass door of the cabinet opens easily. I place Mom's handbell inside. The bare shelf guts me as I think of Cora on eBay, selling what the fire left to the highest bidder.

For me.

So I can hit my star.

I call Tony to ask if my audition slot is still open.

"Yours if you want it," he says.

I tug up the corners of my eyes in my reflection.

"Yes," I say into the phone. "I want it."

And into the glass, I smile at the girl grinning back.

25

The first person I want to tell is Piper, but since she's still MIA, Cora drives me to her house after school.

Her house is perfect—like straight-out-of-a-sitcom immaculate with a porch wrapping around the side and a cobblestone walkway winding through a manicured yard. The only thing that doesn't fit in the suburban fantasy is the makeshift plywood wheelchair ramp covering the front steps.

I knock three times before Piper answers, red-eyed and wearing a tank top and shorts with no compression garments. Without her pink/zebra/neon skin covering, I can see her scars more clearly. Her right arm and thigh are bright red and purple, much sharper than the muted hues of mine.

I hadn't realized how raw her scars still are, or how much mine have healed.

"*Where* have you been?" I say.

Piper shields the afternoon sun with her hand.

"I told you. Bad day. Wasn't in a headshrinky kind of mood."

She waves me into her house, which is just as perfect on the inside. A marble-floored hallway leads into a foyer with fresh-cut flowers on a table.

"I'm going to audition!" I say, unable to wait a second longer. "And that's not even the best part."

She holds up a finger to stop me, her eyes duller than usual as she turns her chair toward the kitchen, where a woman stands elbow-deep in a sink, scrubbing the stainless steel sides so hard her whole body shakes.

"Mom, this is Ava. From group."

Her mom looks up, eyes redder than Piper's but equally lifeless, then puts her rubber-gloved hands over her heart.

"Oh, you poor thing."

"Wow, Mom. Not cool." Piper rolls down the hallway, waving me after her. "Don't mind her. Her emotional whack-o-meter broke when my leg did. Plus, my ortho appointments always send her into a blubbering cleaning frenzy. She'll be polishing for a week after this last one."

Piper's room is as loud as she is. A hot-pink-and-zebra bedspread contrasts the lime-green shag rug. Fuzzy neon throw pillows line her bed, and fuchsia lava wiggles in blobby waves in a lamp on her desk.

Piper pulls her body out of her chair and onto the bed, her limp legs following reluctantly as she grabs them one by one and flops them onto the bright bedspread. When I try to help her, I notice her cast-free right leg.

"You got it off!"

Piper shrugs and swats me away.

"Forget about my stupid leg; you were about to tell me the best part about the audition," she says. "Is it about your boy toy? You still haven't told me his name, by the way. Don't think I haven't noticed."

I plop myself in her empty wheelchair, rolling back and forth with my legs, grinning wildly. I tell her about the surgery while she thumbs through a health-and-fitness magazine on her bed.

"Haven't you had like twenty?" she says, flipping the pages loudly.

"Yeah but this one's cosmetic—to fix my eyes."

I pull up the corners off both eyelids. Piper purses her lips as she scrutinizes my face.

"Sounds pricey."

"It is. And the craziest part is, I think Cora and Glenn sold Sara's dolls to pay for it."

Piper lies back on her pillows, focused on the ceiling instead of me.

"Sounds like everything's coming up Ava." She turns to me, her eyebrows furrowed. "Where's your wig?"

"I don't need it anymore. That's what I'm telling you. This surgery is what I need."

Piper turns back to the ceiling, nonplussed. Shouldn't she be excited? She's the one who pushed so hard for me to do the play.

A glint of light catches my eyes, and I notice pieces of glass in the corner of her room. I pick up a pointy shard, and the remnants of a smashed picture frame along with a picture of a volleyball team crumpled below the wheel of the wheelchair. In it, Piper stands front and center, smiling, burn-free on two legs.

She watches me pick through the debris, and I notice again the pink puffiness around her eyes.

"What happened?"

She shrugs. "Little setback at physical therapy."

I hold up the mangled frame.

"This doesn't seem like a *little* setback."

Piper reaches out to grab it, almost toppling off her bed.

"Okay, *big* setback, then. Massive, colossal setback. Is that what you want to hear?"

"I'm sorry, I didn't know."

"It's fine. *I'm* fine. I just don't need you going all Spanish Inquisition about it. But if you must know, I spent yesterday trying to walk. And failing. And listening to doctors tell me my temporary paralysis might not be so temporary." Piper scrunches a shaggy pillow into a ball. "Stupid doctors don't know their butts from their elbows."

"Is that why your mom was crying?" I don't dare mention that her eyes betray her, too, for fear I'll go the way of the picture frame.

Piper laughs, not like ha-ha funny, but more like an isn't-life-a-kick-in-the-pants, cut-you-open-and-squeeze-lemons-in-the-wound kind of way.

"She hasn't stopped crying since the crash. Mom cries and cleans. Dad drinks. Everyone has their inebriation of choice."

I wheel myself to the foot of her bed.

"Are *you* okay?"

"Yeah, I've got my coping strategies, too." She smiles for the first time since I got here. "Close the door."

Piper leans forward on her bed, her arms wrapped around her waist, trying to pull up her shirt. "Help me."

I lift the back of her shirt, revealing two feathery, rainbow-hued wings on each shoulder blade and a long line of black letters that start at the first vertebrae on her neck and run all the way down to two little pelvic-bone divots in the small of her back.

she
conquered
her
demons
and
wore
her
scars
like
wings

"Did you write that?" I ask.

Piper looks up at me, annoyed.

"Did you even listen to my Fire Mix? It's the main line from that Atticus song—my anthem?" She arches her back slightly so the wings move with her shoulder blades. "I'm officially a phoenix."

She tells me how Asad took her to a tattoo parlor after school yesterday. A niggling feeling works its way into my chest, and I'm not sure if I'm more jealous of Asad for going with her or of Piper for hanging out with Asad.

"I would have gone with you."

"Except you don't drive. And I distinctly remember you saying that you would never intentionally scar your body. Besides, Asad's such a chump, he'll do anything for anyone," she says. "So what do you think?"

I touch the warm pink skin around the ink.

"I think it looks painful."

"I've been through worse," she says. "It's good, though, right? Now even if I can't walk, I can fly."

"You're going to walk."

She flinches slightly when I touch the wing of the phoenix.

"You have to walk because I'm going to get up on a stage, and you're going to give me a standing ovation."

She cranes her neck to look at me.

"Someone's been drinking the BS therapy Kool-Aid," she says. "Next you'll be telling me you've found your new normal."

I kneel on the floor, picking up the biggest shards of glass with my pincer hand and dumping them in the trash.

"Not yet. But for the first time in a long time, I hope it even exists." I smooth the volleyball picture on Piper's desk. "I had to learn to walk again, too, you know. After the coma *and* after they plucked off my big toe. Both times, I wanted to give up. Know why I didn't?"

"Because your spine wasn't broken?"

"Because I wasn't going to add walking to the list of things I lost in the fire."

I leave out the part about Nurse Linda, with her thick Southern accent and her boobs as enormous as her attitude, trying to make me walk for weeks. I also don't mention how excruciating those first steps were, the blood rushing to fill veins and capillaries that had lain dormant for months, like someone poured fire straight into my bloodstream and whooshed it downward in a burst of searing life.

"The point is, I believed I could do it, and I believe in you, too."

Piper looks at me like I've grown a second head.

"Could I speak with Ava, please? You know, my glass-is-half-empty friend who throws a kick-ass pity party. Is she available? Because I don't know this Little Miss Sunshine with rainbows shooting out her butt."

Piper's smirk falls the instant the door flings open. She tugs her shirt down as her mom strides into the room, but it's too late.

Her mom jerks up Piper's tank top. "On your spine? Seriously? After what the doctors said yesterday and you go stick needles in your *spine*? Are you trying to kill me? Or yourself?"

Piper tugs down her shirt.

"It's *my* body."

This doesn't seem like a satisfactory answer to her mom, who starts to yell for someone named Frank, who stumbles into the room with bleary eyes and pillow-tousled hair.

"Look. Just look at what your daughter did to herself now."

She pulls up the shirt again despite Piper's best efforts to keep it down. He looks at her with vacant eyes and then turns back toward the hallway.

"Wake me when she gets an infection."

Her mom says it's time for me to leave. Piper wiggles herself down to her chair and wheels me to the front door. Her mom stands in the hallway, arms folded, and I feel like I'm watching one of Dad's National Geographic shows where two alpha females are about to embark on an epic battle for the pride lands.

"Life's not a musical, right?" Piper says as I walk down the ramp, careful not to slip on the dusting of late-winter snow that's started falling.

"Trust me, Piper. Things are going to work out, I just—"

I turn around, but she doesn't hear me.

She's already closed the door.

April 3

I walked for the first time
because someone else died.
Morbid, I know.
But true.

Nurse Linda tried to get me on my feet every day.
"Not today," I'd say.
"Then when?" she'd say.
"When I'm ready."
"I won't hold my breath."
And repeat.

Then, Bobby died.

Screams woke me in the night.
"He stopped fighting," Linda said.
I'd hardly known him.
The mummy next door.

White coats wheeled Bobby away.
A white sheet covered his face.
A woman clutched his "personal belongings."

I didn't know he was right there next to me
giving up.

I didn't want to give up.
I wanted to fight—
So I started with this:
I would not be wheeled out
in the middle of the night,
an anonymous face under a white sheet.
I would walk out
on my own two feet.

When Linda came in the next day,
I was already on the edge of my bed.
"I'm ready."

26

I have less than a week to prep for my audition.

Cora helps me practice, telling me to *feel* the lyrics and let the words sing through me. I remind her it's high school, not Broadway.

"I'm sorry, I'm just so happy you asked me." She plays a scale on the piano. "You've been so busy since going back to school. I started to feel pretty useless around here."

"Useless? You're a one-woman pep squad."

She laughs. I leave out the part where I only asked for her help because Piper is indefinitely grounded for her tattoo treachery. So Cora helps me practice my audition.

When I sing it for Cora, she stops playing midsong to grab a tissue.

"I'm sorry," she says. "It's just . . . Glenn used to sing that to Sara when she was little. I guess your grandmother used to sing it to him."

A flash of memory takes me back to my bedroom, Mom stroking my arm.

"My mom sang it to me." I sit down on the piano bench next to Cora. She dabs at the bottom of her eyelids, careful not to smudge her mascara.

"You sound just like her."

"I do?" I tap a key lightly with my finger, trying to remember the exact pitch of her voice. "Sometimes I worry I'm forgetting. Like one day I'm going to wake up and her voice will just be gone. She'll be gone."

Cora taps a key in time with mine.

"Me too."

"I do have a voice mail she left me," I say. "A deeply profound message about deodorant."

Cora laughs and grabs her phone off the top of the piano. Sara pops up on her screen in a shaky, selfie video.

"Mom. Pick me up at the south entrance today," she says. "Don't forget. Sooouth. Opposite of north. You'll know it's me because I'll look like this—" Sara makes a ridiculous duckface with her lips in a mock-sexy pout. "Also, you gave birth to me, so there's that."

The video stops, freezing Sara as she blows a kiss into the camera.

"You wouldn't believe how many times I've watched that," Cora says.

I can't help smiling.

"I bet I would."

She lost a daughter. I lost a mother. But as we sit there side by side, the differences don't matter.

Pain is pain.

Cora starts playing again, and I finish the chorus, her notes and mine mingling in the air, and for once, it feels like we're singing the same song.

———

On the day of the audition, Piper skips volleyball to wait with me outside the auditorium. She hasn't donned her compression garments since the tattoo, and her tops get progressively smaller by the day. It's easy now to see her scars and her phoenix wings, flapping through the hallways like she might fly away any second.

"Aren't you worried about how they'll look?" I point to the scars on her arm that will probably heal all puffy without the tight grip of her garments.

She shrugs. "I'm gonna be messed up no matter what." She looks at my bandana like it's a betrayal. "Still no wig, huh?"

"Kenzie said I looked like a Troll doll."

Piper groans.

"She's the troll, and since when do we care what *she* thinks?"

Inside the stage door, a girl does a truly horrible falsetto at the top of her register. Asad waves as he comes down the hallway.

He squats down where I'm sitting on the floor, leaning against Piper's wheelchair, trying to get through my history homework while I wait. Out of his backpack, he produces Dorothy's ruby-red shoes.

"A little good-luck charm for your audition?" His black eyes capture mine. "Click your heels three times and all that jazz?"

I take the shoes and run my fingers over the bedazzled surface. Stupid Asad with his dimply smile and thoughtful gestures, constantly punching holes in my foolproof no-more-boys-for-Ava plan.

When he smiles at me like that, an insidious thought creeps in—the same barely budding idea that started when Dr. Sharp lifted my eyes: maybe after this surgery, getting on the stage won't be the only thing that comes off my list of Things I Lost in the Fire.

Piper stiffens next to me, tossing the shoes back at Asad.

"Ava doesn't need luck."

But when they call my name, Piper yells at me to wait. She unclasps her phoenix necklace and beckons for me to lean down. "I have my ink wings now anyway."

"Wait. Is this a moment of genuine Piper affection?" I say.

She pretends to punch me in the shoulder. "Yeah, I'm all broken up about it." She wipes away fake tears. "Just look, Asad, our little girl's all grown up."

Asad puts one hand down on Piper's shoulder and his other across his heart. I pick up the ruby shoes from the floor and stuff them into my bag.

A little luck never hurt anyone.

A semicircle of casting directors awaits me on the stage: Tony sits on an elevated director's chair between a middle-aged woman who is apparently the drama adviser and the girl playing the part of the Wicked Witch. Kenzie stands in front of them, hand on hip, ready to do an audition scene together with me as Glinda and her as Dorothy.

She hands me a script and we run through about ten lines. Then, it's time to sing.

I stand in front of the circle, trying to ignore the icy looks from Kenzie, who clearly hasn't forgiven or forgotten my involvement in Asad's curtain bombing. I'm singing a cappella, which makes me feel even more alone and naked.

The only way I'm doing this is to shut out the eyes staring at me, so I close my own, swallowing the growing lump in my throat. Just like in the debridement tank, I detach from my body, and before I know it, I'm whispering the final lines.

> *Birds fly over the rainbow*
> *Why, then,*
> *Oh, why*
> *Can't I?*

My final note lingers in the air when I open my eyes. The drama teacher holds her glasses as she swipes a tissue under her eyes in a way that makes me feel even more exposed.

Tony breaks the hush, clattering his clipboard to the floor. I'm pretty sure he also swears under his breath by the way the teacher shushes him.

"Well, I'm sorry, but I'm pissed," he says. He turns to me, like I owe him an explanation. "Why didn't you try out at the *actual* auditions? I would have given you the le—"

Kenzie stands up abruptly, cutting him off midword.

"He'll let you know," she says to me curtly. Tony continues to speak in hushed, hot tones to the teacher as I gather up my stuff.

If my life were a musical, this would be the scene where the judges and I break into a choreographed dance. They'd lift me on their shoulders while actual bluebirds soared over rainbowed skies.

Instead, Kenzie swings the door open and gestures for me to leave.

Life is *not* a musical.

———

Piper and I are sitting on the curb, waiting for our rides, when Tony comes up behind us.

"Ava?"

"Yeah." I stand up but still only come to his chest.

"The part is yours," he says. "It's not a huge role, of course, but it will be good experience for next year when you try out at the *real* auditions."

I smile and shake my head.

"One step at a time."

"So are you in?" He sticks out his hand. "And you do realize you can't sing with your eyes closed in the play, though, right?"

"Definitely," I say, shaking his hand. "I'm in."

Piper shrieks so loud I have to shush her.

I stop him as he turns to leave.

"Just so you know, I'm having surgery. On my eyes. So by opening night, things will be a little . . . better."

Tony's lips slope downward beneath his goatee into the same miffed expression from the audition room.

"With *that* voice, no one's going to be thinking about your face," he says. "And neither should you."

Piper slaps my butt after Tony walks away. I shield my eyes from the slanting afternoon light so I can see more than her silhouette. She's smiling wide, bigger than I've seen her smile in a while, actually.

So even though I'm terrified about what I've just agreed to, I slap on a smile, too.

"You know what this means, don't you?" I say.

"That Kenzie's gonna have a coronary?"

"That. And you have seven weeks to perfect your standing ovation."

27

Tony assigns the girl with the pixie hair to run lines with me for the next few weeks at rehearsal. Her name is Sage and she has the exact same temperament as a Labradoodle—bouncy, energetic, and so eager to please that you kind of want to turn a hose on her.

Turns out, when she's not in Kenzie's shadow, she's nice and way too enthusiastic about helping me learn my lines. She says she's glad to be doing something other than sitting around as Kenzie's understudy.

"She likes me as her backup so she doesn't have to worry about someone poisoning her lunch to get her part," she says.

Lethal lunch? What kind of drama have I jumped into here? On the stage, Asad hammers together Dorothy's farmhouse. Part of me wishes I were still black-shirted, helping behind the curtains and swapping old-school Broadway lines instead of learning my own.

But with Sage's endless energy as my guide, I learn my songs (a hyperactive version of "Welcome to Munchkinland" and a cheesy-to-the-max song called "Already Home") in a few weeks, and melt into the flow of rehearsal. Taking my mark, reading my lines, everything comes whooshing back to me like a wake-up call from my old life. Even Kenzie stays mostly out of my way, minus the occasional snide remark about how much I'm "improving" or how I'm "trying real hard."

Sage tells me Kenzie fumed for a week over Asad's curtain-plummeting trick.

"Not that we didn't deserve it," she says. She smiles genuinely, sitting cross-legged on the stage. "Of course, it doesn't help that you stole her friend or that Tony's been telling everyone you should have been Dorothy."

She leans in closer to me, her eyes darting around for spies.

"Before the accident, she wasn't quite so—"

"Demonic?" I offer.

"Intense," Sage whispers. "I guess that crash kind of changed all of us."

She pulls up her sleeve, showing a thick, wrinkled purply line wrapping around her forearm.

"You were in the car, too?"

"Yeah. Piper got it the worst, obviously. But we all have scars."

———

As the surgery date nears on my calendar and the ground outside begins to thaw, I feel more like myself than I have since I woke up. Cora even tells me one night during lotioning hour that I've been singing in the shower. I mutter an embarrassed apology, but she just laughs.

"Don't you dare stop," she says. "It's nice to have music in this house again."

One afternoon in mid-April, Piper and I huddle over a round table in the library during study hall. She's whizzing through her precalculus homework, and I'm trying to figure out how to write a five-page paper about a five-line sonnet for English, when Asad slaps a flyer down on the table between us.

"Saturday night, ladies. Drama event of the season."

A girl at the table next to us whispers, "Shhh . . ."

Piper shushes her back and snaps up the paper, takes one look and pushes it toward Asad, shaking her head.

"I'm not really in a partying kind of mood," she says. "Especially one at Kenzie's house."

Piper hasn't been in the mood for anything lately. Like yesterday, when a boy in the hall whistled and made some bestiality joke about her bird tattoo, she barely noticed. I mean, she rammed her wheelchair into his calf, but her heart wasn't in it.

I pick up the flyer. PRESHOW SOIREE. This party could be just the thing to bring back the go-ahead-I-dare-ya, middle-finger-to-the-universe Piper, who would go to the party for no other reason than to screw with Kenzie.

"Sounds fun," I say.

Piper cocks her eyebrow at me.

"You? Wallflower Ava wants to go to a party?"

I nod as the girl at the other table shushes us again and shoots Piper some serious side-eye.

"It's your funeral," Piper says, clearly talking louder on purpose. "Besides, Asad hasn't told you the worst part yet."

Asad's eyes dance and he doesn't even try to suppress his spirit fingers.

"Costumes!"

———

After school, Piper explains the annual ritual of the cast and crew party while she rifles through my closet.

Everyone dresses as a Broadway character to compete for tickets to a play at the downtown Eccles Theater. Last year, Piper, Kenzie, and Sage won as dancers from *Chicago,* with fishnets, black blazers, leotards, and top hats.

"It was epic. Of course, we had an edge since Kenzie's parents buy the tickets." Piper pauses to hold up a long-sleeved dress with a high collar. "I'm sorry. You do realize you're a sixteen-year-old girl with decent C cups, right? Why do I feel like I'm going through the closet of a middle-aged widow?"

I grab the dress and toss it into a growing pile of castoffs.

"It's not that bad."

Piper holds up another frock. "Oh, it's *that* bad."

"Cora bought a bunch of stuff for me at a secondhand store. I mostly just wear the stuff I inherited from Sara."

Piper pauses her search, eyeing my clothes. I bury my hands inside the front pockets of the sweatshirt I'm wearing, which reads *San Diego* in swirly letters. I've never been.

"You wear a dead girl's clothes?"

I try to explain that it's not that weird. Sara and I had an open-door borrowing policy. Every time I'd visit, I'd go home with an overnight bag filled with half my clothes and half hers.

I take an arguably hideous paisley shirt from Piper's lap and stuff it in the back of my closet with the rest of the thrift-store atrocities.

"What are you looking for, anyway?"

"Inspiration."

Piper yanks a formal gown from the depths of the closet and hands it to me. "This is a maybe."

My fingers run down the satin fabric of the green dress Sara wore to her sophomore homecoming dance. I did her hair in spiraled curls, and Cora took about a million pictures of Sara's date awkwardly pinning on her corsage, and we all pretended not to notice his fingers "accidentally" brushing her boob. Twice.

"This is it!" Piper squeals. She holds my silicone mask over her face. "I saw people in the unit with these and I thought they were so weird, but for this, it's perfect!"

"For what exactly?"

"Helloooo. The most iconic Broadway character of all time?"

My brain catches up to her. She's had some out-there ideas, but this . . . this is asking for a train wreck.

"Noooo."

"Yes. The Phantom!"

"Like *The Phantom of the Opera* phantom?"

"No, like tollbooth phantom. Of course opera phantom." She grabs the green homecoming dress I'm about to throw into the discard pile. "And I'll go as Christine!"

I take the mask and hold it up to my face so Piper can see exactly what she's suggesting.

"You want me to go as a deformed psychopathic hermit to my first party at this school?"

Piper nods.

"It's social suicide," I say.

"It's a stroke of genius!" she says. "Like when you have a zit on your face and you don't want anyone to make fun of it, so you talk about it first so no one else can."

I snap the elastic rubber band around my head, feeling the familiar claustrophobia of my hot breath trapped beneath the plastic.

"I'm not dealing with an acne blemish here, Piper."

"Listen, you show up as the Phantom, it's like daring people to mock you, and if they do, they're total losers because you already made the joke. You *own* it."

"I own my scars?"

Piper picks up a scarf from the pile of clothes on the floor and slings it around her neck.

"Yes, dahling, you make your scars work for you. They are fabulous because you are fabulous."

"And *you* are crazy."

But it feels so good to see her smile that I don't even try to fight her. Piper wheels herself around the room, singing at the top of her lungs, her tattoo moving with her shoulder blades like a phoenix in flight.

" 'The Phantom of the Opera is here . . . inside my mind!' "

———

On Saturday night, I get ready in front of Cora's bathroom mirror, fastening on my mask, which Piper and I painted half white to look more Phantomesque. Cora, who thinks the whole idea is morbid, helps me put on a black cape and wig Glenn once wore as Dracula.

She stands behind me, brushing out the strands of the wig just like my mom used to do with my own hair.

"Are you sure about this?" she asks for the twentieth time.

In the mirror, the painted portion of the mask covers half my face, while the other half flattens my skin slightly, smoothing and blanching it uniformly.

With my black wig slicked into a low ponytail and the white button-up shirt and cape, I actually look like the infamously disfigured Broadway recluse. Perhaps even more surprisingly, I look like a normal girl dressed up in a costume. Sure, half the costume is my own personal permanent Halloween, but tonight, I let myself believe the lie.

Just a girl in a costume going to a party.

"Yeah, I'm sure."

I feel pretty good about myself until I see Piper on my doorstep. Instead of being up in her usual ponytail, her hair flows over her shoulders in tiny, tight tendrils framing her face and completely covering the scars on her neck. Nude compression garments cover the rest of her scars beneath the fragile straps of Sara's green dress.

I fight the urge to rip off my mask and shut the door.

"You look amazing," I force myself to say instead.

Glenn lifts Piper's wheelchair over the front step and then stands back to admire us.

"You girls clean up nice." His smile falters when his eyes land on Piper. "That's Sara's dress."

Piper smooths out the satin fabric on her lap.

"Is it okay?" Piper asks.

Glenn smiles again, but this time only with his lips, his mind floated elsewhere.

"Do you remember when that son-of-a-gun couldn't get that corsage pin on her?"

Cora laughs.

"He almost stabbed her to death right in front of us." She wipes her eyes, wet from laughing, and then all three of us are laughing together, and even though the memory stings a little, it feels good to remember.

Cora reaches out her hand to Piper.

"Of course you can wear it," she says. "Sara would want someone Ava loves to use it."

Glenn pulls Cora tight against his side in a half hug. She's so petite next to him, like she could hop right into his shirt pocket.

Piper thanks him and then announces she has a surprise. She tells us all to watch her thighs closely, where after a few seconds of intense armrest grabbing, Piper lifts one thigh upward like she's marching in place.

She beams up at me as her leg flops back to the seat.

"You may just get your standing O yet."

———

Glenn carries Piper to the car, and Cora drives us to the party, talking nonstop about the size of the houses, which inflate into mansions as we get farther from our neighborhood. Carports give way to four-car garages, and pickup trucks become BMWs until we reach Kenzie's house, a colossal modern atrocity with sharp angles built into a hill overlooking the lights of the valley.

Cora reminds us for the one-billionth time that we can call her at any time and she'll be here ASAP to pick us up.

I bump Piper's chair up the steep gravel path toward the front door, which is twice as tall as I am. She picks at the cuff of her compression garments, fraying it more each time she fidgets.

"Are you nervous?" I ask.

"Of course not. I just don't usually wear these ones," she says, tugging the arm of her garments down before putting her hands in her lap.

Her fingers find the frayed edge again.

"Okay. Maybe a little nervous."

My own stomach tangles into knots when we reach the door. Music blares from inside, and I smooth my hair back one more time, hoping I'm not committing the party foul of the century by showing up as a disfigured man.

"Hey." Piper snaps her fingers at me. The daffodil green of the dress matches her eyes. "We can do this. It's a party. It's supposed to be fun."

I laugh. "Right. Just two carefree crippled girls out on the town. What could possibly go wrong?"

Piper laughs with me as she reaches for the doorbell.

"Let's find out, shall we?"

28

Kenzie answers the door as some sort of slutty feline.

She stands with her hand on her hip for a second, her long tail extending from her skintight leopard-print leotard. The fuzzy ears on her head wiggle as she shakes her head and finger in unison at Piper.

"Uh-uh. No way. Drama cast and crew only, and you made it crystal clear that you want nothing to do with us."

"She's with me," I say, stronger than I feel.

Kenzie looks me up and down.

"What is on your face?"

I try to stand straighter despite the rising desire to run after Cora's car and go home, where girls dressed as sexy cats with razor-sharp claws can't get me.

"My costume."

Piper jumps in.

"She's from a little musical you may have heard of called *The Phantom of the Opera*."

Kenzie folds her arms, her painted black cat nose turned up, watching me struggle to maneuver Piper's chair up the doorstep. With an audible huff, she scurries down the hall into the family room to sit on the lap of the massive football player who knocked Asad down in earth science and clearly violates Kenzie's drama-kids-only rule. He's dressed like a puppy, which makes zero sense, because there are no dogs in *Cats*.

Asad waves to us as he makes his way from the kitchen into the foyer.

"Piper, you look amazing, as always," he says. "And, Ava, *ho-ly crap*. Hands down the best Phantom costume I've ever seen."

"Hamilton, I presume?" I say, motioning toward his bright blue topcoat, complete with shiny brass buttons and a white ruffly scarf-type thing around his neck. He's even drawn on a mustache and goatee.

"At your service!" he says, raising his Solo cup into the air.

Asad pushes Piper's wheelchair with his free hand, guiding us into the kitchen, where people in various stages of costume commitment stand around drinking out of red cups. Guys dressed as French revolutionaries, girls with bouffant *Hairspray* hairdos, and six other guys dressed exactly like Asad and a few more with blue-striped polo shirts and arm casts masquerading as Evan Hansen.

It's like a Broadway dressing room exploded.

The red sparkle of a pair of shoes on a miniskirted Dorothy reminds me that I still need to return the good-luck pair to the closet before Kenzie finds yet another reason to hate me.

Asad hands Piper and me each a cup, instructing us to only

drink out of the large white cooler and not the orange one, unless we want a "little something extra."

"Which we do not," Piper says, pointing to the spokes of her wheelchair. "As I am already a rolling public service announcement on underage drinking."

Asad dances with some equally rhythm-deficient crew people while Piper and I stand by the wall, nursing our drinks, trying to look completely occupied by our liquid consumption.

"Are we doing it? Are we normal teenagers yet?" I ask.

Piper laughs.

"Let's see . . . standing awkwardly against a wall at a party. We're on our way!"

In the middle of the room, Asad gyrates in a dance move that can only be described as a robot undergoing an exorcism. He doesn't seem to notice or care about the girls next to me laughing at him. He jerks and twitches until his grand finale lands him on his knees on the floor, hands up toward the ceiling.

He reaches out to me. I shake my head.

"I don't think so."

Piper hands me her cup.

"Why not. It *is* a party, after all."

Asad wheels her out into the middle of the room, where he continues his gyrations and Piper does a hind jive from her seat. She squeals like a kid when Asad whips her chair in a circle.

Sage makes her way toward me, also dressed in skintight jungle spandex with cat ears.

"Ava. That is the *best* costume."

"Thanks," I say. "I figure why not use my natural talents, right?"

"You've got my vote!" She holds her cup to me in celebration but lowers it as Piper rolls next to us. Sage's eyes—and smile—shift to the floor.

"Hey, Pipe," she says. "How are you?"

Piper cuts her off, raising her hand between them.

"Careful. You're under strict Kenzie surveillance." She nods over to the other room, where Kenzie watches us from her perch atop her puppy/boyfriend.

Sage shakes her head.

"It's not like that. Maybe you guys can still work this out."

"No thanks," Piper says. "Life's much better out of that particular shadow. You should try it. You'd be amazed at how little you care about what she thinks once you get a mind of your own."

Piper grabs both my hands, spinning us into the middle of the room and away from Sage. I hold tight to her, knowing if I let go I'll slink back toward the wall.

"So, is *he* here?" Piper asks.

"Who?"

"Don't play coy with me, Ava Lee. *The* drama boy."

I shake my head, still not ready to tell Piper it's Asad, or even admit it out loud at all.

"Don't see him."

When the song stops, Asad beckons us into the hallway to tell us that I'm in the lead by a long shot in costume votes.

"And guess what. The costume prize is two *Wicked* tickets!"

Excitement lights up his eyes. "As you know, *Wicked* was one of the most influential plays of my young life."

"Who talks like that?" Piper asks. "Seriously, were you born a fifty-year-old man-child or is this something you've fine-tuned over the years?"

Asad laughs.

"Life's full of mysteries, Piper. Like how someone so beautiful can be so cruel."

A group of *Lion King* lionesses squeeze past us in the hallway.

Asad whispers, "Okay, you didn't hear it from me. Act surprised!"

A gong sounds from the living room, prompting a migration. I move with the wave, telling myself to ignore the excitement welling in my chest. It's just a silly contest.

On the fireplace ledge, Kenzie holds a glass bowl filled with pieces of paper and two *Wicked* tickets. Asad shoots me a thumbs-up.

"Okay, everybody. As you all know, the costume contest is judged by your peers." She shakes the bowl. "We've tallied all these votes and the winner is—" Kenzie nudges her puppy, who perks up and does a drumroll on the coffee table.

"Riley Jones!"

The room erupts into applause as a girl in a brightly colored toucan costume stands to shake her tail feathers. Asad holds up his hands in disbelief. I sink against the wall.

It doesn't matter, I tell myself.

I turn to tell Piper the same thing, but she's already halfway through the crowd, pumping her wheels toward Kenzie. I want to yell at her to let it go, but the red in her cheeks tells me the Piper ship has already sailed.

"Liar!" she yells.

"Excuse me?" Kenzie answers demurely, adjusting her kitty ears. "Last time I checked, you quit the drama club."

"Kenzie, don't play with me. I *know* Ava won."

"And how do you know that?"

"Asad told us."

Her head snaps toward Asad, who appears to be trying as hard as I am to melt into the drywall. Kenzie narrows her eyes at him and then turns back to Piper.

"Ava was disqualified."

"Why?"

Kenzie toys with her long black tail, letting it slide between her fingers.

"Because it's a *costume* contest. She already looks like that."

A low murmur passes through the crowd as everyone in the room turns to look at me. I shrink as far back as I can, the normal in tonight's normal high school party fading fast. I inch behind the drinks table, feeling like I might choke on the suddenly thick air.

"Are you really going to take out our problems on her? Are you that selfish?" Piper is seething.

Kenzie's face flashes red as she drops her tail.

"*I'm* selfish? You're the one using her to get back at me because you think I ruined your life."

"You did!" Piper yells back.

Kenzie scoffs. "Sure. Blame me for everything. Convenient how you always forget who was supposed to be driving that night. Why didn't you, again? Oh yeah, you were too much of a drunken coward."

In one move, Piper reaches up and grabs the votes bowl from Kenzie, who yanks back on it hard, pulling Piper forward in her chair. Kenzie gives it one more strong tug, lifting Piper up like she's sitting on a spring, and onto the carpet. The bowl flies out of both their hands, shattering on the stone fireplace.

The low back of Piper's dress reveals her entire phoenix as she lies motionless on the floor. I want to help her, but I have become one with the wall. Asad has managed to break free, though, and reaches for Piper.

"I'm fine!" she screams. "Leave me alone!"

He lifts her anyway, placing her back in her chair. Kenzie steps toward her, but Asad wedges himself between them, pushing Kenzie back by her shoulders.

"Get off me!" she yells at the same moment her boyfriend's fist lands on Asad's chin, sending him reeling backward. Asad stands in the middle of the room, rubbing his face, the confusion in his eyes quickly changing to anger as he charges back toward the boy, fists swinging.

I swear the football boy laughs as he half throws, half pushes Asad off him, sending him slightly airborne across the room, directly into the card table holding the drink coolers. I watch him spiral toward them—and me—like I'm watching a slow-motion movie scene where each person's head turns, mouth agape, as the moment of impact nears.

You just know it ends badly.

Asad's body hits the table, tipping it and the coolers over. They fall, liquid sloshing, then flying in freeze-framed droplets through the air.

Toward me.

29

The cold is immediate and everywhere, soaking through my shirt, splattering my mask.

Worse than the cold are their eyes.

All of them.

Staring at me as punch drips in front of my face.

I rip off my mask to wipe away the liquid seeping into my eyes. Asad scrambles to his feet.

"Ava, I'm so sorry. Are you okay?"

I choke back the tears. "I want to go home."

Piper tugs me by my hand away from the flurry of whispers and raised cell phones into a bathroom with monogrammed towels and potpourri. She flips the toilet lid down for me to sit while she runs my mask under the sink, red punch spiraling down the drain along with white paint and fantasies of a normal night.

"If you want to go, we'll go. But let me fix you up before you make up your mind." She dabs at my face with a moistened wad of toilet paper. I push her hand away.

"I can't keep getting caught between you and Kenzie," I say. "You have to tell me what happened. Were you really supposed to be driving?"

Piper doesn't meet my eyes. She drops her hands to her lap.

"Yes, okay? I was the designated driver. I should have been sober. *I* should have been the one behind the wheel. All of this"— she points to her wheelchair and then to her burned neck—"it's all my fault. I did this."

The door swings open and Asad inches his way into the bathroom, which is already tight quarters with Piper's wheelchair.

"Everybody okay in here?"

I nod. "Yeah, just trying to figure out how this night unraveled into a total disaster."

Asad clicks the door shut behind him and I can't help but notice his knee pressed up against mine.

"Well, I wouldn't call it a *total* disaster."

"Oh really?" I say. "Name one part that wasn't an epic fail— and I warn you that if you say the part where you attempted to dance, I'm calling BS."

Asad raises his eyebrows and puts his fists up like he's about to hit a punching bag. He swings a right hook into the air.

"What about the part where I took a jab at that football Neanderthal?"

"You mean when he walloped you?" Piper says.

"I got in a few good blows."

"I didn't need you to fight for me."

Asad lowers his fists, deflated. "I thought I was fighting with you."

I point to the juice stains bleeding into my white shirt, already drying with deep purple rings. "And I came out on the losing end of a battle with a cooler." I grab the toilet paper Piper twists in her hands. "She can't treat us this way because you were supposed to be driving or because I'm your friend now. She's the one who sabotaged your friendship in the first place."

Asad interrupts us. "That's not exact—"

Piper cuts him off. "She blames me. I blame her. Vicious cycle of hate that ends in Ava getting punch-doused at her first party. End scene."

"I don't care whose fault everything was," I say. "*This* is not right."

"And what are *you* going to do?" She stares at me, daring me to reply. "I saw you in there, camouflaging into the wall like usual."

"Maybe we should just go home," Asad offers. "Cool off. I can drive."

"Fine," Piper says. She wheels toward the front door, but I don't follow. She's right. I did nothing. Like always.

I tell Asad to get Piper in the car and I'll be right behind him. Then I turn my sights on Kenzie.

She sits atop her puppy-dog boyfriend's lap, the *Wicked* tickets next to her on the couch. Her eyeliner kitty whiskers streak down her face, and tears smudge her black-tipped nose onto her cheek.

"If you're here to tell me this is my fault, keep walking," she says. "I'm getting pretty tired of Piper's blame-everything-on-Kenzie game." When I don't say anything, she keeps going. "You know, I felt sorry for you when you first got here. I really did. But it's like you *want* me to hate you. You're trying to upstage me in the play, you steal my friend and then come to my home with her just to . . . what? Flaunt it in my face? I'm sorry your life sucks, but could you please stop trying to ruin mine?"

For a half second, I almost feel bad for her. She must be buried alive in guilt for the crash, and she'd do anything to shovel some of it on Piper.

She sniffles and stares at me, waiting for me to say something.

"What? No curtains nearby to drop on my head this time?" she says, sucking away my temporary sympathy.

I want to say something witty to sting her back. I want to tell her she can't treat Piper like a castoff and me like a leper. But with everyone's eyes on me, my words dry up in my throat.

Without thinking, I grab the tickets off the couch and run from the room. I don't stop until I'm out the front door, down the gravel driveway, and slamming the door behind me in the back seat of Asad's car.

"Go, go, go!" I shout, hitting the back of his seat.

Asad hits the gas as Kenzie barrels out of the house, red-faced.

"What did you do?" Piper stares at me from the front seat.

I hold up the tickets.

"Something wicked."

———

My heart races for at least ten blocks, slowing only when the Mc-Mansions give way to carports. Piper's laugh fills the car and wafts out the window with the night air.

"Ava! Who knew you had such big cojones hidden under those compression garments," she says.

Asad grimaces. "That's a visual I could live without."

Piper's hand floats outside her window, soaring like the girl in her "Phoenix in a Flame" anthem, which she cranks to max volume, the synthesized piano beat filling the car.

We stop for Froyo rather than go home and explain to our parents why our big night out ended at nine-thirty. I unload the wheelchair from the trunk and hold it steady while Asad scoops Piper from the front seat, placing her in the wheelchair so tenderly that I want to tell him to stop. Stop being so nice. Stop being so cute. Stop being so cluelessly endearing with your dorky dance moves.

Stop making me feel.

Inside Froyo Heaven, Asad fills a half dozen tiny paper cups with yogurt samples while Piper loads up on nothing but gummy worms. Adrenaline still pumps through my veins, making my skin buzz with energy instead of itch.

A woman taps me on the shoulder.

"Excuse me?" She yanks a redheaded boy up next to her by his arm. "I'm sorry to put you on the spot, but my son has an unhealthy fondness of playing with matches, and we've tried everything we can think of to teach him how dangerous it is."

The boy twists his arm, trying to free his wrist from his mother's grip. She holds tight.

"Maybe you can get through to him."

Piper pushes me out of the way, a half-masticated gummy worm hanging from her mouth.

"Are you for real, lady?"

The woman looks down at Piper in surprise.

"Well, I just thought—"

"You just thought my friend was a walking public service announcement to help your dumb pyro kid?"

I put my hand on Piper's shoulder.

"It's okay." I squat down slightly so I'm face to face with the boy, my second wicked idea tonight coalescing in my head. "Do you see these scars?"

The boy nods.

"Do you know how I got them?"

He shakes his fiery hair.

"I have a rare condition called vegetitis," I say, trying not to glance up at his mother because I know I'll stop if I do. "My mom made me eat all the veggies on my plate, and I told her they made me sick, but she made me eat them and my skin just changed."

I turn the side of my face so he can see my scars better. The boy's eyes widen as he turns to his mother.

"Veggies make *me* sick, too!" he yells.

His mother snaps him from me, her face crinkled in a scowl. "You should know better."

I stand as I cut off her rant. "So should you."

The lady huffs away with her child straggling behind her. Asad laughs behind his yogurt bowl, and Piper gapes at me.

"Seriously. *Who* are you? Is this the old Ava we've all heard so little about?"

I swirl Oreo frozen yogurt into my cup.

"I'm not sure who this is exactly," I say. All I know is some-where between the punch and busybody ladies using me for life lessons for their bratty kids, I cracked.

I'm tired of being the Burned Girl.

30

Piper texts me Sunday night to remind me about Color Day, a Crossroads High tradition to promote school spirit and good old-fashioned Viking solidarity.

Don't forget your class T-shirt tomorrow. The last thing you want to be right now is tribeless

Why? You think Kenzie will still be mad?

You bested the queen of the theater in front of everyone. This is NOT over

Riiiight . . . and *she's* the drama queen here?

Trust me. Yellow shirt. Balls-out attitude from last night. Bring both

Monday morning, I walk to my locker in my chick-yellow shirt and matching bandana to declare my undying allegiance to the junior class. As far as I can tell, Color Day is much like any other costume-centered high school event—an excuse for girls to wear less and boys to act like toddlers. My suspicions on this matter are immediately confirmed as Piper and I venture down Senior Hall, passing a variety of girls dressed in red cheerleader booty shorts, some with red tights, others with red-and-white thigh-high socks. Many of them have devil's horns and red-hued hair, while several boys with completely red faces spray Silly String everywhere.

I'm beginning to think half of teenagerdom at Crossroads High involves pretending to be someone else.

"Seniors only," a bedeviled girl says, blocking our path. She shrinks when she sees beyond our yellow shirts to my face and Piper's wheelchair.

"Oh, sorry. You're fine." She bites her upper lip and turns back to her huddle of sexy devils.

Piper pumps her fist into the air. "Disability bonus!" she shouts above the noise in the hallway. "Score!"

"I thought today was all about school unity," I say as we navigate through the sea of red, narrowly dodging a squirt of red ketchup flying toward a wayward freshman.

"Different kind of unity," Piper says before going into her math class. "You dress like everyone in your class, swear a blood oath, and then mercilessly persecute anyone who looks different. It's the Viking way."

Before I get to earth science, Sage scurries up to me, her books clasped tight against her chest and her eyes blinking rapidly.

"Kenzie's out for blood," she says. "*Your* blood."

I try to act unfazed.

"So what? She's going to ghost me like she did Piper? We weren't that close anyway."

Sage tilts her head to the side like she's trying to figure me out.

"Kenzie didn't ghost Piper," she says. "Piper cut *her* off. When we went to visit her in the hospital, she wouldn't see us."

I stare at her. "Wait, what?"

"Acted like we died in the crash. Kenzie took it the worst, obviously, because she thought Piper blamed her. Now they're both too busy blaming each other to ever back down."

Her voice trails off just as Kenzie turns the corner toward us. I brace myself for a showdown right here in the middle of the science corridor. Shouting match? Hair pulling? Girls don't actually throw punches, do they?

I force my spine a little straighter as Kenzie nears, feigning a fraction of the boldness I felt Saturday night. My hand balls into a fist, my fingernails digging into my palm.

Kenzie looks past me.

"Sage." She says her name flatly, like she's summoning a schnauzer. Sage heels, crinkling her eyebrows together to show me she has no choice but to follow.

I hurry to class, jumping at the sound of slamming lockers and checking over my shoulder. When Asad slaps me on the back, I almost leap out of my skin.

"Whoa, settle down there, killer," he says, helping me steady the tray of mealworms.

I write our daily worm report, describing the dry, discarded skin because Magical Mr. Mistoffelees and Macavity are molting again. What if I could crawl out of my skin, shed it behind me like these disgusterous guys like it's no big deal?

Do they even realize the incredible gift of starting over?

Wearing the same-color T-shirt suddenly makes everyone completely focus-impaired, but Mr. Bernard makes a good effort to use our color identification system as an object lesson for biological survival.

"As humans, we form communities based on similar attributes. Your shirts show to which community you belong," he says. "For every species on the planet, finding this community is not a luxury; it's an essential element of survival."

His object lesson disintegrates when he makes the mistake of involving Kenzie's jockface boyfriend as an example, since he is the only red in a sea of yellows. Either way, he doesn't seem to understand that he's the loner in Mr. Bernard's analogy and takes the opportunity to stand on one of the lab tables, shouting, "Seniors rule!"

Asad leans close to me. He smells like vanilla and coconuts, which is a decidedly feminine aroma, probably from his mother's or his sister's shampoo, and somehow the idea that he uses their products makes him even more adorable.

I force myself to look at the squiggling mealworms to get my mind off the idea of him in the shower. Rum Tum Tugger, the smallest of the bunch, has already scrunched himself into a little alien-like ball. I mark "pupa stage" on our observation sheet.

"Okay, so here's the skinny from the drama grapevine," Asad says. The fluorescent lights illuminate a deep bruise running purple along his jaw and fading yellow into his cheek. "First, my social capital is through the roof. My fight has catapulted me to the top of the stage-crew social ladder, which is admittedly about three rungs high, but still, I'm like a drama-geek hero. Tony even high-fived me in the hallway this morning." Asad beams at me, leaning closer. I try not to inhale. "Oh, and second, Kenzie wants you gone."

"I know. My existence offends her."

Asad shakes his head and explains he doesn't mean in some existential way. She's started a petition to remove me from the play because I'm not a "team player."

That's why she ignored me this morning. She's got bigger plans than a little hair pulling in the hallway.

"Ugh," I groan. "I'd rather just get this over with by slapping each other around a bit and calling it good."

"Is that an option?" Asad says. "That's definitely something I'd like to see."

"Perv."

He holds his hands up guiltily. "What? What red-blooded American boy can pass up a girl fight?"

I hide my smile by pretending to search for something in my backpack.

"Don't worry, Ava," he says. "A lot of people are on your side."

"I have a side?"

"Oh yeah, I haven't seen the drama club so divided since the great orchestra/a cappella debacle of freshman year. A lot of people believe you should have won those tickets and you have every right to stay."

The thought of the cast and crew deciding whether I stay or go twists my stomach. I've only been here two months. If people are picking sides, who will pick mine?

I get through the morning, still expecting a Kenzie attack every time I cross her path. When a food fight breaks out between the ketchup-throwing seniors and the mustard-wielding juniors at lunch, I'm sure she'll condiment-slosh me from behind.

But she doesn't. She keeps her distance, and by the end of the day, I figure this petition is the worst Kenzie has in store.

Asad meets me at my locker so I don't have to face drama alone today, and Piper joins us because she doesn't feel like going to volleyball. Between Asad and Piper in the hall, I feel stronger. Like everything's going to be okay because no matter who is on my "side," I can count on these two people *by* my side.

I've just about convinced myself that I should walk right up to Kenzie and tell her to take her little petition and shove it, when Asad stops in front of the auditorium doors, staring down at the phone in his hands. His face drains.

"What?" I say, grabbing for his phone. He tries to snatch it back, but I flip it around before he can.

My face fills his screen.

31

Piper gasps.

The photo shows me dripping with red punch, one hand holding my mask, the other wiping my eye, pulling it down in a way that disfigures me even more than normal.

I zoom in on the picture, fighting back tears. Someone's drawn a black, pointy hat on my head along with a word bubble by my face that says, "I'm melting. I'm melting!" Below, bold red letters: "Do *you* want this wicked witch on our stage?"

Asad yanks back the phone and shuts off the screen, mumbling under his breath. Paralyzed, I hold on to Piper's wheelchair as people file past us into the auditorium. A boy looking at his phone sniggers loudly before he notices me and turns his laugh into a cough, hurrying through the doors.

Time moves in slow-mo just like it did in this hideous moment someone captured on film. All around me, people look at the melting face on their phones, at me, then away. It's like the first day of school again, everyone seeing the Burned Girl for the first time.

"Kenzie's right," I say. "I'm a joke."

Asad waves his phone at me.

"*This* says nothing about who you are, but it screams volumes about who she is."

"But it's *my* face everyone is looking at," I say. "Did she send it to everyone?"

Asad confirms that the text came from an unknown number to everyone in drama. Except me.

VP Lynch walks out the auditorium doors with his usual somebody's-doing-something-bad hunting scowl. Piper wheels up to him, shoving Asad's phone in his face. He looks from the image to me three times before saying anything.

"Who did this?"

"Kenzie King," Piper says. "I mean, she clearly used a new number because she's evil, not stupid, but it was definitely her. Are you going to suspend her? You should totally suspend her. Don't we have a zero-tolerance policy?"

Lynch asks Asad if he can borrow his phone. Then he nods curtly in my direction. "Follow me."

He doesn't say a word all the way to the front office. He doesn't even acknowledge me until we get to Principal D's door, where Kenzie sits on a folding chair. How did they already know?

Kenzie smiles at me, except it isn't a real smile, just loathing concealed behind upturned lips. Mr. Lynch tells me to wait while he goes into the office, leaving me with Kenzie and her dishonest smile.

I want to yell at her. I want to tell her *she's* the wicked witch, not me.

Instead, in true girl fashion, I grin back.

We sit there with our dueling smiles until Lynch pokes his head out and beckons to Kenzie. Behind the door, Lynch's muffled voice rises, and I hear a thud like maybe he's dropped a book on a table. He exits, red-faced with that forehead vein bulging in full force. He stomps off as Mr. D yells for me to come in.

Inside, I catch a glimpse of my face on Asad's phone on Mr. D's desk. His eyes look tired when they catch mine.

"I'd like to give you a chance to tell your side of things, Ava."

Kenzie uncrosses and recrosses her legs three times waiting for me to speak.

"Well, Asad got the text first. I know Kenzie sent—"

Mr. D cuts me off, shaking his head. "No, Ava. I'm not talking about this." He holds up the phone. "We will get to the bottom of who did this, but Kenzie has assured us she was not involved in this prank."

Prank? Like she short-sheeted my bed at camp? She blasted my deepest fears to everyone in the one place that even came close to feeling like home again.

This was no prank. This was pure hatred funneled into action.

Mr. D sits, folds his arms on his desk, and turns to me again. "What we are talking about is the trouble you've been having in drama."

"The trouble you've been *causing* in drama," Kenzie clarifies.

Mr. D stares at me. Kenzie smirks. This isn't a fact-finding mission about Kenzie's bullying, it's an ambush—on me.

"I haven't done anything," I say.

"Not even steal school property?" Mr. D asks.

I blink, confused. "No, of course not."

He leans back in his chair.

"Not even theater tickets?"

Oh. I swallow hard. "I took them, yes, but—"

"I told you," Kenzie says, smiling.

Mr. D shakes his head. "Ava, we can't tolerate that kind of behavior. Theft. Bullying. None of it."

"I haven't bullied anyone." In what bizarro world am *I* the bully?

Kenzie laughs again, her hatred once again wrapped up in a merry disguise.

"You dropped a massive curtain on my head."

Mr. D rubs his forehead like he'd rather be anywhere but here.

I dig into the front pocket of my bag. "I'll give them back," I say. "I can make this right."

As I look for the tickets, the ruby slippers tumble out. Before I can hide them, Kenzie grabs them off the floor.

"Are those my shoes?"

"I didn't take those." I sound guilty even to myself. "Someone gave them to me. For good luck."

She doesn't even bother to accuse me, just holds the shoes up like Exhibits A and B in this rigged trial on my integrity. I hold out the tickets to Mr. D, but Kenzie snaps them from me, careful to use only two fingers to avoid my skin.

Her eyes rest just above my shoulder like Mr. D's did the first day I met him.

"Mr. D, I just don't think she's a good fit for the drama club," Kenzie says as if I'm not in the room. Her flower perfume chokes out any breathable air as she leans toward me, pointing to the picture of my face on Mr. D's desk. "She's just going to end up getting hurt."

She won't look directly at me but has no problem pretending she cares about me.

"You're trying to get me to quit," I say. "Because of the way I look?"

I didn't even want to do this play. But now everyone has seen me, and I've seen them, and I want more than my sad impostor bedroom and half a life. I want to get on that stage and see if Ava Before the Fire is still up there.

I have just as much right to that theater as Kenzie does.

I force myself to sit up straight in my chair, my eyes level with hers.

"I'm not quitting."

Mr. D sighs heavily as he puts Asad's phone in his desk. I can't shake the feeling he has effectively closed the drawer on his investigation as well. Kenzie stares daggers at him; the look in her eyes tells me she's used to getting her way in this office. And Mr. D no doubt is used to getting a big fat donation from Kenzie's family. . . .

A knock breaks the tense silence. Without waiting for a reply, Tony swings the door open, ducks through the doorway, and strides across the room in one step to slam a clipboard down. He looks as out of place in this small office as he does in the red senior's shirt he's wearing instead of his usual black director's getup. Behind him, Asad wheels in Piper.

"That's almost half the cast and crew," Tony says, pointing to the clipboard. He's out of breath. "Every one of them will vouch for Ava and will walk if you force her out."

Tony's face is stern to Mr. D, but when he turns to me, he winks. Kenzie stands up.

"This is ridiculous. She only got the part because of the way she looks."

Tony laughs. "She got the part because she was the best one for it. She was the best one period. And that kills you."

"Kenzie is the one who should go," Piper declares, narrowing her eyes at her.

Kenzie rolls her eyes. "This isn't about *us,* Piper."

Mr. D stands, too, motioning for everyone to stop talking.

"Yes, let's not wander into *that* minefield." He scans the list on the clipboard. Who was willing to put their name out for me?

"Sage recounted the votes," Asad says. "Ava didn't steal those tickets. She won them fair and square."

Kenzie balks. "Sage wouldn't do that. She's on *my* side."

Tony picks up the clipboard and waves it in her face. "Well, these people are on Ava's side. Are you gonna take her word or theirs?"

"Well, we certainly can't have a spring play without half the cast," he says. "But if I hear of any sort of misbehavior"—he looks from me to Kenzie—"from anyone, that's it. Understood?"

I nod, and he waves us toward the door. I can't get out of there fast enough.

I know I should just walk away, but with my friends beside me, I feel stronger. Kenzie steps back as I get close to her and say the words I couldn't muster at the party.

"In one week, I'm getting surgery and I will look slightly less ugly. But you? You will still be hideous."

Kenzie recoils from me, mouth agape, and for once—speechless.

In the hallway, Asad pushes Piper's wheelchair, jumping onto the pegs in the back with one foot, kicking the other behind him as they speed down the hallway. I have to half run to keep up with them and Tony, who takes one step for every two of mine.

"That was amazeballs," I say. "How did you all even know?"

"Lynch," Asad says. "Told us you were about to be railroaded."

"You should have seen how fast people signed that petition." Piper pumps her fists high in the air and yells down the hallway, happier than I've seen her in weeks. "Drama geeks, unite!"

I'm not sure if I'm more surprised by the list of names or that Mr. Lynch helped me.

"I can't believe people really did that," I say.

Tony bends slightly to put his arm around my shoulder as we walk down the hall, four of us side by side.

"Of course we did," he says. "You're one of us."

April 23

Orphan.

An ugly word.

A word
for
tear-soaked faces
in
faraway countries
on
infomercials.

Not me.

Before,
I had
a mother
a father
a home.

After,
I
was
a
star

with
no
constellation.

A
bird
with
no
flock.

A
child
who
didn't
belong

anywhere

to
anyone.

Until now.

32

Kenzie has mastered the art of the sour-faced silent treatment. She aggressively ignores me at rehearsal for a few days; then one afternoon when Tony's gone, she calls everyone up on the stage for an announcement.

I brace for the worst.

"As you all know, Ava and I have had our differences." She looks from face to face as she speaks, finally landing on mine. "But I want to end all this ugliness. I'm glad Ava is part of our cast, and as a show of friendship, I would like to give her these two *Wicked* tickets."

Whispers rocket through the circle as she offers the tickets to me. I'm too blindsided to do anything until Asad nudges me with his elbow, and I stand up to claim the peace offering. Everyone claps slowly, like they're waiting for the punch line.

As I'm about to make my escape from the center of the circle, Kenzie grabs my sleeve. "While you're here," she says, "and since so many of you clearly feel strongly about Ava, let's do an extra trust circle today."

Kenzie snakes her arm through mine. "You don't usually come to the circle, do you?" she says, knowing good and well I do not. "We all close our eyes and say one thing about our MVP. It can be good or bad, something they've done, a personality trait or a physical one."

Kenzie holds my right hand, and I don't even try to offer my toe-hand to anyone.

Asad scoops it up anyway.

"I'll go first," he says, closing his eyes so quickly that Kenzie can't argue. I close mine, too, but peek at the circle. Kenzie has her eyes closed. If she thinks this is going to break me, she's dead wrong.

I've fought worse things than Kenzie King.

I squeeze my eyes tight.

"Ava was burned," Asad begins. "In a house fire. She has scars on her face, I think mostly on the left side? There's something weird about her ear but I can't remember which one. Oh, and she has this really cool scar halfway down her neck that looks like a shooting star."

Sage goes next.

"Ava is not a very good dancer," she starts with a giggle. "But she is always nice."

A boy next to her says I learned my lines quickly. Someone says I have a pretty voice.

The boy who plays the Tin Man says I have a weird hand. "I think maybe it's her toe?"

The Wicked Witch says she likes my colorful bandanas. Another says I've made drama more interesting. I smile a lot. I'm sarcastic, in a funny way.

When it gets to Kenzie, I hold my breath.

"Ava is so strong." She pauses. "She gets up every day and faces her life with bravery. She inspires me, and no matter what anyone else says, *I* think she's beautiful."

She stretches out the final word into a breathy compliment that is clearly nothing but poison dipped in sugar.

After we open our eyes, Kenzie hugs me dramatically. Someone get this girl an Oscar. She dabs fake tears from her eyes as the circle disintegrates.

Asad hands me the end of a roll of masking tape to help him mark the stage for dress rehearsal.

"I hope you didn't mind what I said." He stretches the tape out between us, motioning me to stick it down on center stage. "I mean, someone had to say it, right? I figured it was better if I just got it out of the way."

"It's fine," I tell him. "I liked the part where you pretended not to remember where my scars are. Spoiler alert: they're ev-er-y-where."

"I wasn't pretending," he says. "Straight up, at first, your scars were all I could see. Now, you're just my friend Ava, who, by the way, was burned."

I scoff. "Don't feed me the 'you're not your body' speech. I get enough of that at home and group."

Asad rips the tape with his teeth. "Who else can say they have a shooting star on their skin?"

My fingers trace the scar that stretches across my collarbone and collides with the starburst tracheotomy scar at the base of my neck. I've always hated the way it cuts across my chest. Through Asad's eyes, everything looks different—better.

"But you're more than your body," he says. "Just like everyone else."

He heads up the auditorium aisle toward his lighting booth.

"Asad?" I half yell after him. When he turns around, I hold up the tickets.

"You free next Friday?"

I bite my lip as Asad smiles wide.

"I thought you'd never ask."

33

Piper groans when I tell her about Kenzie's center-stage apology.

"Tell me you're not buying it," she says before group.

"No, of course not. I'm sure she's just trying to keep her enemies close and all that," I say. "But she *did* give me the tickets. How nuts would it be if we end up being friends after all this? Not *actual* friends, obviously, but maybe we can coexist in the same room without seething hatred."

Piper's eyes go wide before she spins her wheelchair abruptly, so her phoenix faces me.

"Can you see it?"

"What?"

"The knife."

I spin her back around by her chair handle. "Dramatic much? Besides, you used to be friends with her, so she can't be all bad."

Piper's usual smirk falls and she leans in closer to me so Layne can't eavesdrop from where she's still laying out refreshments.

"*Used to be* is the key. After the crash, she became this bitter version of the girl who *used to be* my friend. This new Kenzie is incapable of being actual friends with anyone," she says. "She and I used to do this stupid thing where we'd ask each other if we'd still be friends 'if.' Like, 'Would you still be my friend if I had a nose on my forehead?' or 'If I stole your boyfriend?' Of course the answer was always yes. Turns out, our friendship had some serious fine print and a gaping drunken-crash-that-lands-me-in-a-wheelchair loophole."

Piper grabs my hand tightly. "Just promise me you won't fall for it like I did."

I mutter my commitment as Dr. Layne takes command of the group.

"People don't always know how to react to your burns. They may feel nervous or scared, just like you," she says. "Does anyone have examples of someone saying the wrong thing?"

I tell about a time an old lady stopped me at the post office to tell me that God still loves me, no matter what I look like. Olivia talks about how some girls on her second-grade swim team wouldn't get in the pool with her because they were afraid they'd catch her "disease."

"I've worn a full cover-up ever since," she says.

Braden says his friends call him Stumps.

"I hate it. But it's just a joke, so I laugh along. It makes people feel better about it, I guess?"

Piper jumps in. "You gotta tell people to buzz off." She then details my run-in with the lady at the ice-cream store. "You should have seen her face. Vegetitis. It was awesome."

Dr. Layne seems less than impressed.

"I know none of you asked for this, and it's not fair, but you are an ambassador for all burn survivors," she says, pacing in the middle of our therapy circle. "People can be cruel and ignorant, as you all clearly know. But the way you react reflects not just on you, but on all of us. You should certainly stand up for yourself, but in an appropriate way."

She gives us a three-point method for responding to invasive questions:

1. Briefly say what happened.
2. Say how you are doing now.
3. Close the conversation politely.

Layne makes a note on her clipboard, and I swear she keeps her eye on me the whole time we practice our responses.

"I'm Piper. I was burned in a car accident caused by my sadistic ex–best friend. I'm probably never going to walk again, and thank you so much for sticking your big, fat nose in my personal business."

When the hour is up, Dr. Layne snags me before I leave, to give me a pamphlet with a burned boy swimming in a lake on the front.

"I already told Cora," I say, pushing the paper back toward her. "I'm not interested."

Instead of taking it back, Dr. Layne regales me with how burn camp is for survivors like me. A place where we can talk and bond and sing "Kumbaya" about our scars.

"All I'm asking is you think about it, and whether you're getting all the support you need." She looks at me earnestly for a minute. "Telling a little boy your scars are from vegetables doesn't sound like the Ava I know."

I toss the pamphlet in the trash on the way out.

———

At our postgroup study date, Piper shoves her phone between me and my math textbook.

"More anonymous cruelty from the queen of drama," she says.

Three texts fill the screen:

> You know it was your fault.

> How do you even get up in the morning?

> Everyone would be better off without you.

Piper rolls back and forth in swift, jerky movements.

"Just want to show you that Kenzie King is more likely to burst into flames than be anyone's friend."

"Are you sure they're from her?"

Piper nods and takes the phone back.

"Anonymous text bullying? Sounds like Kenzie's style to me. Probably got one of those untraceable numbers to route through her phone like with that picture of you. Guess it wasn't enough to just cut me out of her life."

Piper clicks off the screen, but I can't help asking the question that's been bothering me since Color Day.

"Sage told me *you* cut Kenzie out first," I say. "That they tried to visit you in the hospital."

Piper stops rocking her chair as her eyes flash toward mine and then away just as quickly.

"The friendship was over. Who cares who made the first strike? We're not friends now, and that's all that matters, okay? The past is the past."

"But—"

Piper throws her head back, heaving an exasperated sigh.

"I'd think you'd be the last person to lecture me on facing the past." She picks her phone back up, taps it, and when she flips it around, my Ava Before the Fire photo wall stares at me. "That's right, I found your abandoned account growing weeds out in cyberspace. But you don't see me interrogating you about it, because clearly you want to forget it. So could you *please* do me the same favor?"

Piper plops the phone back in her lap.

"Now can we stop talking about this, because I have something way more important than Kenzie King to show you."

Piper insists I wheel her out to the trampoline and help her hoist out of her chair. I put my arm out like a ballet barre so she can grab on to me as she plants her feet on the ground and rises, shakily. I steady her until she's almost completely upright.

"Piper! You're doing it!" I can hardly keep from screaming.

She wobbles, her body half leaning on me, until she teeters

slightly and lets herself collapse onto the trampoline with an "oomph."

Her forehead glistens with sweat. I flop down beside her, pretending not to notice when she takes a pill from her pocket and swallows it whole. She's been popping pain meds like candy since the cast came off.

"Well," she says. "I may have that standing ovation in time for your play, but definitely not in time for *Wicked*. What day is it again?"

I turn my face away from Piper, toward the sky, bathed in fading pink light. The setting sun illuminates the eastern mountains in coral hues.

"Well, actually, I was thinking of taking Asad," I say.

"That's cool. I can put up with him for an evening for free Broadway."

"Well, there's only two tickets." I pick at the sleeve of my compression garments as I spell it out for her. "So I mean *just* Asad."

Piper sits up abruptly, sending the trampoline rolling.

"Like a date?"

"No. I don't know. Maybe?"

Piper's eyes light with realization. "Wait. Is Asad *the* boy?"

I try not to smile like a middle school girl at a sleepover. Piper throws her hands in the air.

"Are you for real? Asad. Dorky, jazz-fingers, lighting-nerd Asad? He's the boy you've been crushing on this whole time? Does he like you?"

"Sometimes I think he could." My mind shoots back to his

fingers wrapped around mine. The way he talked about my star scar. The way he does everything.

Piper clucks her tongue as she shakes her head. "I don't know. Asad seems like a prime candidate for the friend zone."

"You don't think he could like me?"

"No, that's not what I'm—"

"'Cause who could possibly be into me, right?"

A lump forms in my throat. Piper holds up her hands to me. "Whoa, chill out. Date whoever you want. Doesn't matter to me. I'm just trying to protect you."

I turn away from her, back to the stars starting to punch through the sky as teary pinpricks threaten to dribble out of my busted eyes. I shouldn't have told her.

"Your protection feels a lot like a hostage situation. Don't be friends with Kenzie. Don't like Asad. You have a lot of rules for my life lately."

Even without looking, I can feel her staring at me.

"I didn't know this friendship was such a burden," she says, a sharp edge to her words.

The silence between us thickens with each second that I don't dispute her. The trampoline rocks us slowly as we look away from each other. Finally, her mom blares her car horn when she pulls into the driveway.

Piper inches herself to the edge of the trampoline. I balance myself on the waving net and try to help her up, but she brushes away my hand.

"Don't want to be a burden."

I stand there like a useless moron as Piper struggles to flop herself into her chair, which she finally does with a lot of contorting. She pushes herself through my house with me walking behind her, bounces down the front step without my help and almost spills herself onto the concrete.

"It's just one night," I say as she wheels toward her mom's car, her inky wings flapping wildly.

She doesn't look back, so I shut the door.

34

Piper wheels beside me in the hall the next day as usual, but we travel in near silence. The only thing I say to her all day is that I like her haircut, which I do just to be nice, because, in truth, it looks like she took a weed whacker to her head.

The ragged bob makes her tattoo and scars even more visible, not that her barely there tank tops weren't already handling that task.

She says she needed a change.

I don't invite her over Friday night to help me get ready for *Wicked*. Cora does her darnedest as girlfriend stand-in while I try on my fifth outfit. She tells me I look "charming" in a pencil skirt and pumps. I take it off and start over.

I settle on a pair of black pants and a silvery blouse, mostly because it covers a good chunk of me. Piper would probably say I look like a sixteen-year-old cougar who belongs in the friend zone for life.

Asad probably isn't giving two seconds to his attire.

I tighten a green bandana around my head that completely clashes with my outfit, but it's the same daffodil-shoot green as the Wicked Witch of the West, and if I know Asad at all, a subtle Broadway reference is right up his alley.

I pull up the corner of my eyes in the mirror.

"Three more days."

Cora answers the door and interrogates Asad about how long he's had his license and what his cell number is and when he'll have me home.

When I walk into the room, there's an awkward silence when a boy would normally say, "You look beautiful." But since this isn't actually a date, and since I am me and Asad isn't the shoveling-BS type, he just says, "Wicked bandana."

After Asad signs in blood to have me home no later than 11:00 p.m., Cora allows us to leave. Asad talks about *Wicked* the whole way to the theater. How he was twelve when he first saw it. How it was *the* reason he got into drama.

"It was one of those pivotal moments, you know?"

I nod along, letting him talk, relishing that we're talking about anything other than my scars or Kenzie or Piper. Tonight is about us—two normal high school kids on a date, or an outing, or whatever this is.

When we pull up to the new downtown theater, I crane my neck to see the orblike chandeliers blinking behind tall glass windows.

"First time?" Asad asks.

"Yeah. My parents used to take me to the old theater across town."

Asad parks the car, hops out, and opens my door. I place my right hand in his, not even caring that my compression garments and overcooked fingers don't fit into this normal teenage story line.

"New theater. New play. *You* are going to remember tonight."

The rainbow reflections from the chandelier scatter across his face when we enter the lobby, and I know—without a doubt—he's right.

———

Inside the theater, the ceiling stretches away from us, making the massive room even more grand. Men and women in suits and satin dresses speckle the seats, and it's like I'm eight years old again, walking into my first Broadway theater with my mom to see *Jersey Boys*.

Asad and I settle into velvety seats behind a girl who can't be more than ten, with her hair pinned up like she's going to prom. Every few minutes, she turns around like she's looking for some-one, but it's clear she's sneaking peeks at me. Her mother leans down and whispers, and the girl whispers back, one eye on me.

"Go ahead, then," the woman says. The girl turns around in her chair so she's sitting on her knees, looking at me straight on.

"What happened to your face?" she says quietly.

"I was burned," I say, trying to recall Dr. Layne's steps. Say what happened. Say how I'm doing. Close the conversation.

"How?" she says.

"In a house fire," I say. "But I'm doing much better now, even though I know it looks a little scary."

Hey eyes wander around my face. "Does it hurt?"

"It did. A lot. But not as much anymore."

"Can I touch it?"

"Joslyn!" her mother scolds.

"It's okay," I say. I reach out my hand to her, and she strokes her pointer finger along mine.

"It's bumpy."

"Weird, huh?"

"But it feels like skin."

"Did you expect reptile scales?"

She laughs and shakes her head.

"Show her the other one," Asad says. "Wait until you see this!"

I pull up my left hand and the girl gasps a little at the misshapen fingers and enormous thumb.

"That looks really weird," she says.

"Yeah, but who else do you know that can scratch their head with their toe!" Asad says.

The girl laughs again when I scratch my scalp.

"And pick your nose with your toe!" she says.

"Yeah, I'm not doing that one," I say. "But thank you for asking me about my scars. That was brave of you."

She beams and flips back around in her seat, smiling up at her mom. Her mom smiles back, and for a second I feel another twinge of a memory: a velvet dress with a taffeta skirt that made me feel so fancy that I had to twirl in it at least every thirty seconds. Mom bought Junior Mints at intermission for ten dollars a box, which seemed extravagantly wonderful.

"Do you get sick of it?" Asad whispers to me as the lights dim in the theater and the orchestra crescendos a warm-up note, releasing the butterflies in my stomach that I get every time a performance begins.

"What?"

Asad nods toward the girl.

"That."

"Nah. Questions aren't bad. It's the silent starers that get old. Like my skin somehow makes me unapproachably subhuman," I say. "It's just skin, people; it's not me."

Asad smiles, his teeth white against his skin and the darkened room.

"What's so funny?" I ask.

"Nothing. I was just thinking how much you're going to love this."

35

The gist of the play is this: shunned from society for her green skin, Elphaba becomes best frenemies with her roommate, Glinda.

Elphaba becomes the infamous Wicked Witch because she fights cruel discrimination, and Glinda becomes the Good Witch because she lacks the courage to defy the all-powerful Wizard.

But it's not the plot that keeps Asad on the edge of his seat, mouthing along with the words, and me entranced beside him.

It's the music, thick with life.

I lose myself in each song.

My heart aches when Elphaba sings about how she's not the kind of girl boys love. I'm glad Asad doesn't look at me during that one.

Then Elphaba flies on a broomstick, soaring higher and higher, her black cloak floating behind her as she tries "Defying Gravity."

The notes reverberate through the theater, her voice rising

along with the orchestra, the pulsing beat rushing through me. I'm that eight-year-old girl again sitting by my mother, wrapped up tight in the music.

When Asad turns to me, I realize I've been death-gripping the armrest between us.

"Right?" he says.

When Glinda and Elphaba reconcile toward the end, thoughts of Piper and our fight needle me. I touch the phoenix around my neck as Glinda sings of how their friendship has changed her for good.

When the stage lights fall, the reality of the houselights hits me hard. I stand to leave with the rest of the row, but Asad puts his hand on my arm.

"I always stay until they kick me out." He jerks his head toward the exit sign. "Once we go through those doors, the magic ends."

The ringleted girl in front of us waves as she files out of her row.

"Toes-up!" I say, sticking up my thumb. She laughs and gives me a thumbs-up before she disappears into the aisle.

"You liked it, right?" Asad says.

"For lack of a more sophisticated term, it was amazeballs," I say.

Asad laughs lightly and kicks his feet up on the chair in front of him like he has no intention of ever leaving.

"I knew it. Of all people, I knew you especially would get it."

"*Especially* me?"

"Yeah, especially you," Asad says unapologetically. "Because you're different, and that's the point of the whole thing. The world casts us into roles based on snap judgments. We look at people, but we don't see them."

The stragglers dotting the nearly empty theater are getting up now, putting on spring jackets and shoulder shawls. Asad makes no move to leave, even when it's just us and a few men in white blouses and black vests sweeping up ten-dollar Junior Mints boxes.

"So when you look at me, what do you see?" I ask.

"Oh, you're a tough one. Closed up like the final curtain," he says. "But the thing I see most is how you've changed everything since you got here."

I laugh, and the towering room swallows up my voice.

"Me? How could I possibly change anything?"

"It's like the song in the play—people change us," he says. "Like we're all just pool balls, bouncing around a table. Some balls are random, but some balls find a pattern in the chaos, and when they hit us, they change our trajectory. And you, Ava Lee, are a big fat eight ball. You slammed into me and into that school and you've inspir—"

I hold out my hand to still Asad's, which he waves around as he talks.

"Don't say it," I say. "Don't you dare say it."

Asad frowns and his hands fall. "What's so wrong with being an inspiration?"

"Because real inspiration is Elphaba, fighting corruption and evil. Not me."

"Hello? We're in high school. Our demons may be smaller, but that doesn't make the fight—or the bravery—any less real."

A man in a vest tells us we need to go. Asad stands up reluctantly and stretches before hooking his arm through mine to escort me down the long aisle. At the end of the red carpet, he turns and looks back at the theater, rows and rows of empty seats, now somehow a little less magical with the lights on and a woman with a jet-pack vacuum sucking up stray Junior Mints.

"All I'm saying is I'm braver just from knowing you. I got into a fight, for crying out loud. I dropped a curtain on Kenzie's head and threatened the principal. I don't do things like that," he says. "At least, I didn't. Until you. So I'm glad I could be here with you tonight, and I'm glad your ball hit my ball."

I try not to laugh at his quasi-sexual metaphor. His cheeks burn red in a way that makes me want to both pinch and kiss them.

"You know what I mean," he says. "You say words now before I make an even bigger fool of myself."

I try to think of something to say as we walk to the car, past the shining chandeliers and back into real life.

"I'm getting surgery on Monday."

"So Piper tells me. Which hospital? I'll come see you."

"No, don't!" I say quickly. The last thing I want is for him to see me wrapped in gauze like a half human.

Asad opens the car door for me, taking my hand again as he helps me in.

"I was different before, you know," I say before he closes it. "A normal girl who had both her ears and all her fingers and toes in the right places. You would have liked her."

Standing in the open door, he smiles, the glow of the streetlights shining from his eyes.

"I do."

36

Two days later, on the morning of surgery, I get up early, too ramped up to sleep. Glenn is already outside, his cowboy boots deep in dirt as he mulches a row of tulips. The earthy smell triggers a memory of Mom and me planting bulbs in front of our house, our fingers and knees caked with earth.

"Your mom sure loved the spring." Glenn reaches down to dust off a sunset-orange tulip. "As a kid, she thought it was magic how the flowers would shoot up as soon as the snow was gone. She'd forget they'd been under there working like the dickens all winter, growing toward the light."

He shades his eyes with his hand as he looks east toward the mountains, where green spreads beneath the shrinking snowcap like the mountain is waging a civil war with itself over what season it is. "Although as long as there's snow on those peaks, winter still has a few tricks up her sleeve."

He clips the bright tulip at the base, handing it to me.

"Check on your aunt Cora for me?" he says. "Make sure she doesn't pack the whole house in that bag of hers."

I find Cora in her room trying to jam a pair of slippers into a too-full suitcase.

I sit on the bed next to her, eyeing a pile of shoeboxes wrapped in brown shipping paper just inside her open closet door. Each one has an address penned in Cora's curly handwriting, and even though she's tried to hide them from me, I know exactly what's in each box. I imagine the hours she spent carefully wrapping and addressing each doll. I picture her dropping them into a package bin at the post office, shipping off little pieces of Sara. She probably sneaks them out while I'm at school so I won't feel guilty.

"You don't have to stay the whole time," I say after she exhales in frustration at her overstuffed suitcase and takes everything back out to start again.

She pauses, her toiletry bag in one hand. "Where else would I be? It's only a week. I'll be with you every minute."

I don't doubt it. Cora rarely left my bedside in the months after the fire. She slept on couches and chairs, eating cafeteria food and peppering the nurses with questions every time they checked on me. No matter what, Cora stayed. Like both our lives depended on it.

And now we're headed back in. Back to hoping. Back to crossing fingers that the graft "takes" so Dr. Sharp doesn't have to rip it off and try again. Back to living in fear of the almighty infection we talk about in the same hushed tones as pubescent wizards at Hogwarts speak of He-Who-Must-Not-Be-Named.

She crams her slippers into the suitcase, which pops open as Cora throws her hands up like she's just remembered something.

"Oh, I got you something!" She removes a square, wrapped present from her bedside drawer, and smiles as she hands it to me.

A DVD of *The Wizard of Oz*.

"And I downloaded all the songs for you to listen to in recovery. Help you get ready for the play," she says.

I turn the case over in my hand, pretending to read the back, but actually thinking through all the things Cora has done for me. Taking me in. Selling the dolls. Working to pay off my bills. What have I ever given her?

I jump off the bed and run into my room to grab the piece of butterfly wallpaper.

"It's not a big deal or anything." I hand her the small square of Sara's childhood. "And I need to get a frame so we can hang it on the wall. And I guess technically it was already yours and I'm just giving it back—"

Cora cuts off my rambling.

"Thank you, Ava." She wipes her eyes, trying to laugh off her crying. "You'd think I'd be all out of tears by now, huh? But I just can't get used to her being gone."

She lays the butterfly paper on the bed.

"Like in the middle of the night, Sara used to squish between us, and we'd wake up with her feet up our noses. I always told Glenn we needed a bigger bed. We needed more space." She runs her fingers across the top of the mattress. "Now all I have is space," she says. "And it will never feel normal."

I lean on the suitcase so Cora can zip it up.

"Dr. Layne says we have to find a new normal."

"A new normal." Cora says each word individually, as if she's chewing them over, digesting them. "I like that."

———

When the three of us walk into the burn unit, Nurse Linda's ample bosom practically bowls me over as she hug-attacks me. You tend to bond with someone after they change your diaper and crusty bandages. Nothin' says lovin' like a little skin sloughin'.

The smell of her perfume—lilacs—whisks me immediately back to my bedbound days, fantasizing about when I could go home.

Now I'm heading back in.

I glance behind me at the exit. One week.

In the pre-op room, Dr. Sharp runs through the procedure with me while Linda inserts an IV into my arm.

"Now, this one's going to be a little different," Dr. Sharp says. "When you wake up, your eyes will be sewn shut. This will allow the skin to heal, but it will feel very strange."

Different. Strange. Got it.

Nineteen surgeries. I've been down this path nineteen times, but Dr. Sharp is right: This one is different. He's not just patching up the empty places.

He's giving me back a piece of what the fire stole.

Cora smiles at me, gripping my hand before they wheel me away. I grip her back.

Linda switches out the saline for the good stuff, the clear elixir that transports me out of this bed while doctors work on my body. I count backward from ten until the numbers blur like the ceiling tiles above my head.

And everything fades to black.

37

A boy screams.

Loud, terrified, gut-punch hollers that echo through my dreams.

I jolt awake.

Darkness grips me. I, too, scream into the nothingness.

A touch on my arm.

"Ava, it's Cora. You're in the hospital. Your eyes are sewn shut. Do you remember?"

My memory slowly coalesces. My breathing slows. The screaming boy continues.

"Who is that?" I croak.

"A boy down the hall, that's all."

I'm in the burn unit, where pain is background noise.

I hear Cora's feet on the linoleum, followed by the click of the door, which muffles the boy only slightly.

"I'm just here for a week, right?"

"One week. And then you've got the play in a few weeks. Your drama crew sent over some balloons for you. Oh, and your friends from back home sent flowers. Your favorite—orange and pink gerbera daisies."

I think of all the unanswered messages they've sent since I left.

"How did they know?"

"Oh, they check in with me now and again. They love you, Ava."

I feel sleep pulling me under.

"I think I'll rest now."

Cora is so quiet I'm not even sure she's still there until I ask and she says, "I'm right here, honey."

It used to make me anxious, Cora always by my bed, checking my stats, asking if I was okay. But now, each time I wake up, I'm glad she's there, like an anchor in the darkness.

The hours melt into each other without light or dark to define them. When a nurse brings pain pills every four hours, I try in vain to keep track of the time.

Cora casually mentions what time of day it is often. She did the same thing when I first came out of the coma, too. Huge sheets of paper on the wall so the first thing I'd see each time I woke up was the date and a list of surgeries I had while I slept.

It almost feels like I never left. Cora by my bed, the same antiseptic hospital smell in the air, a nauseating blend of anti-bacterial soap, latex, and optimism. The same muffled screams from the tank. And always, the beeping of the machines in time with my body.

Soon, the days start to melt, too. Cora tries to distract me by reading my earth science homework out loud and talking about how it's time to start thinking about college applications. She plays *The Wizard of Oz* when I get restless, and even holds up my phone to my ear so I can hear my mom's cheerful "Call me ba-ack." Her voice helps, but not enough.

My mind spins. I jump at every noise. I panic when I think I'm alone.

The claustrophobic darkness pins me in.

"Are you okay?" Linda asks when she pauses from what sounds and feels like she's changing my catheter bag.

"Yeah. Why?"

I feel her dab at my face with a tissue.

"You're crying."

"Oh."

"You've got an hour till your next pill."

"It's not that," I say. "It's just I hate it here. No offense."

Linda laughs. "None taken, sweetheart. You'll be home in a few days."

I nod. That's what they told me last time.

Home.

Click your heels three times.

It's been a year.

Am I there yet?

The darkness shrouds my vision *and* my mind. I think about the night of the fire, when Sara said she smelled something and went downstairs to check. I think about Dad's face, all contorted through the flames as he ran to shove me out my window. I feel the heat pushing me down, filling my lungs, closing me in.

Cora pats a wet washcloth on my head and tells me I'm screaming in my sleep.

She reads me a card from Asad after assuring me five times that he did *not* see me.

" 'Hope your surgery went WICKED awesome. See what I did there? I'm so punny. Love, Asad.' "

Cora puts the card in my hand and I hold it, letting the good thoughts flood in through the dark. I have people now. Asad. My drama friends. I guess even cantankerous Mr. Lynch.

And Piper.

In the blackness, I allow myself to admit how much I've missed her since our stupid argument.

Then, one morning (at least I think it's morning, judging by the sound of the food cart and the smell of eggs), Piper's there.

"Ava?"

I don't know why, but I revert to one of my postfire avoidance tactics. I pretend to be asleep, making my breathing extra heavy and long as Piper parks her wheelchair next to me, banging into my bed rail.

"Well, I wanted to tell you some things, and maybe you being asleep will make it easier," she says.

I stay quiet as Piper draws in a big breath.

"Before you got here, my life sucked. I mean, it kind of still sucks, but it like colossally blew the big one." She pauses, breathing heavily. "You were right: I pushed everyone away after the crash. I was the one who cut out Kenzie. But I knew she blamed me because I should have been driving. I blame me, too."

Her voice quavers. I know I should say something, but I'm not sure what.

"I've messed up everyone's lives. My parents treat me like I'm a broken piece of their perfect puzzle. My friends all hate me. So I'm a pariah at school, and a parasite at home, always needing to be carried and helped. Do you know what they call handicapped people? Invalids. In. Valids. Which sometimes doesn't feel entirely In. Accurate. But then you came, and for the first time since the crash, I didn't feel like just a leech. For once, I felt good instead of guilty." Her voice shakes more, and she pauses. "So I'm not trying to run your life, Ava. But don't forget that I need you in mine."

Her breath gets closer, and I imagine her leaning over the bed rail.

"I have one last thing to tell you, and this may be the hardest to hear," she says. "You are truly the most terrible fake sleeper I've ever met. Seriously the worst. How you even got into that play with this level of acting skills is beyond me."

I smile despite my best efforts to stay stone-faced.

She squeezes my hand. I squeeze hers back.

But I don't say anything—not because I can't, but because I don't have to.

Best friends never do.

———

At the end of the week, Dr. Sharp removes my stitches.

"Let there be light," he says.

I blink rapidly, a thick gel still blurring my vision.

The light floods my retinas, washing away the darkness.

Dr. Sharp comes into focus first, then Glenn and Cora, who leans into my range of vision with a big smile.

Dr. Sharp pokes around with his cold fingertips, talking about how my vision will improve, and how the pink around the edges will fade but I have to be extra vigilant with the tube of thick gel he gives me.

"These are your eyes we're talking about," he says. "Can't grow a new pair of those."

He hands me a small mirror.

A twinge of memory grips me, remembering the first time I saw my face, thinking it would be like that time Sara double-bounced me off the trampoline and the doctors gave me a row of stitches on my chin. A little scar. But still me.

This time, I'm not so naive. I expect the girl in the glass.

My scars are still there. My mouth still seeps beyond its bounds, and the skin grafts still chop my cheeks into light and dark meat.

But instead of the droopy, half-brain-dead sag of my eyelids, my eyes look like normal eyes.

My eyes.

I find myself in the blue and let the rest of my face wash away.

The girl in the mirror sees me for the first time, too.

Hello in there.

I've been looking for you.

May 7

Four months
    after the fire,
I walked out
    on my own two feet.

I said goodbye
    to nurses morphine beeping screaming
infection transfusions terry tweezers surgery
gauze catheters balloons visitors linda torture
bedsores bedpans cafeterias jell-o crying code-
blue gowns vaseline mood-music stitches
post-op IVs sepsis bacitracin amputations
debridement hydrotherapy g-tubes rounds lab-
coats pain

sayonara
auf Wiedersehen
adios

I was going
    home.

38

Cora drops me off at school a few days later, after most of the swelling subsides. By the curb, like always, Piper waits. But this time, she's standing, not exactly on her own, but with the help of a walker-style contraption in front of her. A long plastic-looking brace runs down both legs and into her shoes.

Her chopped hair blows wildly in the wind. In the distance, a cloud thick with snow compresses against the mountains.

"Been working on my standing ovation," she says as I run to hug her, which I accomplish awkwardly over her walker.

"This is incredible," I say. "No more wheelchair?"

"I've got old wheelie in the office on standby, but it's a start." She leans heavily on the walker like she's already tired. "Plus, I couldn't let you take *all* the recovery glory."

She motions for me to come closer.

"Speaking of, let's see this new and improved you." She taps her chin with her fingertips, deliberating, as I lean forward. "Good job, Dr. Cold Fingers."

"Really? Do you think people will notice?"

"And by people do you mean Asad?" she says, cocking her eyebrow.

"I mean people."

"I think 'people'"—Piper holds up her finger in air quotes—"don't matter. I thought this surgery was for you."

"It is." I hold the door open for Piper. "And I like it."

"Then I pronounce it a success!"

In science, I pretend to read my textbook when Asad walks in. I'm being ridiculous—I know this—like there's going to be a classic meet-cute moment when the girl looks up from reading and the boy sees her eyes for the first time, or when the studious librarian takes down her hair and the boy realizes she's been a stone-cold fox the whole time.

It's not like I think Asad is going to take me right here next to the mealworm habitats, but today feels like it could be the start of something. New eyes. New me.

"She's back," he says, bouncing his closed fist on my desk.

I look up. He feigns surprise with that contagious, dimpled grin.

"Hey! It's still you!"

I laugh.

"I was a little pissed because I clearly said 'Make me look like Beyoncé' as I was going under the anesthesia. But when I woke up, I was not even mildly bootylicious."

Asad shakes his head and clicks his tongue.

"Doctors these days. No skills."

"Thanks for your card, by the way."

"Least I could do. I don't know how you did it. I would go crazy having my eyes sewn shut."

"It was pretty much horrific. But you do what you got to do, right?"

Asad nods. "Ah yes, the price of beauty."

The word hangs in the air as Asad lifts the lid off our mealworms.

"Well, while you were undergoing your transformation, our little guys had one of their own." Inside, instead of worms, three white beetles crawl around. "And that's not all. I also had a mildly soul-changing epiphany. After our talk on bravery, I realized I've been totally throwing away my shot."

"*Hamilton.*"

"Yes, yes, you know *all* the songs. But my point is that I've decided to stop being a colossal coward, and I have you to thank for inspiring me."

I groan, and Asad holds up his hands like I've busted him dealing drugs.

"I know, I know. You hate that word, but it's true. You'll be proud to know that next year I will no longer be the man behind the lights. I will be trying out for an actual, honest-to-goodness part in the play."

"What about dear old dad?"

"I told him straight out that I'm not interested in medical school and that it's my life and I want to play my own role, so I'm doing drama, and that doesn't make me less of a man. And you know what he said?"

I shake my head.

"Nothing. He said absolutely nothing. Not one word to me in three days." He says this like the silent treatment is a victory. "Three days! But guess what. I'm still alive. I didn't die of shame. He didn't die of disappointment. And since that revelation didn't end in a fatality, I'm going to face another fear. It's a doozy, but I think I'm ready."

"Ready for what?"

"To jump. But it all hinges on your answer to a very important question."

"Which is . . . ?"

Asad scans the classroom and leans in close to me.

"Not here. After school, meet me in the lighting booth?"

I nod, pretending to concentrate insanely hard on my journal-entry description of our former mealworms turned beetles. I use tweezers to remove the dead skin they left behind.

Amazing how one week can change everything.

———

Getting through the rest of the day is basically torture. A few people comment on my eyes. Sage tells me she can better imagine what I used to look like, which I think she means as a compliment.

Kenzie tells me at lunch that drama hasn't been the same without me. I don't think she means it as a compliment.

Even Vice Principal Lynch stops me in the hall to say it's good to see me back. He actually smiles, which is kind of amazing considering I've never seen him do that before to anyone. His lips snap back into his usual perma-scowl after approximately one-tenth of a second, but still, I saw it.

By lunchtime, Piper's given up her walker and resigned herself to her wheelchair.

"Not bad for the first day," she says, trying to smile while rubbing her legs and sneaking a pain pill. She tells me about all the slings and bars and crazy contraptions the physical therapist uses to help her walk farther each session. She taps the spokes of her wheelchair. "I bet I'll make it a full day without this baby soon."

All I can think about, though, is Asad and his question that only I can answer.

Maybe it's something silly. Like do I think he should experiment with different-colored spotlights. My gut tells me it's bigger, though, the way his eyes came alive.

When the afternoon bell rings, I reach the booth before Asad, which only makes the suspense more unbearable because the first thing I see when I walk in—right there on top of all his switches and dimmers and control panels—is a bouquet of bright pink gerbera daisies. Did I tell him they were my favorite? Who knows. Who cares. My chest tightens, almost like it used to in the burn unit, like there's not enough oxygen and too much oxygen at the same time.

A small card peeks out from the stems of the flowers. Should I look?

No. Definitely not.

I'm just about to look anyway when the door flies open. Asad skids into the room, plunks himself down in his rolling chair, crossing his feet up on a control panel while he leans back with his hands behind his head.

"Here's the thing, Ava Lee. I'm tired of waiting and wishing. I want to be like you—go out and grab life."

My eyes flick between Asad's face and the bouquet. How is he acting so calm with those flowers sitting right there? With "the question" looming between us?

"Okay, so what exactly are you grabbing?" I say.

He puts his feet on the ground and inches toward me, his dark pupils dancing.

"So remember how I told you one time that quantity is not key when it comes to chicks?"

"Right, right, your dubious chick count of girls you've invited to your lighting booth seduction lair."

Asad scoops up the flowers next to him.

"Exactly. Because I've been waiting for the right one. And I think I found her—actually I found her a while ago." His smile drops slightly. "But I've been too scared to tell her because she's . . . well . . . it's like in *The Phantom of the Opera,* where Leroux writes love is only unhappy when the lover isn't sure their love will be returned. And right now, I'm unsure to the max."

I push myself off the control panel, filling the space between us. "You should just tell her."

I take another step closer to him, my skin buzzing, but not with the itch I'm used to. This time, the buzzing is wonderfully alive, electric as it zaps pieces of my skin I thought were long past feeling.

"That's where I need your help," he says with earnest eyes. "You're her closest friend. Do I even have a chance?"

I stop my advance midstep, the buzzing switched off, replacing the electric heat with ice through my veins.

"Piper," I say, more to myself than to him. "This is about Piper."

Asad blinks up at me, confusion clouding his face for a split second as he lowers the flowers between us.

"Of course. Who else?"

39

"The flowers are for Piper."

Asad holds up the bouquet. "Took me forever to find her signature hot pink."

Piper pink.

"I know she busts my balls a lot, but we've been hanging out a lot more this year, and I think maybe she's starting to see me differently. Or see me at all."

I back slowly toward the door, feeling the walls of the already-too-small room closing in. How did I not see it? He took her to get the tattoo. He wanted her to try out for drama. It's always been about Piper.

"You like Piper. She's the one you like," I say, still trying to make sense of the words.

Asad scrunches his eyebrows.

"Why do you keep saying that?" He stops short. Awareness washes away his smile. "Did you think—?"

"No." I cut him off before he can verbalize my embarrassment. "Maybe. I didn't know."

"Oh," he says in a half-breath, half-word sigh. He studies the flowers like he's hoping they'll open a portal out of this awkward moment. When he looks up, his face contorts in a grimace. I can only imagine what mine looks like.

"I like you, too, of course, just not *that* way," he says.

Of course. Not that way. Never *that* way. Not for me.

I nod and reach for the door handle.

"No, it's fine. I—I just have to go."

Asad hits his palm into his forehead.

"Idiot! Idiot!"

He stands close to me, the flowers between us again. Her flowers. In his eyes, something foreign—a look I'm well versed in, just not from him.

Pity.

"I thought you knew. I thought everybody knew. I've had a crush on her since middle school." His face twists like my insides. "It's gonna be weird now, isn't it?"

I shake my head. *Please stop talking.*

"Asad, really. It's fine. I'm fine."

I step back, the door against my heels. I'm out of room to retreat. I grab the door handle behind me as Asad steps closer.

"Seriously, Ava. I meant what I said the other night. I'm so glad you're in my life. When Piper asked me to look out for you, I never would have guessed you'd end up being one of my closest friends. Now I've gone and screwed it all up."

My fingers slide off the knob.

"Wait. What?"

"You are, really. You've got to know how much I value our friendship."

"No. Not that. The other thing. Piper asked you to look out for me? When?"

Asad shrugs. "I don't know, before drama club."

The day I wanted to bolt from the auditorium. He convinced me to stay. Held my hand.

Made me hope.

"You only talked to me because Piper asked you to?"

"No, I also talked to you in class on your first day, remember? You totally shafted me."

I remember. He talked to me. I was rude. And yet he was still nice and welcoming and over-the-top friendly at drama. Because Piper asked him to be my pity friend. Because he'd do anything for her.

And she knew it.

I turn my back to Asad, awkwardly trying to open the door without backing any closer to him or her flowers. He grabs my arm.

"Don't leave it like this, Ava. Who cares how we met? What matters is you're one of my closest friends *now*."

Friends. Of course—the Burned Girl: friend zone for life.

I shake him off. "I have to go."

"Where?"

"Anywhere. Somewhere not here."

He shouts my name as I go, but I ignore him as I run from the lighting booth, down the small staircase, and to the main auditorium. Tears prick my eyes, the saltiness stinging my still-tender skin.

Asad's not the idiot; I am. One little eye surgery and suddenly I'm going to have a happily-ever-after.

The surgery couldn't fix this.

It couldn't fix *me*.

———

As I flee to the parking lot, I almost barrel into Kenzie and Piper.

"Whoa, whoa, where's the fire?" Kenzie immediately covers her mouth, her eyes wide. "I swear I did not mean that."

Piper's still back in her wheelchair, her face red, mascara smeared. The tear streak down Kenzie's cheek tells me I've walked into the middle of an argument. I brush past them both. The last thing I need is to get involved in more drama.

But Kenzie stops me, her hand on my shoulder.

"I think we should talk. Maybe at my house? I can't go into this play with all these bad feelings—"

I shake Kenzie off and start walking. Piper wheels next to me.

"Yeah, Ava and I already have plans."

I stare down at her. Did she know Asad liked her? Does she like him?

I turn back to Kenzie. "Actually, maybe I will come over."

Piper taps hard on my arm and half whispers, "Umm. What are you doing? You are *not* going with her."

I look down at her. "You're not in charge of who I hang out with. I'll go if I want."

Kenzie raises her eyebrows. "I think we all—"

"Butt out," Piper says.

Kenzie holds up her hands and backs away, but not too far, loitering within earshot as Piper tugs my sleeve to bring me closer to her. I resist.

"Ava, what are you doing? We talked about this. She's just using you to get to me."

I yank my arm from her grip. "Right. Because you can't imagine a world where everything doesn't revolve around you."

Piper sits back in her chair, lowering her voice so Kenzie can't hear us. "I thought we were past this. I told you to do whatever you want, just not *her*, okay?"

"Oh, okay. Then how about Asad? You know, the guy who was only my friend as a favor to you."

This piece of information surprises her, judging by her halting response. "No, it was— It wasn't like that. I just asked him—"

"You asked him to take pity on me. And he did it because surprise, surprise, he likes you. But I'm guessing you already knew that."

Piper picks at the wrist of her compression garments.

"You did, didn't you? You knew all along?" I press.

She doesn't look up. "Yes."

All the hurt and embarrassment rushes to my face, making me hot and itchy like I was on the first day of school walking through the halls, everyone staring at me. I thought it couldn't get worse than that.

I was wrong.

"And you didn't bother to mention that?"

Piper's head snaps up. "I tried to stop you. I tried to tell you—"

"You told me he was friend material. You couldn't have been more specific, like, oh I don't know, 'He's been in love with me since we were zygotes.' Then maybe I wouldn't have just made a colossal fool of myself."

Piper furrows her brow. "What happened?"

"*You* happened. You told me in the hospital that you needed me. What you needed was a charity project. But I'm done."

Piper's mouth turns downward. "With what, me?"

"You said yourself I should get my own life."

"You should."

"It's pretty hard to do that from inside your shadow."

Piper straightens up in her chair and glares at me, her face red. I stare right back. When I don't flinch, she throws her hands up.

"Well, there you have it. If I'm such a strain on you, then you're right, it's time to get your own life and stop trying to live mine."

I unclasp the phoenix necklace from my neck and hold it out to her.

She scoffs. "Keep it."

"I don't want it anymore."

Piper grabs the necklace. "Fine!" Curling her fingers into a fist, she stretches back her arm, and when she thrusts it forward, the gold phoenix and chain fly through the air, disappearing into the grass. She turns her wheels away from me and pumps back toward the school, her own wings flapping furiously behind her.

297

Kenzie starts to open the door for Piper, who yells that she doesn't need help and then heaves forward to forcefully push Kenzie out of the way. I walk toward the road. When I reach the intersection, I keep going. The tears I've been holding back finally burst their bounds. Even my newly constructed eyelids are no match.

I fish my headphones from the bottom of my bag and put them on as I walk toward Cora's store, trying to ignore the stares from the people at bus stops and traffic lights who have every right to stare at the crying mutant girl. As I walk, snow flurries begin to fall around me, powdering the ground and the newly blossomed daffodils. In the distance, a white fog conceals the mountains.

Glenn was right: spring is a tease, and winter is never going to end.

By the time I trek the two miles to Smith's, I'm shivering. I roam the aisles, searching for Cora, rubbing my cold hands together. Two elementary-school-aged girls in soccer uniforms hustle out of the cereal aisle with a giggle when I pass them. I hear them in the next aisle over, still whispering, unsuccessfully stifling their laughter.

I imagine Josh Turner holding his Corn Pops, paralyzed with fear at the sight of the girl he used to kiss. I crumple to the floor, the memory crippling me.

The way he looked at me. The horror in his eyes. The pity in Asad's.

Why did I think it could be different?

I don't even try to stop the darkness that swallows me. I sink into it slowly, swimming in it, letting it envelop me in its familiar nothingness.

Just like the black holes Dad used to tell me about, the weight of my own gravity tugs me inward.

Right there next to the Kellogg's, I implode.

At some point, Cora crouches next to me, tugging off my headphones. She pulls me against her, and I bury my face in her shoulder.

"Let's go home," she says.

I shake my head, muttering into her shirtsleeve. She holds my chin up so she can hear me.

"I can't," I say again.

"Sure we can. I'll tell my boss I'm leaving early, and whatever happened, we'll fix it."

"No," I say, the tears stinging me again. "We can't. It's gone."

"What is, honey? What's gone?"

My mouth pressed into her shoulder, I whisper the word that haunts me.

"Home."

May 9

There'snoplacelikehome

There'snoplacelikehome

There'snoplacelikehome

What if

there's just

noplace?

40

Piper calls me three times in the night.

I don't answer.

I don't even hear her final call, and only see the missed call when I wake up to Cora siting on the edge of my bed, where I've wrapped myself up tight in Sara's quilt so not even one speck of light can find me.

She taps me gently.

"Ava, we need to talk to you."

When I open my eyes, the first thing I see are Sara's empty shelves. I flip to the other side, where they can't mock me.

"You shouldn't have wasted Sara's dolls for me," I say, feeling particularly sorry for myself as the memory of yesterday yawns awake in my brain. "For nothing."

Cora doesn't do her usual optimism full-court press, but instead smooths my hair and kisses my forehead.

"I'm not sorry one bit," she says. "Come on out when you're ready. Dr. Layne is here."

Groan.

"You called in professional help? I'm fine."

Cora flicks the switch on my wall, making me blink as she floods the room with light.

"No," she says, more forcefully than normal. "You're not."

An impromptu Committee on Ava's Life sits around the room. Layne sits on the couch, her usual pristine makeup applied sloppily and not at all in some places, so I can see the discoloration of her scars. Glenn leans against the wall, his eyes on the floor, hands shoved deep into his front pockets.

Dr. Layne smiles at me with weary eyes when I enter. Glenn's and Cora's are strained, too. A pang of guilt hits me: they're all worried about the broken girl in aisle seven. I brace myself for the onslaught of encouragements reminding me that everything's going to be okay.

That I'm a survivor.

"Ava, sit down," Dr. Layne says, patting the cushion next to her. "We need to talk."

I shift in the seat, wondering what aspect of yesterday they want to discuss. I am not about to get into my boy drama with them, and how would they even know about my fight with Piper?

Dr. Layne taps her pen quickly on her notepad, a nervous tick that's out of sync with her usually poised, professional demeanor. She should be happy: I finally had the breakdown breakthrough she's always wanted. Surely a public meltdown falls somewhere between guilt and bargaining on the therapy path to healing.

Glenn refuses to make eye contact with me. Cora dabs the corners of her eyes with a tissue.

Something's different.

Something's not right.

"I really am fine," I say, still trying to piece together the weird energy in the room.

Dr. Layne talks slowly, like she's trying to keep me calm, or maybe even stay calm herself.

"Ava, something's happened," she says. "To Piper."

41

Darkness settles in my chest.

"Piper's parents found her early this morning. They think she may have taken too much pain medication."

Cora sniffles and covers her mouth. Glenn looks at his feet. Layne looks at me.

"She overdosed?" I ask.

My anger toward Piper morphs into fear and guilt. She called me three times.

Layne measures her words carefully.

"It's unclear—"

I cut her off. "Is she dead?" My voice rises along with my panic at this all-too-familiar conversation where people dole out truth morsels so I don't flip out—so I choose to live despite the pain. "You have to tell people when people they love die! Just tell me! Dead or alive?"

Layne rests her hand on mine.

"Alive. She's alive."

Air fills my lungs and I put my cheek down on the couch arm-rest, my head suddenly weighing one thousand pounds.

"She wouldn't have done that. Not on purpose."

But even as I say the words, the darkness creeps deeper—not with fear, but affirmation. I knew Piper was in a bad place. *I knew.* But she said things were better since I got here.

Except I wasn't there. Not last night. What did I tell her? That our friendship was a burden? She threw away the necklace.

She called three times.

I threw her away.

"I knew she was struggling, but I didn't think she'd—"

I stop short, afraid speaking it out loud will make it real. Dr. Layne taps my hand again softly.

"This is no one's fault, Ava. But we know you're close with Piper, and we're concerned about you. Cora told me about your episode last night. At the store."

Dark circles hang below Cora's eyes. Did she sleep at all? Glenn looks equally haggard.

"I had a bad day."

"Do you have a lot of bad days?" Layne presses.

"I'm not going to gulp down a bottle of codeine, if that's what you're asking." I try to say this glibly, the way Piper would, but the words catch in my throat.

Dr. Layne leans toward me, the weight of her body on the couch cushion making me fall into her slightly.

"What you girls are going through is more than most people can

305

bear. There's no shame in asking for help. We all wish Piper had." She locks eyes with mine. "How do you really think you're doing?"

I think about yesterday, about how tired I am of fighting the gaping blackness.

Did Piper feel it, too?

She called three times.

"I think—" I look at Cora and Glenn, their dark circles and pink eyes probably matching my own. "I think maybe no one is as fine as they're pretending to be."

Dr. Layne nods. "I think you're right."

"Can I see her? I need to see her," I say.

"Soon. The doctors are helping Piper now, but I would like to help you, if you'd let me."

"How?"

"Well, for starters, I think it's time for a road trip."

———

Dr. Layne won't tell me where we're going, probably for fear I'll tuck and roll out of the moving car on the highway. Once we're about twenty minutes south on the freeway, though, I know exactly where we're headed.

I slouch into my seat as she drives, grateful that she doesn't try to fill the silence with therapy talk. Out the window, huddled farm towns replace sprawling suburbs. The new-spring green rolls out from the highway toward the base of the mountains.

My mind drifts to Piper as the fields and horses and foothills flash past my window.

I should have been fighting the darkness with her.

We could have fought it together.

After about an hour, a lake at the base of the western foothills comes into view.

Home.

My stomach tightens at the familiar crests of the foothills surrounding the farming community. These wide-open pastures dotted with cows and horses used to make me feel limitless, like I was somehow part of the grandeur of the peaks and valleys stretching out into infinity.

Now they fill me with dread.

Dr. Layne exits the highway, heading west toward my old neighborhood.

We pass the orchard where Sara and I used to pluck cherries each summer. We pass kids playing foursquare on the blacktop where I skinned my knee in third grade. The creek with the wooden bridge where Chloe and I carved our initials in middle school. The bleachers where Josh kissed me.

We pass the ice-cream shop where Mom and I inhaled pistachio-almond cones. The hardware store where Dad would pretend he knew the difference between a lug nut and bolt.

My old life passes in front of the window, and as it does, I catch my reflection in the glass. How can home still be the same when I'm so different?

Dr. Layne pulls along a curb and stops the car. Ahead, just beyond a baby-pink cherry tree, is my street.

"I'm not going to force you to do this," she says. "Say the word and I'll turn around right now."

From the sidewalk, Mrs. Heckman waves like she does to

everyone, while wrangling her three corgis on her punctual morning walk. The tulips bloom in straight rows along the edge of Colonel Ashby's military-perfect garden on the corner.

It's like my life is still here. Moving on without me.

Even though part of me wants to turn away, the part that was me for sixteen years wants nothing more than to turn this corner.

"We've already come this far," I say.

Dr. Layne pulls forward, hugging the turn as we start down the street where I once lived.

42

She parks under the maple tree in our front yard.

Behind it, a gaping space.

Demolition crews tore down the straggling remnants, so now there's nothing left but a foundation dug into the earth and a few erratic pieces of rusted rebar sticking out at odd angles.

"Why are we doing this?" I say, turning away from the nothingness formally known as my life. Dr. Layne leans back in her seat, her fingers tapping the wheel. After a minute, she points to my neck.

"You're not wearing that necklace you usually wear. The one Piper gave you?"

I grab at the empty space.

"You know, most people think the phoenix symbolizes survival," Dr. Layne continues.

I picture the wings on Piper's back, angrily flapping away from me yesterday. "I know—rise up from the ashes unharmed and all that motivational mumbo jumbo."

Dr. Layne looks past me to the empty lot out the window.

"Except the flames *do* hurt it. They completely consume it. The magic of the phoenix is not that it's unharmed, but that it's reborn."

I turn to the window again, unsure that visiting these particular ashes will produce any sort of magical transformation. Dr. Layne tries another approach.

"Look at it this way: What was the most painful part about the hospital?"

I don't even have to think.

"The tank."

Just saying the word makes my skin hurt, thinking of the nurses scrubbing off my scabs, picking off my skin in tweeze-size snippets.

"Exactly. But the nurses had to remove the burned areas so the grafts could grow. If you hold on to the old skin, you'll never heal." She leans across me, pulls the shiny handle, and pushes open my door. "Time to let go."

I reluctantly follow her across the front lawn. Mom's tulips burn red and orange along the walkway to where the front door should be. We walk on a soft mix of ash and dirt and random charred bits, maybe something I loved once.

Dr. Layne asks me to describe how the house was laid out, so I try to picture walking in the front door, Mom's handbell curio cabinet straight ahead, a massive leather couch to the right. I walk around the foundation, which seems so much smaller now. You'd never know by looking at it how much life—and love—it once held.

"This was the family room," I say.

I walk across the space into what was the kitchen.

"Our table was kind of right"—I move over a few feet so I'm

square with the multipeaked mountain I could see while eating breakfast—"here."

The wind whips my bandana against my neck. As it blows through the trees, I can almost hear Dad's voice reading the headlines and Mom's laugh on the phone. I close my eyes and hear her singing, Dad clanging pans to make bacon on Sunday morning, Mom yelling at me for missing curfew, Dad sitting at the table crying when his own dad died.

I open my eyes.

The voices leave.

A gust stirs the ashes into a mini dust devil made of my past. Spinning across my old kitchen, the dirt flies with nothing to hold it down, nothing to cling to but air.

"What's the point of all this?" I say. "Is this part of my therapy? Checking off the seven stages?"

Dr. Layne just looks at me.

"Which one am I on now? Anger, right?" I reach down and fill my hands with ashes and dirt, my life sifting between my fingers. I fling it after the dust devil, trying somehow to hit it. To hurt it. To stop it from looking so sad and solitary and pathetic.

I throw another handful.

And another.

Dirt and ash blow back into my face, leaving gritty residue on my lips.

"Now what?" I raise my voice over the wind. "I'm healed? I should just move on and forget my life ever happened?"

I start to throw another handful, but my strength leaves me. I sink to the ground instead, dropping the ashes. Dr. Layne kneels next to me, her arm around my shoulder.

"Moving on doesn't mean forgetting," she says. "It just means letting go of the hurt."

The dust spirals out of existence as I try to find the words to explain the similar twisting in my chest.

"But the hurt is all I have left," I say. "When it's gone, so are they. I'm alone."

Dr. Layne pulls me closer.

"You're not alone."

"Yes, I am. Everyone leaves me. You want to know my first thought when you told me about Piper? I thought, of course. Nobody I love sticks around." I sweep my arm out, gesturing to the emptiness around us. "It's all gone. I. Am. Alone."

"When?" Dr. Layne says, her voice unexpectedly stern. "When have you been alone?"

"Since that very first night. That's kind of what *sole survivor* means."

Dr. Layne's lips scrunch to one side.

"So in the hospital, surrounded by nurses and doctors who worked to save you? When Cora and Glenn sat by your bed around the clock? When Piper—"

"What about Piper?" I interject. "She's running for the exit, too."

"Piper's not trying to abandon you. She's hurting. She needs you. So do Cora and Glenn and all the people who love you. They all need you, just like you need Piper to keep fighting."

"I already told you, I'm not going to do anything drastic."

"I'm not talking life and death, Ava. I'm saying, are your scars going to keep people out, or let people in?" She touches her face. "You didn't choose to be burned. Neither did I. I could have stayed angry. I could have pushed everyone away. But I had a choice, just like you have a choice." She moves her fingers to her chest. "You decide how your scars change you *here*. You decide how much love you let in. You chose to live that night in the fire, and you need to keep choosing it."

I stand from the dirt and walk off the concrete slab into the grass, orienting myself to where my bedroom would have been on the second story. I find the spot in the grass and stand in it, facing Dr. Layne.

"I did not *choose* any of this. My dad pushed me out a window and I landed right here, in a life I did *not* choose."

Dr. Layne's eyebrows furrow, trying to understand.

"You think your dad pushed you?"

I nod. "The last thing I saw before the roof collapsed was him, running toward me. He pushed me, and I fell. Right here."

Dr. Layne stands and folds her arms, her hip jutted out slightly as she considers the grassy spot where my neighbor found me that night.

"Ava. I've seen the police reports. Your dad's body was found in the hallway outside your room. You're right—they think he was trying to get to you. But the ceiling collapse blocked him."

"He pushed me," I say. "How else did I get out that window?

Dirt spirals between us, but Dr. Layne doesn't blink.

"Ava, your dad didn't push you. You jumped."

43

That can't be true.

I crumble to the grass, replaying that night in my mind. The heat crashing down from the ceiling. Snippets of a movie reel— flashes of panic and smoke and burning in my throat. I opened the window to breathe.

Dad's face through the flames. His mouth moved at me. And that's it—the next thing I knew, I was on the ground clinging to the stars and my neighbor's face above me, telling me to hang on.

I lay my head among the cool blades, right where I landed that night. This time, puffy clouds glide above me rather than twinkling stars. Dr. Layne tells me to take as long as I need.

Even if I did jump, I didn't know what I was leaping toward. I didn't know how I'd look, or that when I woke up, I'd be alone.

Even if I chose life in a moment of panic, how do I keep choosing it now?

A silhouette enters my view, backlit by the sun. I think I'm having some majorly realistic déjà vu until the memory speaks.

"As I live and breathe," a woman's voice says.

I shield the sunlight until the shape comes into focus as Mrs. Sullivan, the neighbor who found me that night, burning on the grass. She puts her hand over her heart as I stand. As soon as I'm on my feet, she hugs me tight to her, then holds me at arm's length.

"Let me look at you. You look"—she scans my face, smiling—"wonderful."

I let her hug me again.

She clings to me for a long time, and when she finally lets go, she holds me by the shoulders, searching my eyes. "I can't tell you the good it does my heart to see you standing here. Alive and well."

A tear slides down her wrinkled skin, and she laughs and lets go of me to pull a yellowed hanky with an embroidered pink flower from her shirt pocket. She dabs at her eyes.

"What a silly old ninny I am," she says. She dabs again, starts to put it back, and changes her mind as new tears emerge. "I think about you all the time. We pray for you every week at the Sunday service."

"For me?"

"Of course, dear. All of us." She shakes her head. "You gave me quite the scare that night, you know. A couple of times, I thought I'd lost you for good."

So much of that night is a smoky haze, but I never thought what I must have looked like to her. How frightened she must have been trying to keep me awake as the house burned.

"I never thanked you," I say. "For helping me."

The words seem so small, so wholly inadequate. She laughs and waves her hanky in the air.

"Oh goodness, don't you dare thank me," she says. "To tell the truth of it, I'm not sure I did much to help."

She takes my hand in hers and taps it lightly, not reacting in the slightest to my disproportionate thumb. Her skin is thin and soft against mine.

"I'm not gonna sit here and pretend to know why God lets things happen to good people like you and your folks, but I know this: God puts people in our path, and my path crossed yours that night," she says. "Your story is part of mine now, and I know that's how he wants it—our hearts all jumbled together."

Her eyes fall on the remnants of my life behind me.

"There's always beauty in the ashes. Sometimes we just can't see it yet."

She squeezes me tight one more time, steps back and shakes her head like she still can't believe I'm real.

"God bless," she says. Another dab at both eyes, and then she turns and walks back toward her house. For a moment, I want to call her back, to tell her she saved me that night.

How her voice snatched me back from the darkness.

How she helped me choose to stay.

And when I woke, other voices took her place. Cora with her bedside vigil. Glenn with his soft-spoken reassurances.

Dr. Sharp. Too many nurses to count. Dr. Layne, leaning now against the front of her car, waiting on me like she always has.

She's right: I've never been alone.

Except maybe once.

When I threw myself out that window. The choice I made then—the first of a million choices to live—*that* one I made alone.

But after, someone was always there.

In my path.

Helping me fight.

Linda with her unwavering tough love, yanking me out of bed to walk. Even Terry with his torture devices, making sure I could bend my elbows to dress myself.

Tony pulling me onto the stage. Asad making me believe someone could ever love this face again. Piper making the nightmare less lonely.

Piper.

Flipping off the universe to the beat of her fire music.

How did I not see she was waging her own war against the darkness?

More important, who's helping her fight now?

Who's helping *her* choose to live?

A wind shakes the leaves of the maple tree, and I picture myself running to Dad as he gets out of his car. He tosses me high into the air, then wraps me in his arms as I fall.

I laugh and scream, "Again!" I have no fear—no doubt.

Someone will be there.

I stand and brush the ash from my pants. "We need to go!" I yell to Dr. Layne.

"Take as long as you—"

"The house is gone. I get it." I look once more at the place I called home. "But my best friend is still here, and right now, she needs someone to catch her."

44

Dr. Layne and I stop by the school on our way to the hospital. She helps me comb through the grass for the gold phoenix.

"I was such a jerk," I mumble, pushing aside a clump of newly mowed remnants. "I should have been there for her."

"Well, you can be there now. Is this it?" She holds up the phoenix, whose right wing has been clipped, probably by the steel blade of a lawn mower.

I run my finger along the jagged, broken wing. "What if she hates me?"

Dr. Layne stands up and reaches down to help me to my feet. "Be there anyway."

Piper's parents huddle with a white coat when I walk into the third-floor hospital hallway. Her mom cuts off the doctor and rushes to hug me. She tells me they've moved Piper out of intensive care but still have her on fluids and surveillance. She winces when she says these last words, like the thought of her daughter needing to be watched round the clock physically pains her.

"Can I see her?"

Her mom nods. "But, Ava, she's heavily sedated right now and very tired, so I'm not sure she'll even know you're there."

I pull back the curtain to the room, which is dead quiet except for the beeping of the machine in time with Piper's heart. Behind the curtain, Piper is small and young and impossibly fragile. The massive bed swallows her up, and I feel like I'm seeing her for the first time.

I pull up a chair and lay my hand on hers. It's bruised beneath the surface of the skin, where some nurse with no skills tried to insert her IV.

I'm not sure what to say. I'm used to being the one in the bed. When Cora and Glenn visited me in the burn unit, I watched from my immobile perch as they suited up in booties and scrubs and hairnets so they wouldn't bring the infectious dangers of the outside world into my little reality. I'd lie there like a caged zoo animal.

Now I'm the one tapping on the glass.

"Piper?"

A small sound escapes her lips, but her eyes only flicker slightly.

"You don't have to talk. I just want to say I'm sorry. I wasn't there when you needed me." I choke down the lump in my throat.

Beeping fills the otherwise silent space.

Then I feed her all the same battle language people used to

give me. I hated it then, and I hate myself for saying it now, but it's all I have—the hope that my words will reach her.

"I need you to fight. I need you to wake up so I can tell you something amazing. I found my new normal." I flip her hand over and lay the gold phoenix in her limp palm. "It's you. You and Cora and Glenn, and I almost missed it, searching for someone I used to be. I couldn't see the beauty all around me."

I close her fingers over the bird.

"But I see it now, Pipe. I see you. You're not In. Valid. Not to me. So you have to get better so I can tell you that I'm sorry. I should have been there. But I'm here now, and I'm not going anywhere. You're part of my story, and I'm part of yours."

The antiseptic smell and beeping transports me back to the unit. I used to think Cora had a martyrdom complex, the way she'd stay through the night curled up on the chair, surviving off cafeteria Jell-O.

Did Cora feel the way I do holding Piper's hand? Like there's nowhere else in the world I'd rather be.

Then I do the one thing I know how to do: I sing softly, words about dreams and bluebirds and troubles melting like lemon drops.

Before I leave, I scribble a note on a cafeteria napkin.

You've got lots of flying left to do on this side of the rainbow.

PS If you try to die on me again, I'll kill you myself.

Piper's dad stops me on my way out to offer a supremely awkward apology for when I saw him in all his drunken splendor at his house.

"I haven't always been like that," he says, as if I've asked for an explanation. "Sometimes it feels like the accident happened to all of us. You know?"

I nod like I get it, but I don't: The accident didn't happen to him. It happened to Piper, and then *she* happened to everyone else. It's a feeling I know well, and as I walk away from Piper's bed, I wonder if that's the burden she felt so acutely last night when a bottle of pills looked a lot like relief.

Her dad takes my spot by the bed. A nurse closes the curtains again, and Piper's mom walks with me down the hall, talking in circles the whole way.

"Did Piper tell you anything? About what was wrong? Or that she was thinking about doing something . . . like this?"

Her eyes dart across my face, searching for an answer I don't have.

"I thought she was doing okay. She was walking with that walker thing a little. And helping with the volleyball team," I say.

Her mom's face twists in confusion. "What volleyball team?"

"You know, being an assistant on the team again."

She shakes her head. "No, she wasn't."

I start to argue, but realize I have no evidence. I never actually saw her working with the team. She was always "skipping" practice to come hang out at drama, or didn't have to go because the team was on the road. Did she ever even talk to the coach?

I look back toward Piper's room.

Maybe Asad was right; I've been so busy looking down that I didn't see the pain in the person right beside me. Just like Asad in his lighting booth and me behind my curtains, Piper's been hiding this whole time.

———

At home, Cora and Glenn walk on eggshells, watching me out of the corners of their eyes until it's time for bed. I don't blame them—in the last thirty-six hours, I had an epic meltdown, took a harrowing trip down memory lane, and visited my suicidal friend in the hospital. No wonder they look at me like I'm a bomb about to detonate.

Cora lotions me up in silence, and when I'm rezipped in my second skin, she sits on the edge of the bed. Glenn comes in, too, but stops and leans against the wall to take off his boots. Cora smiles.

"Can't take the cowboy out of that man," she says, half laughing. Then, softer, "Not that I'd ever want to."

Debooted, Glenn bends down to kiss Cora on the part in her hair. She leans into him.

"How is she?" he says.

My voice comes out gravelly with emotion.

"She wasn't really awake when I saw her."

"Are *you* okay?"

"I don't know." My voice vibrates, tightening right at the spot above my star scar. "It was so weird to see her lying there, so small. And all I could think was how I can't lose someone again. My heart can't take it."

Glenn picks up the charred handbell off my dresser and transfers it between his hands.

"It's hard watching someone you love in pain. You'd take their hurt in a heartbeat, but you can't. It's *their* pain."

"How did you guys do it? I mean with me. Sara was gone. I was . . . me. How did you stand it?"

Cora takes the bell from Glenn and rubs her fingers across the blackened surface.

"We had to," she says quietly.

"Because I needed you?"

"Because *we* needed you."

"*You* needed *me*?"

Cora swallows hard, reaching up to hold Glenn's hand. "I was a mother without a child. You were the one thing that kept the weight of that from crushing me. I needed you, Ava."

Cora pauses like she's waiting for more breath.

"I still need you," she says. "If anything ever happened to you—"

I put my hand on her arm.

"I'm not going anywhere."

Cora smiles and slides her thumb along the scarred ridges of my fingers.

"Do you remember each time you would get a new graft? How we knew it was going to take?"

I think back to the white patches of skin sewn into my body. How the nurses would change the dressings, day after day, always checking to see if my body was going to accept or reject this new piece of me.

And then, one day, little pink pinhead dots would appear.

"When the buds appeared, we knew."

Cora nods. "Once it connected to the heart, it had a chance." Her small, manicured fingers envelop my hand, toe and flipper and all. "You're grafted into our hearts now. Permanently stitched together."

Cora hugs me and Glenn kisses me on the top of my head. He stops at my door to flick off the lights like he always does, his profile silhouetted against the light.

In the dark, my mind whirs with thoughts of Piper. How am I going to help her? How can I make up for the terrible things I said? And how can I face the hallways—let alone the stage—without her?

I put on my headphones, hit the Fire Mix and play Piper's self-proclaimed anthem.

> *She's a phoenix in a flame—*
> *a hellfire raging from within,*
> *her story written on her skin.*
> *Once broken, now she flies—*
> *soaring above everything.*
> *She conquered her demons,*
> *and wore her scars like wings.*

An hour later, I still can't sleep. I listen to Mom's deodorant voice mail, but when it's over, I think about Piper, and the darkness creeps in again. I write in my therapy journal, but the dark won't go. Rather than fight it alone, I grab the *Wizard of Oz* DVD and knock on the door across the hall.

When Cora tells me to come in, I find Glenn lying propped up on a pile of pillows with Cora leaning against him, watching some TV documentary.

"You okay, honey?" she says.

Glenn mutes the TV. They both wait for me to say something—anything. But the words get stuck.

I want to tell them I'm scared. I want to tell them about the darkness and that I don't want to stop fighting.

I want to tell them thank you for being there when I woke up.

That I'm a child without a mother.

That I need them, too.

"You guys up for a musical?" I hold up the DVD.

Cora scoots over quickly in the bed, nudging Glenn to make room.

"Of course!" she says. She throws up the covers on her side and pats the bed while Glenn puts in the disc. She fluffs a pillow next to her. "Jump in!"

I slide into the sheets, still toasty from her body heat. Under the covers, Cora's hand finds mine, and when it does, the darkness lifts slightly.

I barely make it to Oz before I drift off.

All I know is it feels good to be there, sharing the same space.

May 10

I don't remember much.
My dad's face
through flame.

Heat crashed down on me.
Dad
disappeared.
An open window
beckoned.

I remember
a thought:

If I jump, I live.

If I stay, I die.

                                        I jumped.

45

Cora and I go by the hospital before school the next morning, but Piper's mom says she's not up for visitors.

"Visitors? Or me?" I want to know as we leave.

When Cora drops me off at school, a major wave of déjà vu from my first day grips me. I walked in alone then, too.

I wave goodbye to Cora and turn, bracing myself to see the empty spot by the door where Piper would normally sit, zebra-striped and ready for the worst the hallways can throw at us. Today, when I turn, no wheelchair waits. But also not the nothing I expect.

Asad stands in Piper's place. He rocks back and forth on his heels when I approach.

"Ava."

"Asad."

Once we establish who we are, we run out of ideas. The memory of our last conversation—the one where I made a total fool of myself—replays in my head.

"I see the wig has returned," he says after what is undoubtedly the longest any two people in the history of earth have gone without speaking.

I instinctively tug at the bobbed strands I donned this morning.

"I wanted to do something for Piper."

"How is she?"

"Okay. I think."

Asad's face is tight.

"Kenzie says you guys had a fight," he says. "Was it because of me—because of what happened with us?"

Us.

I look up at him, which I was trying desperately hard not to do because those deep, black eyes gut me.

"Oh, you mean the time where I thought you liked me but then, oh, no, wait, you're in love with my best friend?"

Asad's face blushes red, but he smiles back at me.

"Yeah, that time." He bites his lower lip. "Is this my fault?"

"No." I leave out the part where if anyone is to blame for the fact that our friend is under suicide watch on the third floor of a hospital, it's me.

Asad nods, studying his feet, then flicks his eyes to me through his thick eyelashes.

"Are *we* okay?"

We.

Another stab.

"We will be."

He exhales like he's been storing up oxygen for a month and opens the door for us to walk through together.

Inside, a staring resurgence has swept Crossroads High. I'd all but forgotten the feel of all eyes on me in these narrow corridors. Except this time it's not about me; it's about Piper.

Some brave souls have the courage to actually ask me how she's doing. Did they ever bother to ask her?

They want to know when she's coming back. What happened, exactly.

I give them all the same answer.

"She's fine."

Others talk behind cupped hands, spinning rumor webs I can practically see threading from mouth to ear, spiraling down the hall, looping back and forth until the whole school is talking about the Girl Who Took the Pills.

Asad walks with me all day in the hallways, which become more unbearable by the minute. When people aren't whispering about Piper, they're making some asinine comment about how worried they are about her. Like they've been up all night pacing about the girl they didn't give the time of day to a week ago.

A boy I've never even seen before stops me in the hall to tell me Piper was always really nice.

"Is," I correct him. "Piper *is* nice." He gives me the universal symbol for sympathy, cocking his head to the side and tucking his lips into a half frown. He nods like we're having a soul-to-soul moment and then walks away, still watching me like I'm made of glass.

A girl in my math class even quotes some psych stats.

"My dad says burn victims are way more likely to have depression," she tells me.

"Survivors," I say.

"Excuse me?"

"You said victims. We are burn *survivors*. We didn't die."

The worst part is when I walk past Piper's locker, a makeshift shrine that looks like a Hallmark card threw up on it. Posters and pictures and sentiments ripped straight from cheesy Internet memes crowd the front of locker 681.

KEEP FIGHTING!

IT GETS BETTER!

WE'RE ALL HERE FOR YOU.

I think of the box of similar empty sentiments sitting in my room. I know everyone means well, but it bothers me anyway. Why couldn't they have meant well a month ago? When Piper was just the girl in a wheelchair.

"Quite the outpouring of support," Mr. Lynch says, stopping next to me in the middle of the hall as I stare at the locker grief vomit.

I nod. "Yeah. Suddenly, Piper has a hundred best friends she never knew existed."

Mr. Lynch steps between me and the locker, meeting my eyes, just like he did on my first day here.

"If you ever need anything. Anything. My door is always open," he says, and I know he means it. Of all the phonies at this school, at least I've always known where I stood with him. "I should have seen what was happening with Piper. I should have seen the signs, but I missed it somehow."

"Everybody did," I say, my own guilt creeping up again.

Mr. Lynch nods and turns to the locker of cards that came too late.

"It's a good reminder: Everyone has scars. Some are just easier to see."

———

Asad and Sage abandon their usual cliques to sit with me at lunch. Sage asks about Piper, and then gets a weird look on her face like maybe she's about to cry or puke. "I should have done more."

"Join the club," I say.

On the far side of the cafeteria, the volleyball team has set up a poster for everyone to sign commanding Piper to GET WELL SOON! I toss my soggy sandwich down on the table.

"We should do more *now*. Something real. Not cards or words or smiley-face hearts on her locker," I say. "You *know* none of these people are going to be here for Piper when she isn't the gossip of the week, and she's going to be right back in all the same old crap. We have to fix it."

"How do you fix this?" Asad asks.

"I don't know. There has to be something we can do. One *actual* thing."

Sage chews slowly, thinking. "What would make Piper do this? Why now?"

Kenzie catches my eye from her table. She watches me with sideways glances, her pink-tinged eyes sparking something in my brain.

"The day Piper took the pills, Piper and Kenzie were fighting outside."

And then—like the jerk I am—I chose Kenzie over Piper.

Sage shakes her head. "Kenzie didn't say anything about a fight with Piper. She barely talks to her."

Kenzie stands and takes a step toward me, but then abruptly sits like she's changed her mind, and as she does, a thought that's been smoldering longer than I realized suddenly catches fire. The anonymous text of me melting. The cruel one-liners on Piper's phone from Kenzie.

Piper said she could handle a few texts. But what if it was more?

I hug Sage.

"You're a genius. Of course Kenzie didn't *talk* to Piper. That's never been her style."

———

After school, I return to the hospital, armed with my wig and a mission.

Piper's mom sits outside the room, bloodshot eyes reading a pamphlet on depression. She tells me again that Piper's not ready to see anyone.

"Where's Piper's phone?" I say.

Her mom rifles through a drawstring personal-belongings bag next to her, finally holding up Piper's hot-pink cell phone.

I enter the passcode I've seen Piper do a thousand times and open her text messages. Just as I thought, four new texts from an unknown number on the night Piper overdosed.

Everyone hates you.

You know you should have been driving.

Why didn't you just die that night?

Maybe you still should.

I turn the screen to Piper's mom. She gasps as she reads them, covering her mouth as she scrolls through.

"Who would do this?" she says.

I put the unknown number into my own cell phone. Piper's mom keeps staring at the texts. She barely responds when I tell her to play Piper's Fire Mix for her.

"And tell her I'm going to fix this. I'm going to fix everything."

46

Asad looks at me like I've lost my mind.

"No way. Taking down Kenzie has kamikaze mission written all over it," he says while prepping our mealworms for the release into the woods today.

I sketch Rum Tum Tugger onto our lab report, making note of the fact that one of his legs somehow broke and now he limps along, dragging his useless limb alongside him. The sight of him heaving his way across the habitat is so pathetically heroic I can barely watch.

"What else *can* I do? I have to fix this, and I need your help."

Asad shakes his head.

"A wise friend of mine once said that in this high school cosmos, bullies are the gravity we count on."

"Well, a wise green-skinned witch once said we should try defying gravity."

Asad sighs, smiling. "Using Broadway to bolster your argument. Tacky."

"I learned from the best."

"Unfortunately, life is not a musical, remember? We can't fight all of Piper's battles for her."

I put my finger into the dish, helping Rum Tum Tugger climb up to the water sponge.

"But we can fight this one."

We follow Mr. Bernard past the football field to the wooded area separating the school from the neighborhood behind it. He turns to us at the edge of the field, his hands raised up dramatically.

"Let us say goodbye to our friends who have led us on this journey of discovery. We have watched them build a community. We have watched them transform. And now, we bid them farewell."

He says an honest-to-goodness prayer, complete with snippets of poetry from Maya Angelou about how nobody makes it through life alone. It's all very dramatic, and after the prayer, he nods solemnly to us as if we're about to send our grandparents out on an iceberg instead of release insects into the field where seniors sometimes pee during gym class.

Asad and I hold the dish together, touching it lightly to the grass. Magical Mr. Mistoffelees and Macavity scurry away, but Rum Tum Tugger won't leave the dish until Asad shakes him out.

Asad puts his arm around my shoulder as we watch the beetles burrow into the mulch.

"Do you think they'll be okay out there in the big, bad world?" he says, pretending to be choked up.

"As long as they have each other," I say. "Someone to count on. No matter how impossible the odds."

Asad rolls his eyes and clutches his chest.

"Break my heart, why don't you?"

When I give him my best pouty face, he throws his hands up in surrender.

"You win. Tell me your plan."

———

My plan is this: if the unknown number is routing through Kenzie's phone, then all we have to do is call the number when we can hear her phone ring. She won't be able to hide anymore from how she's treated Piper.

We make our first attempt during drama. Asad pretends to hang scenery behind where Kenzie rehearses lines, her phone in the front mesh pocket of her backpack. When I call the number, the line rings on my end, over and over. Kenzie's stays silent.

I try again in the hallway the next day.

Nothing.

Asad stands next to Kenzie in the cafeteria while I call.

Nothing.

Asad decides she's turned her ringer off during school.

"Or maybe it's not Kenzie," he says.

"It's her," I say. "I know it."

We even call one time when she's waiting for a ride home, holding her phone right in her hand. Like always, a few rings and a call-ending click.

Each time we fail, I feel like I'm letting Piper down. She leaves the hospital after a week, but she still won't see me. Every day after school I go to her house, and every day her mom tells me she's not up for company.

"Give her time," she says.

One afternoon, I jam my foot in the door before her mom can close it. I crane my head into the dim house and yell: "You're not getting rid of me, Piper! I'm going to fix this."

At home, I scroll through Piper's pictures online, hoping for some sign of life. All I find are more messages from classmates echoing the sentiments from her locker.

I tap on my own profile, where the picture of Sara and me is still my final post. I open my camera roll on my phone to the last picture—Piper and me at the wig store, her cheek against my hot-pink hair.

Before I can second-guess myself, I upload it to my wall. *#scarsistersforlife #keepflying*

I want to say something else, something witty and personal and perfect. Something right. But the words don't come.

I tap submit.

An instant later, the photo appears on my homepage, and just like that, the picture-perfect illusion of Ava Before the Fire is gone.

I tag Piper and shut the screen before anyone can comment.

Without Piper, life hobbles along in a pseudo normal. Homework. Play practice. Failed attempts to catch Kenzie. Cora signs me up to take the SAT, and a huge book called *The College Application Survival Guide* replaces the *Burn Survivor Quarterly* on her nightstand. She even starts dropping hints about visiting a campus or two this summer.

End-of-the-year fever spikes at Crossroads. The hallways are so congested with prom posters advertising the Night of Your Life! and gaggles of girls signing yearbooks that no one notices the pictures and cards shedding off Piper's locker after a few weeks. I watch as someone tramples a picture of her between classes without even seeing it, just like they don't see the Piper-size void walking next to me.

I can face the hallway alone now. I just don't want to.

Just like I don't want to get up on that stage without Piper in the audience. During dress rehearsal, I stand on my mark in my hideously pink Glinda dress, squinting into the spotlight. The play is in one week. This will be my first performance without Mom and Dad. What if Piper isn't there, either?

Every night, I fall asleep to Piper's anthem about turning scars into wings. But as the play zooms closer on my calendar, I begin to doubt I can fix anything for either of us. I ask Cora to drive me to group.

"I think I need it," I say.

In the spacious rec room, our circle of four seems especially small. I stop outside the ring of chairs, staring at where Piper should be.

"She's coming back," Dr. Layne says. She puts her arm around me, pulling me into the circle. "Her place here will be ready when she is."

Piper's empty spot glares at me as we talk about the power of love. How we need it. How we show it. How we deserve it.

For once, when it's my turn to share, I talk. I tell the group about how I'm trying to help Piper by exposing Kenzie.

"I blame myself for not helping Piper before, and I'm sure she does, too. But I'm going to fix all of this for her."

My comment is met with silence, even from Braden, who is amazingly not already crying. He raises his hand hesitantly.

"If you want to talk about blame, I'm kind of an expert. I'm the boy who carried a gas can over an open bonfire. There was no one else to blame but myself. And for a long time, I did. Every surgery, I told myself I deserved the pain. It was my fault when my dad left. My fault for making my mom a single parent buried in medical bills."

He pulls his sleeve up so we can see his splotchy arm, the skin all wrinkled and discolored from his shoulder down to where his forearm cul-de-sacs.

"But after years of blaming myself, guess what." He rubs his other hand up and down his scars. "I'm still burned. Guilt can't unscar my skin. I guess what I'm saying is blame is useless."

"He's right," Olivia chimes in. "I know it's kind of weird I still come to these groups. I should be better by now, right?"

I don't dare nod.

"But I don't come because I need to be fixed. I come because I'm accepted, just the way I am." She looks up at me. "You can't fix Piper. All you can do is be stronger together."

Dr. Layne concludes by telling us to show love to someone today, even if we just love ourselves. I almost laugh out loud thinking of how Piper would have said Braden probably loves himself on the regular.

Then Dr. Layne leads us in a group hug that hits an easy 10.5 on the awkward-o-meter. But when I start to inch away after a quick squeeze, Olivia pulls me back in. She laces her arm through mine as Dr. Layne folds me against her side and Braden props his half arm on Olivia's shoulder.

I let them pull me in, and as I give in to the embrace, the room suddenly doesn't feel so empty. In that vast room, standing skin to skin—scar to scar—our small and slightly broken circle of trust fills the space.

On my way out, Dr. Layne gives me another brochure about burn camp and tells me to "give it some thought."

This time, I take it.

———

I check my post when I get home. No sign of Piper. But I have to scroll through the comments on the #scarsisters picture three times to reach the end.

Queenchloe84 Ava! Where have you been?!

4eva_emma Love the pink hair.

Nightavenger You look great! We miss you down here!

Sttb704 You are an inspiration!

My gut reaction is to scoff at the pages and pages of words. Pathetic. Awkward. Empty.

But then I look next to the words at the profile pics of my old friends, the faces I used to know so well, and a thought hits me: Do they feel like I do with Piper, helpless and unsure what to say or do? How long did they sit with their fingers hovering over the keyboard, waiting for the right words to come? How many times did they type, erase, type, erase before hitting send?

I scroll through the comments again. The girls from drama who tried to be there for me after the fire. I pushed them away, afraid they couldn't handle the new me. Afraid they would find I was unfixable.

Like me, they don't know the perfect thing to say, but here they are, saying something anyway.

Maybe it's never been about the words.

Maybe my therapy group was right: it's about being there—reaching out—even if there's no way in hell to fix it.

I type a quick reply at the top of the thread.

dramagrrl Thanks! Miss you all, too! I'll come visit soon.

To my surprise, I mean every word.

I lie back on my bed and listen to Piper's "Phoenix in a Flame" anthem. While the girl sings about wings, I pick up the burn-camp brochure next to me. On the cover, a man with a hole for an ear like mine carries a laughing little boy. Scars blur both their faces under the words, "Nothing heals people like other people." The pink phoenix symbol soars above the words.

I turn off the Fire Mix and text Asad.

> Remember the tattoo parlor where you took Piper?

Yeah. Why?

> Because you're taking me.

47

Asad drives while I clutch the letter from Cora saying I can deface my body to my heart's content. Cora wasn't crazy about the idea at first. Okay, truth: she said it was *the* craziest idea she'd ever heard.

"Why would you want to *add* scars to your body?" she asked, genuinely puzzled.

I reminded her that it is, in fact, *my* body and that up until now, I've had zero say in my scars.

"But with a tattoo, I get to decide what I look like," I said. "For once."

That got her pretty good.

My announcement that I'm going to burn camp also put her in an especially agreeable mood. So after a quick phone consult with Dr. Sharp, who gave me his medical-degree blessing to ink any nongrafted skin, she signed the form. She also put this in big letters at the top: SOMETHING SMALL! TASTEFUL! THAT WON'T HORRIFY HER GRANDCHILDREN!

As we drive to the parlor, Asad doesn't mention my lack of compression garments, but I'm sure he noticed. My ridging skin-graft scars twist and turn down my arms and legs, and even I'm not used to seeing them so exposed like this outside lotioning hour. But I haven't picked a spot for the tattoo yet, and I don't want to be trying to unzip and shimmy out of my garments in public.

The tattoo parlor is nothing like I expect, which was essentially a cliché movie portrayal of leather-clad biker chicks and dudes getting inked in some dodgy back room. Instead, Asad and I walk into a spotlessly clean store smack-dab in the middle of a suburban strip mall.

With its reclining chairs and sterilized instrument trays, it's more like a dentist's office than my imagined skeezy den of iniquity. I try not to let the reality take anything away from my rebellious act of solidarity. Asad peruses the various images pinned to the wall like a smorgasbord of skin art. He points to one, a zipper, opening up the skin below it.

"You should totally get this one."

I tell him skin zippers most likely violate Cora's "horrifying grandchildren" rule, and besides, I already know what I'm getting.

Asad turns to face me, one eyebrow cocked.

"Please tell me it's not some Chinese proverb. Half the time those don't even say what you think they do and you walk around your whole life thinking your wrist says 'hope and love' but it really says 'Where's the toilet?' "

I unfold the burn-camp brochure from my back pocket and point to the bird.

"I'm getting that," I say. "Like Piper's."

"Piper as in phoenix Piper?" a voice behind us asks. A guy barely older than us rustles through a beaded curtain behind the front desk. He doesn't have the bearded, leather-vested look I hoped for, but with his man bun and thick, black-framed glasses, he does give off a certain just-got-high-on-my-hookah-in-the-storage-room vibe that will have to do. On his bicep, a colorful dragon tattoo curls around his arm down to his wrist.

"You know Piper?" I ask.

"You bet. I did her ink." He reaches his hand out to me. "Gabriel."

"Ava."

"Well, Ava. Any friend of Piper is welcome here. A fellow Viking, I presume?"

I nod.

"Me too. Graduated last year. Your girl Piper was my first solo job, actually. She came in here demanding something majestic, something out-of-this-world—" He smiles at me. "Something to give her wings. So I did. How is she?"

I pause.

"Not great, actually. Kind of why I'm here." I hold out the burn-camp brochure. "I want to get a phoenix like hers. But not my whole back or anything."

Gabriel leans against a vinyl reclining chair, his chin propped on his fingers, his eyes searching my body. If he's shocked by my scars, he doesn't show it. He just keeps scanning me, inch by inch.

"I'm going to tell you the same thing I told Piper, then," he says finally. "You don't need a tattoo."

"You're not much of a salesman," I say.

"Hear me out. Everybody comes in here, picks an image off that wall to tell the world who they are. Express themselves." He reaches out to me, but stops right before he touches my skin. "May I?

I nod. He grabs both my hands, seemingly unfazed by them, and holds my arms out wide.

"But you? Your scars tell your story."

"And what story is that?" I say.

He looks right at me with true-blue intensity.

"That you're stronger than whatever tried to kill you."

Even though I can barely feel his touch through my numb skin, shivers squiggle through me.

"Forget the ink," he says. "You're already a walking piece of badass art."

Asad rolls his eyes behind the guy. I ignore his mockery, although I have to admit this guy is out there. I stand mesmerized for a minute until Asad waves his hand between us.

"So are we doing this or what?"

"Yes, yes, we're doing this," I say. "This tattoo isn't just about me; it's about Piper. She needs to know I'm on her side, no matter what."

Gabriel studies the bird on the paper again and pulls a pen out of his man bun.

"Okay, but if we're doing a phoenix, we're not doing this sad sketch. We're gonna do it right."

Like magic, he transforms the bird with ink, turning the small image into a masterpiece.

"I love it," I say.

He vanishes behind the beaded curtain again for a minute and comes out with a woman whose arms are covered shoulder to wrist with colorful ink.

"Technically, I'm still an apprentice so the boss-woman's gotta babysit me," Gabriel says. The woman smiles and shakes my hand, her eyes roving over my scars in a way that feels like when Tony looked at me after my audition, a kind of wonder mixed with—respect?

Gabriel ushers me to a reclining chair, where he pulls up on a wheeled stool just like the one Dr. Sharp uses. Between the antiseptic smell and vinyl chair, I almost feel like I'm back in his office, about to go under the knife again.

But like I told Cora, this time, I choose the scar.

Gabriel spends a few minutes trying to find a good piece of skin as his canvas. I'm too nervous and excited to even care when he and the woman scrutinize every inch of my exposed body. We narrow it down to a spot on my ankle right between where the scar-free skin of my feet bleeds into the roughness of my calves.

"I can do half the bird in the ankle, kind of flying up into the scars," he says. "Like it's rocketing through them."

"Let's do it," I say.

I lean back in the chair as he props my ankle up and draws an outline of his creation on my leg. When I approve, the boss-woman gives a nod and Gabriel gets to work. Asad holds my hand.

"Oh, it's not so bad." I unclench all my muscles as the little drill nips at my skin like a series of tiny rubber-band snaps that sting and fade, sting and fade.

"After what you've been through, I'm sure this is a walk in the park," Gabriel says. He talks while he draws, asking about how I like Crossroads and how I got burned. Even though I've never met this guy before, I talk, too. When I tell him about Piper, he pauses.

"That's rough. She's a cool girl."

I love him for using the present tense.

Before I can stop myself, I've basically told him everything about my life. About the fire. How I'm in *The Wizard of Oz*, and how it's my first time onstage since the scars and how much I've missed singing and all things Broadway.

He tells me the only musical he's ever seen is *Cats*, but he loved it. He keeps working, his lips moving slightly and I realize he's singing softly beneath the whir of the drill. When I recognize the tune, I join in, and we sing the final chorus of "Memory" together.

Asad shakes his head.

"*Cats*? Seriously, dude?"

Gabriel shrugs, eyes still trained on my ankle. "What can I say? I'm a sucker for the classics." He smiles up at me. "Killer voice, by the way. That auditorium won't know what hit 'em."

I fight the urge to flick my eyes away from his.

"Thanks. You too."

Gabriel holds his rubber-gloved hands in the air triumphantly like he's about to launch into an encore: "Voilà!"

He points to my skin, where he's captured a phoenix in mid-flight, her wings stretched out on either side, blazing red and orange and yellow just like Piper's. Straight as an arrow, her head and beak point fixedly at my scars.

Gabriel reaches out his hand for mine to help me up, and when I'm on my feet, he spins me beneath his arm slowly.

"She conquered her demons and wore her scars like wings," he says as I complete my rotation. "Piper's lucky to have a friend like you."

"I'm pretty lucky, too."

Before we leave, Gabriel writes a number on a business card.

"I added my cell. Call me if you have any inflammation or questions or if there are any local high school drama productions I shouldn't miss." He winks at me when he hands me the card. "I promise not to break into song."

Outside, I stop to admire his handiwork one more time in the dusky light.

"Piper's gonna love it," Asad says definitively. "The perfect way for you to welcome her back."

"Okay, so what about you?"

Asad laughs as he opens the car door for me. "Yeah, right. My dad just barely started acknowledging me again after the convo about doing curtain calls rather than being on call. A tattoo will not help."

"No, I mean about Piper. Are you planning to declare your undying love when she gets back?"

Asad closes the door before he answers, walks around the front of the car, and when he gets in, he stares at the steering wheel a minute.

"Someday, maybe. I think you were right—what Piper needs right now is a friend."

I raise my hand over the center console between us.

"Friend zone for life! Welcome to the club."

Asad doesn't hit my palm. He points to the tattoo parlor, where Gabriel waves to us through the glass.

"Hello? Were you not in there just now? That hippy-dippy tattoo guy was totally flirting with you." He bats his eyelashes at me. "Let me twirl you across the strip mall, my lady."

I reach across the center console to punch him in the shoulder.

"He was just being nice."

Asad starts the car, reaching his arm behind my seat as he backs up.

"If you didn't know that was flirting, then you're as wacky as he is. I'm not saying it has to be that dude because hello—man bun—but someday, some guy is going to rip you out of the friend zone, kicking and screaming."

"Like a blind guy?"

"Maybe." Asad laughs. "Or maybe just someone who loves your scars because they're part of who you are." He smirks as he turns back to the wheel. "You're a walking piece of art, remember?"

I wave to Gabriel through the window as we pull away. I tuck the card with his number in my purse where I won't lose it. As we drive home, I turn my calf to admire his artwork.

The phoenix tail stretches out below the powerful bird in curly tendrils the same flaming colors as the wings rocketing up toward my scars.

I'm not jumping on the scars-are-awesome bandwagon, but this time last year, I would never have believed any part of me could be so beautiful.

May 22

A story.
A shield.
A star.
What are these scars?

Am I this skin?
All trapped within?
A broken body.
A broken girl.

Or is there more to me than this?
This patchwork quilt
of shame and guilt.

For once, I'm starting to believe,
Beneath this skin,
There's still a me.

Of ash,
Of smoke,
Of scars—
A girl.

Her wings
In waiting
To unfurl.

48

With zero warning, exactly twelve hours before facing down my first postfire audience, Piper returns.

On the morning of the play, as Asad and I leave earth science, I see her at the end of the long science hallway, her face twisting in pain with each scoot-step of her walker.

Piper makes her way slowly through the crowd, her eyes glued to the linoleum as everyone turns in the same not-so-obvious way as on my first run of the hallway gauntlet. Stares. Whispers behind hands.

Rumors about the Girl Who Took the Pills. The girl who is walking, painfully slow, right back into everything she tried to escape. Because I didn't fix it.

When Piper stops at her locker, she balances on one side of the walker to rip off the two straggler cards that have managed to hang on for her less-than-triumphant return. A few feet ahead of us, Kenzie also watches Piper's glacial approach. I nudge Asad when I notice the cell phone in Kenzie's hand. He shakes his head.

"Forget about her," he says. "It'll be a big scene."

A searing flame of anger shoots through me as I think of Kenzie's texts, every nasty word.

Everyone hates you

I grab my own cell from my backpack and pull up the number that's been torturing Piper.

"A big scene is exactly what I want."

I head straight for Kenzie, but she's moving away from me now, threading her way down the hall. She pulls a blue envelope out of her backpack and hands it to Piper.

"... from all of us," I hear her say. "We were so worried about you."

I grab the card before Piper can.

"You were *so* worried about her?" I say. "You can drop the act, Kenzie."

She stares at me, speechless.

"We all know what kind of a friend you've been," I say.

Wildfire itching pours over my body as Kenzie turns to me, along with half the hallway. Another day, another me, I would have run away with my tail between my legs. But not today.

Not when Piper needs me.

You know you should have been driving

"What are you doing?" Piper hisses to me through gritted teeth. "Everyone's staring."

"Let them," I say.

Around us, I can feel bodies closing in, trying to listen. A few boys start chanting, "Fight, fight." Kenzie shifts her weight uncomfortably.

"This isn't my fault," she whispers. "I didn't do this."

"You didn't do what?" I say. "You didn't cause the accident? You didn't try to blame it on Piper? What exactly *didn't* you do?"

Kenzie's eyes widen, nostrils flaring. She shakes her head. "I didn't make her—"

"No," I say. "You didn't give her the pills, but you *did* walk away from the accident, and you've been walking away from Piper ever since."

Kenzie turns toward Piper, who wobbles on unsteady legs.

"You were the one who hated me first," Kenzie says. "Every time I see you in that chair, I wish I could take it back, but I can't. What was I supposed to do?"

I move between them, the fire inside me roaring so loud, I can hardly hear myself think. Asad stands next to Piper, reaching out to steady her.

"Ava, stop," Piper says. Her voice is tiny, almost a whimper.

I step toward Kenzie.

"You were supposed to be her friend. You weren't supposed to text her that she'd be better off dead."

Kenzie recoils from me like I've punched her in the gut as a wave of whispering surges through the crowd. "I didn't do that," she says. "I swear, Piper, I wouldn't."

"Just like you didn't send that picture of me?" I say.

Kenzie glances around the crowd, down at the floor, anywhere but at me. She doesn't answer.

"That's what I thought," I say.

I start dialing.

I feel a hand on my arm and turn to see Piper, eyes pleading, face white.

"Let it go," she says. "It doesn't matter."

Why didn't you just die that night?

"Yes. It does," I say. "And so do you."

I press send.

My phone rings, and my eyes—all eyes—are on Kenzie's pink cell, waiting for it to light up.

Beside me, Piper makes a choking sound as she twists backward, reaching into her backpack.

A familiar ringtone of synthesized piano breaks the silence, turning my insides to ice. I look toward the phone—not the one sitting dead silent in Kenzie's hand but the one that's halfway out of Piper's backpack, ringing in time with my own.

Maybe you still should

49

Piper silences the phone, but it's too late.

"I told you to let it go," she hisses under her breath.

A hundred other pairs of eyes watch me, but mine are stuck to Piper. She looks again like the fragile girl in the hospital bed. And now I've pulled back her curtain in front of everyone.

"It was you?" I whisper.

The crowd melts away one by one. No fight today, folks. Just a broken girl in the middle of a hallway, trying to disappear. A few people loiter, watching, whispering, waiting to see what happens next. Kenzie stares at Piper, and I wait for some triumphant display or Kenzie-style verbal judo. Instead, Kenzie reaches out to Piper, placing her hand on the walker.

"I had no idea things were so bad," she says. "If I had known—"

Piper swats her away, and as she does, Kenzie tilts her head toward the ceiling, trying to stop a tear that escapes defiantly, streaking down to her neck along a jagged pink line I've never noticed before. A scar, the same still-healing hue as Piper's, slices from her jaw to her collarbone.

When she catches me looking, Kenzie flips her hair back in front of her shoulder, hiding the scar no one can see, the one she let make her ugly anyway.

Piper yanks her walker away from both of us, teetering unsteadily. Dr. Layne's words ring in my head: you can let people in or you can let your scars push people away. Piper pushed Kenzie away. Kenzie pushed back. And they both ended up alone.

Now Piper's cutting me out, too.

She glances up at me with empty eyes, and when she does, a realization settles on me: I can't fix this.

No more than I can fix the scars on my face.

But there's something I *can* do.

I turn so I'm next to Piper, keeping my steps in line with hers.

"You're making it worse. Just go away," she whispers, her voice tight. "I don't need you to stand up for me."

"I'm not. I'm standing up with you."

Piper lifts one hand from her walker, wobbling to the side as she pushes me away from her.

"Just go!" Her words ring loud even above the noise of the hallway. "Everyone is looking at us. You hate that. So Just. Walk. Away."

"No."

Piper's face flushes red as she stops again, midstep, and raises her hands wildly in the air.

"It's a freak parade, then! Hey, everybody. Step right up to see the show."

Half the people around us turn away in embarrassment. The other half can't look away.

"The burned girl and the psychopath, for your viewing pleasure!" she yells.

"It won't work this time," I say. "You can't cut me off before I leave, because *I'm* not leaving."

Piper groans and continues to scoot-step her way down the hall, edging her way through clusters of people who jostle her and her walker. When she veers into the bathroom, I veer, too.

"You've got to be kidding me," she says.

She turns to me inside the bathroom, yelling so loud that a terrified freshman drops her paper towel on the floor and scurries between us to escape.

"What do you want, Ava? An explanation? Is that it? I lied, okay? I sent those text messages so you'd stay away from Kenzie. Congratulations—you were right! I'm possessive and needy and jealous, and I couldn't stand the thought of you being friends with her."

"I don't—"

"And then, guess what." She cuts me off. "I liked it. It felt good to put down the truth of what everyone thinks."

"You think everyone wishes you were dead?"

She pulls away from me when I try to touch her shoulder.

"I *know* they do."

"You're wrong."

"And you're stupid. Didn't you hear what I said? I lied. I used you. I am a crazy, pill-guzzling maniac, and you should get as far away from me as possible."

When I don't move, she maneuvers her walker into the handicapped stall and slams the door, locking it tight.

"Go away!" she yells through the barricade. "You can't fix me!"

I sink onto the tiled floor next to an overflowing trash can and pull my knees to my chest.

"I'm not trying to fix you," I say. "I'm trying to tell you I love you. Scars and all."

The kind of love I thought died with my parents. The kind I thought was gone forever when I saw my face.

Love without fine print.

Under the gap of the stall door, I see Piper flop to the floor, rubbing her thigh like she's kneading sore muscles.

"Does it hurt?" I say.

"I'm fine."

The bell rings, eliciting a sneaker squeak from the hall as kids hurry to class. Then it's quiet. A sink drips deafeningly loud in the space between us. What would Dr. Layne do right now? What would Cora do?

Then it hits me: What would Piper do?

" 'She's a phoenix in a flame,' " I say in half speech, half song.

"Don't you dare use my Fire Mix against me," Piper growls through the door.

I sing a little louder, pretending I don't hear her.

" 'A hellfire raging from within—' "

Piper groans.

"We are *way* beyond cheesy fire songs. So. Just. Stop."

I stand in the corner, my head titled back so my voice echoes through the bathroom.

"'Her story written on her skin.'"

Piper pounds on the stall wall, shaking the whole row.

"Stop singing! Stop pretending like everything is okay. Nothing is okay!"

My voice smashes out of me. "'Once broken, now she flies.'"

While I sing, she screams.

And screams.

And when the scream runs out of air, she screams some more.

"They hate you! They won't even touch you! You're a joke. We both are."

"'Soaring—'"

"Freddy Krueger!" Piper shrieks. "Roadkill!"

"'—above everything.'"

I'm scream-singing now, too. My voice barrels into the space between us.

"'She conquered her demons'"—hot waves of silence billow from the stall as my voice bounces off the tiles—"'and wore her scars like wings.'"

I sing the *oh-oh-ohhh*s, and when I hit my last *oh,* a broken whisper—almost inaudible—comes from behind the door.

"Your best friend tried to kill herself."

I lean my hand against the door, Piper's words echoing louder than my song.

"I know."

Piper's voice almost isn't there. "Don't you get it? It's never going to be okay."

"I never said it's going to be okay. I said I'm not leaving."

Piper's legs stretch into the next stall, reminding me of how I hid backstage on my first day, terrified of being seen. I half laugh despite myself.

"Three months ago, I actually broke my skin trying so hard to fade away behind a curtain," I say. "Because I thought I deserved to be alone. That no one could look at me, let alone love me. Then a girl with hot-pink appendages and seriously questionable taste in wigs showed up."

I try to turn the lock from the outside. I can't.

"Let me in, Piper. I needed that girl. I still need her. I'm not leaving here without her."

Piper doesn't say anything, so I clear my throat and begin to sing another fire song even louder. " 'This girl is on fi—' "

The door swings open.

"You win! Just shut up!"

On the floor, Piper leans back with a huff.

"You're the worst," she says without looking at me.

I sit next to her and shove her softly.

"You love me."

Piper rests her head on the wall. A tear streaks from the corner of her eye, down her face, dissolving into the scars on her neck.

"I didn't want to die, you know," she says. "Not really. I just didn't want to live anymore."

More tears fill Piper's heavy eyes, like she's holding them in by sheer will.

"I thought if I could just walk, things would be magically better. But I was still me. Still this." She gestures to the burns visible on her legs behind her plastic braces. "And I was so tired of pretending to be stronger than I feel."

"Then don't," I say. "Not with me."

I put my arm around Piper and she folds into me, her scars against my second skin. Leaning on me, she deflates, letting out an echoing sob that reverberates in the small stall.

I hold her shaking shoulders on that tiled bathroom floor as we both stop fighting the tears.

After a few minutes, she sits up and wipes her eyes with her sleeve. I pull up my pant leg and unzip the bottom of my compression garments to reveal the bright-winged phoenix on my ankle. Piper sniffles and touches my skin.

"Ms. I'm-Never-Intentionally-Scarring-My-Body got a tattoo? I don't believe it."

"I don't mind this scar," I say. "It reminds me that you're a part of me, now. That we're stronger together."

I pull toilet paper out of the dispenser and hand a wad to Piper so she can blot the tears on her face.

"Dr. Layne has me doing one-on-ones twice a week now," she says. "I've graduated to big-girl therapy."

"Good."

She reaches out to wipe a tear dangling from my chin.

"Are you sure you want to be part of this?" she says. "It's not going to be pretty."

I point to my face.

"Hello? That happens to be my expertise."

Piper laughs weakly. She blows her nose in the paper and then puts both hands in the air, shooting the wad into the small trash can on the wall. "So what do we do now?"

"Well, for starters, we get out of the bathroom before people start to wonder about our digestive health."

Piper shakes her head.

"Too late. I'm already the butt of every joke out there."

I stand and offer her my hand.

"I'm kind of over what they think. Besides, we'll go together. My best friend told me no one can face high school alone."

"She sounds smart." Piper lets me help her to her feet, leaning on the wall and me for balance. "And hot."

"And outrageously humble." I hook my arm through hers. "We can handle it. High school is no match for two bona fide phoenixes. Phoenexii?"

"Phoenixens."

I push her walker contraption to her, and she struggles to make her legs line up beneath her. When she finally straightens out, she pumps one fist in the air.

"I'm an inspiration!"

"And unbelievably brave!" I say.

"A living, breathing miracle," Piper says, half laughing now.

"The luckiest survivor that ever chuckled in the face of death."

Piper steadies herself on the walker, wincing as she pulls her feet up to it like she's moving through wet concrete. She breathes heavily, and reaches out for my hand again.

"I'm scared," she whispers.

I steady her with my arm around her waist. "Me too."

I open the door, and we walk out.

Together.

50

That night, I stuff myself into my monstrosity of a Glinda dress while Cora reaches DEFCON 1 panic status.

Glenn and I stay clear while she whirls around the house, making sure she has not only her phone but also her big-lens-for-momentous-occasions camera, her power cord, and a backup battery just in case there's a citywide power outage during which she—and she alone—can memorialize the splendor of my high school musical.

She used to do the same thing for Sara's ballets, her purse bulging like she just robbed an audiovisual store. Glenn stands by the door per Cora's strict instructions that we absolutely cannot be late. He holds the camera bag, trapped on the welcome mat with his boots while Cora zips my dress.

"Been a long time since I helped a girl get gussied up for the stage," she says, not even bothering to wipe away the tear that smudges her mascara.

"I look like a Pepto-Bismol commercial," I say.

"You look like your mother," Glenn says.

I smooth out the pink satin ruffles of my dress. They bounce back defiantly.

"Yeah, right."

He steps off the mat, closing the space between us with two long strides.

"You do," he says. "The way she used to light up before your plays. Her eyes came alive watching you on the stage. Tonight, you have that same look—you look just like her."

Cora hugs Glenn and he puts his arm around me and we lean on each other, a trio of broken hearts huddled tight together—cowboy boots on the carpet and all.

———

In the packed auditorium, Cora and Glenn manage to snag a few seats halfway up on the left side unclaimed by jackets and purses. Cora reminds me to look for her and smile when I get onstage. She pats her bag, as if I could forget that she is armed with a plethora of memory-making devices.

I scan the rows for Piper.

"Save a seat for her," I tell Cora, who obediently slings her camera bag onto an empty chair.

"Are you sure she's coming?"

I nod despite the sinking feeling in my stomach. Today was rough, but she *has* to come. I need her.

"Ava!"

Sage squeals and waves from the stage, grinning from ear to ear, dressed in Kenzie's Dorothy costume down to her ruby-red slippers.

"So you really did it?" I say as she runs down the aisle toward me. "You poisoned Kenzie in the greatest understudy long game of all time."

Sage laughs loudly and hugs me.

"Better!" she says, looking over her shoulder to where Kenzie, costume-free in jeans and a T-shirt, walks down the aisle. "After what happened with Piper today, Kenzie told Tony she was the one who sent that picture of you. They met with Mr. D and decided Kenzie shouldn't be in the play this year."

"You're kidding."

Kenzie shakes her head when she gets to us. "Nope."

"But you're the lead."

Kenzie shrugs. "We both know I don't deserve it. I was just so mad. You'd taken my place with Piper and then came into drama and—" She stops, breathing heavily. "It doesn't matter. I should never have sent that picture. I should have been there for you like I should have been there for Piper. The way you were today. You were so inspir—"

I hold my hands out.

"I gotta stop you right there. Being burned doesn't make me an inspiration."

"I meant the way you stood by Piper. I knew I had to make things right, too," she says.

Part of me wants to tell her it's far too late and much too little, but Kenzie's face, a softened version of the one who exposed me backstage months ago, stops me. After all, who am I to begrudge second chances?

I shake my head and tell her the past is the past. "You're here now."

Kenzie tells me I'm going to do great before she walks away, Sage at her side practically skipping the whole way.

Before I go backstage, Cora takes roughly twenty pictures in a row until my cheeks hurt from smiling. She pauses and reaches out like she's about to adjust my wig but seems to change her mind.

"It's perfect," she says, and then hugs me so tight it almost hurts, but in a good way. Tony taps me on the shoulder, half bowing to Cora and Glenn, clearly trying not to have an opening-night coronary.

"I know she's your daughter, but tonight, she's my Glinda, and I need her backstage *prontissimo*."

"Oh, no, these aren't my—" I start to correct him, but stop midsentence. Cora's camera is poised in midair with Glenn's arm around her. "These are my people."

Before I go, I remind Cora to save Piper's seat.

"She'll be here," I say, more to myself than anyone.

Complete mayhem reigns backstage. A half-dressed Tin Man barrels past me, yelling about face makeup. The Wicked Witch can't find her broom, and Toto, our live prop, has run off after relieving himself on the Scarecrow.

From behind the curtains, I peek out, my heart racing at the sight of the jam-packed theater. I run my fingers over the soft satin of my dress again, and then run them across the bumps of my face.

Asad finds me there, gripping the black curtain.

"Earth to Ava." He waves his hand between my eyes and the audience. "You okay? You've got that 'help, I'm drowning' look going on."

His voice brings me slightly back into orbit. He's black-clad from head to toe, including a black headset that screams CIA agent or employee of the month at the Gap. He holds a box with a big pink bow.

"I'm kind of freaking out," I say.

"Well, this probably won't help, but a certain tattoo artist with an atrocity of a man bun is here."

"He came?" I search the crowd. Cora spots me and holds up her camera, pointing to her smile. Piper's seat sits vacant beside her. From the back row, Gabriel gives a half-wave.

"Why, Ava Lee. You surprising little minx," Asad says. "You totally invited him."

"What?" I try to say it nonchalantly despite Asad's suggestive grin. "He was nice. He likes theater."

"Right." Asad draws out the vowel until my cheeks get hot and my nerves go haywire again. I take another glance toward the room full of people. Am I really doing this?

"Tell me the truth: This is crazy, right? Getting up on this stage, playing the part of a beautiful fairy."

Asad lifts the headset off his ear and pushes it back on his head, but I hear the person on the other end going off about a burned-out light bulb backstage.

"Life is not a musical, Ava, but it is *your* life. No one can cast you in a role unless you let them." He catches my eyes with his. "So what part do you want to play?"

In the audience, Cora chatters to Glenn as she rechecks all her camera equipment.

"It's not like I can back out now. Cora is so excited. And Tony has worked—"

Asad snaps the curtain shut.

"Forget them. What do *you* want?"

His eyes reflect me as I consider this question. In his black irises, I see the shape of me—not the scars—just me. What do I want? And even though part of me wants to run from this, the real answer bubbles up in me strong and sure.

"I want to sing."

Asad adjusts his headpiece back in place.

"So what are we still talking about?" Then, like he's just remembered he's holding it, he holds up the box in his hand. "I almost forgot, this is from Piper."

I tug the pink ribbon to release the lid, and pull a light brown wig from the bottom of the box. Underneath, a note:

This one seems a little more you. Break a leg tonight. (Not a spine.)

"She was here?" I ask. "Is she coming back?"

He shrugs. "Dropped it off earlier on her way to get her head shrunk. Her words, not mine." The earpiece voice rises as Asad puts the set back on his ear. He points two fingers to his eyes, and then turns his fingertips toward me. "Remember, it's just you on the stage and me in the booth, making lighting magic. Forget all these other people."

In the mirror backstage, I swap out my pink hair for the new wig. The strands are almost the color mine used to be, coming to a slight curl right above my star scar. In the glass, a girl with a bulbous nose, no ear and countless scars, but her eyes are a familiar blue.

As the houselights start to dim, I peek out one more time, trying to memorize where Cora and Glenn are in the cavernous space.

The last thing I see before the lights go out is the empty chair beside them.

———

Before I know it, Tony is telling me to get on my mark. Through the crack in the curtain, I see only the faces of the first few rows, then head-shaped silhouettes back to the wall. I can't see Cora and Glenn in the darkness, but I imagine them like I used to picture Mom and Dad, their unseen strength helping me face the crowd.

"Glinda, go!" a crew member shout-whispers to me.

As I step onto the stage, Asad's massive spotlight finds me, and when it does, an instant gasp surges through the audience.

And then, silence.

Standing in the beam of light, I feel every eye on me, the light revealing every inch, every burn, every scar.

My neck itches white-hot as I eke out a single, shaky note. But fear chokes off my voice. I look to the right, trying to find where Cora and Glenn should be. And Piper.

A whispering from the darkness crescendos. I close my eyes, trying to shut out the people, the eyes. I try to envision my parents and Sara, lifting me up from the darkness. But fear flicks my eyelids back open.

I seriously consider darting offstage, when suddenly, like someone flipped a switch, the spotlight goes out.

Black.

Through the darkness, all I can see is Asad, backlit by a flickering fluorescent ceiling light in his booth, giving me a thumbs-up.

He's taken away the crowd.

Just me and him.

And then, to the right, a single, small beam of light pierces the darkness. A voice splits the air.

"Keep flying, Ava!"

Piper.

I turn toward the light that looks like a cell phone. Two other lights flick on beside her, and I imagine Glenn and Cora holding their phones high in the air. Bright stars cutting through the darkness.

Pinpricks tingle my skin. Air fills my lungs.

A new strength courses through my body, which as sure as I'm alive is part of who I am.

But as I cling to those three stars, I am more than my body.

More than my scars.

One by one, more lights blink on, like a smartphone Milky Way punching through the black, reaching the part of me the fire couldn't touch.

I breathe deep.

My voice finds the words.

Through the darkness, buoyed by the glow of countless tiny lights, I sing.

Acknowledgments

This book would not have been possible without the burn survivors who shared their stories—and scars—to help me tell *this* story.

Marius Woodward, you were my first inspiration, with your courage and humor and absolute knowledge that you are so much more than your scars. Thank you for being you. To Elizabeth Watson and Hope VanderToolen-Thatcher, you helped bring Ava to life by sharing your own pain and triumphs. Amy Farnsworth and Stephanie Nielson, thank you for reading and for being examples of strength to so many.

The joy, power, and beauty in the burn survivor community continues to overwhelm me. To all the survivors, whether you're already soaring or still fighting the darkness, thank you. Keep flying.

Thank you also to all the organizations and people who support burn survivors every day and helped with my research, particularly Dr. Katherine Au at Shriners Hospitals for Children, Kristen C. Quinn at the University of Utah Burn Center, Kristen Black-Bain at Sugar House Rehab Clinic, Lynne Woodward, and everyone at the Phoenix Society for Burn Survivors.

I am beyond grateful to my superstar agent, Brianne Johnson, for seeing the beauty in Ava's story. You are the best agent/cheerleader/therapist a writer could have. Thank you also to Allie Levick for plucking me from the slush and Cecilia de la Campa for sharing my words with the world. To the amazing team at Delacorte Press, thank you for bringing this book to life. Wendy Loggia, your keen eye as my editor and your belief in this novel made all the difference. Thank you Jennifer Heuer for working to get the perfect cover for Ava, and to Colleen Fellingham and your team for your mad editing skills.

I am lucky to live among an outrageously talented and generous writing community. I started on this journey thanks to the time and love of Carol Lynch Williams and the WIFYR conference. I found my tribe at Storymakers. And of course, I couldn't survive without the brilliant insights of my critique partners, Kim, LoriAnne, Cheryl, Michelle, and Matt, a wordsmith extraordinaire who turned my rough drafts into things of beauty. To the Knuckles critique group—Jaime, Brekke, Jessica, Crystal, and Taffy—you have the golden touch. Thank you to all my writer friends who read early drafts, particularly Shannon, Debbie, Lisa, and Rebekah.

To Atticus, thank you for loaning me a taste of your brief and beautiful poetry.

This book also would not have been possible without my people, the ones who never gave up on me as I pursued this dream.

Andrea Christensen, thank you for letting me live in your basement, where I wrote the first words of this story, and for being my friend through all the ups and downs of life. To Catherine Dunn, you are my forever writing buddy and the pride to my joy, or the joy to my pride, I can never remember which.

To my sisters, Katie and Jenny, you are my best friends and lifelong allies. To Don and Kathie Stewart, I'm grateful every day to have you in my corner. A huge hug to my backyardigan ladies, who help me raise my kids, babysit so I can write, and generally keep me sane. I'd be lost without you.

I wish I could sign a book for my grandparents Glendon and Bobette, who are undoubtedly tromping through heaven in cowboy boots, still cheering for me.

Thank you to my parents, Woody and Page Johnson, for raising me in a home with books and stories and imagination. You were always out there in the crowd—cameras ready—making me believe I could do and be anything.

To Ellie, Avery, and Cayden, a million thank-yous for being my biggest fans and for putting up with Mommy when I "zone out" during drafting or when we eat takeout for three weeks straight during revision. You've given me the time to pursue this dream, but know that you are *the* dream. You are each so kind, brave, and beautiful.

To my husband, Kyle: You had faith in me and in this book when it was just a bunch of random Post-it notes on the office wall. You believed in me even when I didn't, and you loved me with all my flaws. None of this is possible without you.

Finally, I am forever grateful for a God who has given me more stars in the darkness than I deserve or could ever count.

Erin Stewart grew up in the woods of Virginia catching fireflies. She now makes her home in the shadow of the Rocky Mountains with her husband and their three children. Erin loves using her background in journalism to research and write fiction based on real life. A heart failure survivor and adoptive mother, she believes life throws plot twists and people in our path for a reason—always. *Scars Like Wings* is her debut novel.

erinstewartbooks.com

@Erin_N_Stewart